The Unwelcome Visitor
at
Grey Sage

The Unwelcome Visitor
at
Grey Sage

Phyllis Clark Nichols

Southern
Stories
Publishing

THE UNWELCOME VISITOR AT GREY SAGE
Copyright © 2025 by Phyllis Clark Nichols

 outhern
tories
ublishing

Published by Southern Stories Publishing

ISBN: 979-8-9888854-7-4 (paperback)
ISBN: 979-8-9888854-6-7 (ebook)
Print Edition

Cover art from an original oil painting by George W. Nichols

For

Jan Patterson, M.D.

who cares for the least of these and champions the rights of
the underserved,

who has the brilliant mind of a scientist and the
compassionate heart of a healer,

who is a professor and continual learner,

who has walked her path of grief with grace,

and

who is my treasured friend.

Chapter One

Wednesday, September 20, 2006
Grey Sage Inn near Santa Fe

⟨*T*⟩he slanting rays of sun flickered through the ponderosa pines as the gusting winds transported a late-afternoon September chill. Alo dropped the last log onto the woodpile, brushed his hands, and looked at his watch. There was still time. He had an hour to start splitting and stacking the cottonwood. They'd need it. All the signs his Hopi father and grandfather had taught him indicated an unusually cold winter coming soon.

He closed the tailgate of his truck and headed to the barn for the axe. Warm from the work of unloading half a cord of wood, he removed his gloves and wiped his damp brow with his handkerchief as he walked and inhaled the cool air that smelled of juniper.

Inside, Alo went to the corner of the barn where he kept all his tools hanging on the wall. That was another thing his father had taught him: take care of the tools of your work, keep them clean and sharp, and either have them in your hand or in their place. As property manager at Grey Sage, Alo avoided clutter, preferring order. Even the woodpile looked measured. Silas, the inn's owner, had often accused Alo of having the tidiest barn in the Sangre de Cristo Mountains.

Alo smoothed his shoulder-length sable hair away from

his face and was about to reach for the axe when he noticed the empty spot on the wall. No axe. Only he and Silas frequented the barn, and Silas, a retired doctor, hadn't picked up an axe in years. Standing as motionless as the boulders bordering Wild Horse Creek, Alo's eyes surveyed the wall for anything else that was missing.

Only the axe.

Strange. He had used the tool Monday afternoon and was certain he had cleaned it and put it away. He would ask Silas.

Maude, holding the phone in one hand and tapping her pencil in rhythm to Lily's sputtering with the other, sat at the kitchen counter with her notebook. She watched Silas pour himself a cup of coffee and head toward his chair in the gathering room adjacent to the kitchen. She scribbled another note and attempted a question, but once Lily's On button was pushed, she barely breathed. Maude had never been one for interrupting, especially not her old college roommate and friend for almost fifty years. So she waited until Lily was saying goodbye.

"Wait, Lily. Just a reminder. Alo will pick you and your group up at the airport Friday midday. We have the flight number, and he'll be driving the van. Oh, and I heard this morning from Emily. The newlyweds will be driving up just for the weekend. Should be here for dinner on Friday. They want to tell us all about their honeymoon and their move to Albuquerque. They didn't want to miss seeing all of you." Maude hesitated. "And one other thing, just as a warning, Lily: we do have other guests. Professor Marshall Boone, but he likes to be called Boots—"

Lily didn't mind interrupting. "A professor calling himself Boots. Aha, is he an old cad or a young Adonis?"

"Neither. Maybe somewhere in between. He and his wife, Clara, have been with us for two weeks and will be here through October. He's on sabbatical and doing research in the area, something to do with tribal folklore. So he's often out and about while she knits the day away on one of the portales. And we have another writer-in-residence, Drake Dodson, working on a movie script. He's actually a novelist turned screenwriter and a friend and former student of Professor Boone's. They've taken over the library, but I'm working on an alternative place for them to work while you're here. The good news is they're mostly quiet and focused, and they'll make for interesting conversation around the table with all your artist friends. That's all. I think I have everything I need from you, and we'll see you on Friday."

"Wait, Maude. Might I assume the novelist is much younger and single?"

Maude cleared her throat. "You might, although I can assure you he is quite focused on his work. Deadlines do that."

Lily giggled coyly. "I've been known to change a man's focus a few times."

"Umm, I seem to have lived through some of those times." Maude saw Silas waving his hand. "Wait, Lily. Silas wants to say something." Maude grinned as Silas spoke quietly to her. She translated Silas's words in friendlier terms. "He just wanted me to remind you that if you bring that infernal whistle you use to gather your troops, he will dispose of it permanently this time."

"You tell Silas the whistle is already packed. I never lead a group without my whistle, because it works. It'll be around my neck."

"Goodbye, Lily. See you Friday."

Hanging up, Maude turned to Silas. "Sorry. Lily says the whistle is packed for the trip and will be around her neck. You'll do what you must, Silas. You always do."

Lita trudged through the kitchen, mop and bucket in hand. "Did I hear something about Lily and her whistle and her neck? I threatened the last time to set her red hair on fire if she blew that whistle one more time. Silas rescued her when he hid it. She may not be so lucky this time."

Still holding the mop and bucket, Lita stopped in her tracks on her way to the mudroom.

"Maude, how long have Alo and I been here with you?"

Maude raised her eyebrows. "I think it's been close to forty years, but why are you asking me that question now?"

Lita continued her walk to the mudroom, her voice trailing like her apron strings. "In all those years, I've never seen such a mess in your studio. You're usually fastidious about cleaning up after yourself, but I wiped and scraped more red paint this afternoon than I have in . . . what'd you say? Forty years."

Maude's eyebrows moved farther north. "Red paint?"

Lita returned from the mudroom and went straight to the sink and began washing her hands. "It wasn't blue. Go look at the mop water. I haven't dumped it yet. I'll get Alo to dump it in the outside sink and clean the bucket when he comes in. Trying to get rid of the evidence. Looks like there was a bloody crime committed in the studio." Lita laughed.

Maude was puzzled. She was aware that she was a bit more forgetful these days. But . . . "Lita, I thought I did clean up when I finished painting yesterday and washed my brushes and put them away. I knew I'd have no time to paint again this week with Lily's group coming in. And to my knowledge no one else has been in the studio." She perked her head toward Lita. "And what were you doing cleaning the studio anyway? I thought you hired Kyah to do those chores. Why didn't you have her clean the studio?"

Lita wiped her hands and turned to Maude. "Because there was much to do. Today was cleaning day, and tomorrow is for shopping and food preparation. And honestly, cleaning up after you in your studio has always been a next-to-nothing job. Kyah was cleaning the common areas except for the library, sprucing up the suites, refreshing linens, and getting everything ready for Lily's gaggle. And don't forget Kyah has the cleaning and laundry responsibilities for our other three guests."

"I'm sorry. You should have come and gotten me. I am quite skilled at cleaning up paint."

"It's done, but you may need some more tubes of red paint. Might want to put that on the shopping list for tomorrow when we go into town." Lita went to the pantry and removed the clipboard hanging on the nail next to the door. "I have the basic grocery list. I'm guessing you went over things with Lily. Anyone of her entourage have food allergies or dietary restrictions?"

"Two. It seems that Henry, our retired colonel friend, has developed late-onset diabetes, so he needs to watch the sweet stuff. And Lily has a new traveler who doesn't eat anything in the nightshade family."

Lita stopped in her tracks. "Can't or won't?"

"I'm not quite sure, but it sounded closer to can't without consequences."

Lita plopped her clipboard on the counter and joined Maude. "And did Lily bother to tell you what the nightshade family is and what happens if this traveler eats them?"

"Now what do you think? Of course, she told me. The woman doesn't eat potatoes, tomatoes, eggplants, or any kind of peppers or red spices."

Lita rolled her eyes. "Does this woman know she's coming to Santa Fe?" She looked back at her shopping list. "Sounds like I need to double the salad fixings and load up on corn and beans. I'll make special desserts for our dear Henry. Oh, but Laura's coming, isn't she?"

Maude nodded in agreement.

"Since I made a baker out of her last Christmas, I'll get her to help me. Now maybe you could tell me what would happen if the no-nightshade-woman ate my chili."

A quiet giggle slipped from Maude. "Lily said the woman is a recently retired professor of forensic psychology, looking forward to her first artists' retreat." She looked at her notes. "I'm quoting Lily now. 'Sarki prefers not to spend her week at Grey Sage conjoined to the toilet, so tell Lita no nightshades.'"

Lita hung her head. "Nothing's ever easy or normal with that red-haired, man-chasing artist friend of yours, Maude. Always puzzles me that you two made friends in college and still speak to each other."

"We do know to expect the unexpected with Lily, but somehow it seems to be enjoyable, Lita. At least most of the time." Maude hung her chin and looked sheepishly over her glasses. "Besides, you and I are so straitlaced and predictable that a little of Lily is good for us. We've gotten old and set in our ways. She'll bring out the eighteen-year-olds in us again."

"A little? Of Lily? Lily's a lot, and you know it. She's not changed in all these years, and she's not likely to have a personality adjustment before Friday. I'll strap myself in and get Alo to put a muzzle on me while she's here."

Maude tapped her pencil on her notebook. "I hope you have secured Kyah for some extra hours. Maybe we should go over the menus for the week. I'm thinking more snacks than usual since the artists will be in the studio most days."

"A basket of fruit, a bowl of nuts, and cookies. I can

handle that. What else?"

"There will be an outing or two for some plein-air painting, weather permitting. Remind me to check with Alo on the weather. Might need to think picnic or bagged lunches for a couple of those days. And Lily did mention going into Santa Fe for an excursion and a ride through the mountains to see the aspens. But again, all that depends upon the weather."

"I'll be flexible. I can bend, but I'm telling you, I won't be bowing to that woman's spur-of-the-moment whims."

Maude watched Silas heading in for the coffee pot again. She turned to Lita and whispered. "It's nearly five o'clock, and that's his fourth cup since lunch, and he'll sleep like he's been drinking warm milk all afternoon."

"Alo's the same way. Bleeds dark roast or chicory." Lita gazed out the kitchen window. "He's driving up now. The sight of that man still makes my heart flutter. Look at him. Looks like he stepped off a movie set."

Maude chuckled as she stood, walked to the coffee bar, and took the coffee pot. "How about a half a cup, Silas?" She poured his coffee. "Alo's coming in, and he might like a cup. And besides, you'll want another cup after dinner."

"I can always make a fresh pot for dinner." He sauntered back to his chair.

Lita added. "Speaking of dinner, I told our guests at lunchtime I'd have something light and ready for them at six thirty in the library. I'll remind them to remove their books and papers tomorrow and work in their rooms while our other guests are here."

"Thank you, Lita, but allow me to take their dinner to them tonight. I'll do the explaining about the need to remove their books and papers from the library for the convenience of our arriving guests. That should get things cleaned up. And what if I tell them that we'll all have our dinners together starting tomorrow night? You and Alo should join us. Around the dining table, I can tell them about our friends who are coming and what their schedule might be."

Lita agreed. "I think the professor and his wife will appreciate that. But Double D, as I call him, won't care. That is if he even hears what you say. He could very well hibernate in his room for a week, and that's perfectly fine with me. He's worn the same clothes for the last three days. If he comes out in those crusty jeans and blue plaid shirt tomorrow, I'm thinking of handing him a can of shaving cream and a bottle of shampoo."

Maude chuckled. "And I thought artists were messy and eccentric. I agree that he is slightly different. So, you've given him a nickname now?"

"Double D, not because he's Drake Dodson but because he's distracted and more than a little disturbed. I hear Alo coming in now."

Alo took off his light jacket and hung it on its hook in the mudroom. He walked through the kitchen without speaking and poured himself a cup of coffee.

"Did you get the wood?" Lita asked.

"I did. Just half a cord of cottonwood today, and another half tomorrow. Pine and mesquite next week." Alo took his normal armchair next to the fireplace. Silas sat quietly reading only a few feet away, his silhouette highlighted by the afternoon sun cascading through the window. Neither of them spoke.

Alo studied the way Silas seemed more bent, perhaps from many years of leaning over an operating table or from the weight of caring for hundreds of suffering people. His thinning white hair glistened in the incoming light. Alo thought of the many late afternoons over the last forty years when these four had come together in the kitchen or sat around the fireplace in the gathering room or hovered over a game of Scrabble in the evenings or just in conversation about plans for the next day.

Alo had considered Maude and Silas Thornhill family since his and Lita's first daughter was born and he came to work for them. The Thornhills, native Texans, had settled in Santa Fe after medical school. Maude had searched longer than a year for land and found this property, close to fifty acres with a stream and one small adobe structure. When she brought Silas out to see it and told him she had named it Grey Sage, he could not refuse her.

To pay Silas's bills for taking care of Lita and the delivery of Catori, Alo had offered to work to help Silas and Maude clear their land. Maude was a dreamer and designer, and Alo quickly became her right-hand man, as he knew about constructing adobe structures and land preservation. Silas had managed the births of their daughters, and Alo managed the birth of Maude's plans, replacing the piñon grove with walls, doors, floors, and portales held up by the very pine trees that were cut down from the property.

Over the next five years, the small adobe building had become a sprawling structure encompassing Maude's art studio, five bathrooms, four bedrooms, a library, a large kitchen, and a gathering room. Alo and Lita had been surprised when Silas announced that the last structure would be a casita down by the creek just for them and their two daughters. Maude helped with the design, and Alo oversaw the building of the adobe structure, which had become their home for nearly the last four decades. The expansion and reconstruction had started again when they decided to open the inn for artist and writer retreats.

Alo's daughters had grown up with Elan, Silas and Maude's son. They'd wept with them after Elan died in an accident over twenty years ago when Elan was only seventeen. They had been and would always be family.

Alo had noticed the changes in Silas over the last year—slight cognitive changes—and he hesitated to bring up the missing axe but thought he must. "Silas, the half cord of cottonwood is in a pile at the barn, and I'll pick up the rest of it tomorrow. When I finished unloading, I intended to start splitting and stacking the wood, but the axe wasn't in the barn. Do you have any idea where it might be?"

Silas looked up from his book. "I can't say as I do. Now, if you asked me about my scalpel, I could tell you exactly where it is, but I don't have much to do with axes and hatchets. That's your department. Maybe Jedediah borrowed it."

"Doesn't sound like Jedediah. In all these years as neighbors, he's never borrowed anything without asking first." Alo paused. "I used the axe Monday to split up the limbs I trimmed from the piñon tree next to the bedroom window on the north side. But I was certain I cleaned the axe and put it back in its place. I'll take another look around."

Maude and Lita walked into the gathering room and sat down with their notebooks. Lita responded. "Could have been Double D." She looked at Maude and grinned. "I meant to say Mr. Dodson. I saw him out wandering around the barn yesterday, just nosing around. Looked like he was talking to himself and doing a lot of head scratching."

Alo's face never showed expression. "He has no need of an axe. As I said, I'll take a closer look around."

The four of them chatted about the group coming in and what the schedule might be and what weather was coming. Alo was the one who always gave the best weather predictions. His Hopi ways were more accurate than the local meteorologist's. He had a better understanding of the signs the forests and animals gave and of the local terrain, especially the elevations around Grey Sage. "Coming weather is cooler and dry. Weekend will be sunny and breezy. Maybe some rain by midweek, and a fire will feel mighty fine in the evenings."

The thought of the fire alerted Alo's unsettledness about the axe. "What time is supper?"

Lita answered. "The guests are eating at six thirty, then we'll have a bite with Maude and Silas."

"I'll be in at six thirty." Alo stood from his chair, took the last swallow of coffee, and put his mug on the kitchen counter.

"I know you're going to look for that axe," Lita said. "Would you empty the mop bucket in the outside sink please? And the mop could stand a good rinsing too."

"I will." Alo grabbed his jacket on his way out the mudroom door. Another good hour of daylight. He walked the pine straw–covered path to the barn and opened the barn doors wide to let in all the light. He went straight to the corner wall where all his tools hung. The only empty spot was where the axe should be.

He next walked the interior perimeter to see if he had laid it down somewhere. Not on the worktable. Same with the wheelbarrow he had used to haul the piñon limbs Monday. Clean as a whistle. Nothing was out of place.

Until he saw the tracks in the wood shavings on the concrete floor. Not his size 11 tracks but smaller. He knelt to look closer, the angled sunlight making them easier to see.

Like he was tracking a mountain lion, Alo trailed the footprints to the back entrance of the barn and opened the doors. No discernable tracks marred the packed earth and pine straw.

As he pulled the doors shut again, a glint of white caught his eye. The axe, as though someone had hurled it, was lodged in the trunk of the chinquapin oak and impaled a piece of paper.

Alo walked slowly to the tree, moving its nearly bare branches away from the axe. The axe head was buried deep into the scaly, gray bark. Saddened at the sight of the wound in this century-old oak, he removed the axe carefully so as not to cause any more injury. It would take fifteen to twenty years to heal.

He held the axe, looked at the blade, and picked up the piece of paper that had floated to the ground in the nippy breeze. The red-painted drawing gave him a sudden chill.

Chapter Two

Wednesday afternoon
Chicago

*S*ince retiring from the School of Art Institute of Chicago eight years ago, Lily had taught small group art classes in her apartment. Her eccentric ways made her acutely selective about the students she accepted. In this season of her life, she had no desire to spend time with conventional humans.

No longer needing to live near the campus for convenience, she had found an apartment with walls of windows that satisfied her craving for natural afternoon light and gave her magnificent views of the shoreline and beaches of Lake Michigan. She had waited two months for an apartment that faced southwest. Sunsets had more appeal than sunrises, since she often painted into the wee hours and slept until noon. Dotted with overstuffed chairs and occasional tables holding quirky lamps and stacks of art books and magazines, the spacious living area was also her studio. She never cooked, so the kitchen area had become the storage space for art supplies and the place to mix paints and clean brushes.

Since she didn't cook, she had no need for dishes—only salad and cereal bowls, a stack of paper plates for serving takeout, a few utensils, and a dozen stems of Waterford crystal given to her years ago by a gentleman friend who despised drinking out of mugs and paper cups. Lily drank and served all beverages from mugs. The many she had collected from her world travels were displayed and easily accessible on four open shelves next to the sink.

Reba and Sarki had finished their art class and were already seated at the corner mahogany table near the window, waiting for Lily. Lily chose three mugs and filled them with coffee from a pot that never seemed empty. "Great session today. And when you return from the retreat next week, you will see your paintings differently."

She set the mugs down on the table. "You ladies have balcony seats for the encore appearance this time of afternoon, ever changing and always spectacular. The sun is setting on schedule, and I'm providing you a light dinner to add to your enjoyment."

Lily stepped away to the kitchen area and returned with a bakery box, paper napkins, a stick of room-temperature butter on a paper plate, and a knife. She opened the box and handed each of them a croissant on a napkin. "Sorry, we'll have to share the butter knife."

Sarki, a woman of slight but muscular build, ebony skin, and a chiseled profile that belonged on a cameo brooch, reached for her mug of coffee. "Lily, you're unbelievable. How many brushes and paint knives do you own?" She paused. "That was rhetorical. I know you don't count that high. But you own only one butter knife? You're a real case study, my friend."

"Oh, I have more, but they're not clean." Lily looked askance. "I don't remember the last time I ran the dishwasher." She pointed to the window. "Sunset, girls. Oh, if I could mix color to capture that. I've come close, and better than most, but I'm not certain something so exquisite can be captured. Sort of like me." She slathered butter on her croissant and handed Reba the knife.

Reba took the knife and reached for the butter. "Lily, I'm guessing this is your idea of dinner. No protein and nothing green. How do you stay healthy?"

"Good guesser you are. It is dinner tonight, and probably appetizer for you two, but I'll make up for it when we get to Grey Sage." She turned to Sarki. "I can just imagine Lita is whirling like a dervish trying to come up with a menu to satisfy your needs. She probably had no idea what a nightshade is. You're being deprived of experiencing true southwest cuisine. Food is another fabulous reason to visit Grey Sage."

Reba passed the knife to Sarki. "Lily's right. Three- or four-course dinners. Coffee and dessert in the great room around the fire. And the breakfasts? Nothing like Lita's breakfast burritos and her corn cakes with prickly pear syrup. She even makes the syrup, jellies, and fruit spreads."

Sarki buttered her croissant. "Tell me about this Lita. And tell me about the other travelers. You two are the only ones I know."

Lily wiped her mouth. "I've told you all about Maude and Silas, my forever friends. Lita is the cook, and Alo manages the property. They're of Hopi Indian descent. Wouldn't you agree, Reba, that Alo looks like the wooden Indian in front of the proverbial general store—ruggedly handsome?"

Reba, her mouth full of day-old croissant, nodded in agreement.

Lily continued. "They're both sixtyish. Deep, earth-toned skin and not the hint of a wrinkle. And they're pleasant and efficient." She paused. "Oh, Lita can get a burr under her saddle sometimes, but they're family to Maude and Silas. They've been there since the beginning. In fact, Alo built much of what you will see at the inn. They have their own home on the property down by the creek. There would be no operating inn if there were no Alo and Lita."

"Noted. Other family members there?"

Lily's facial muscles changed. "Silas and Maude lost their only son in a climbing accident when he was almost seventeen. He was attempting to rescue another climber. And Lita and Alo's two daughters are grown, and neither lives there."

"Noted. Now what about our other travelers?" inquired Sarki.

Lily responded. "All of them have been to Grey Sage. We made our first trip last Christmas and were stuck there for days in a snowstorm. But as uncomfortable as those experiences were, they created a bond. The bus wreck, the wolf attack . . . But then came an unforgettable Christmas morning and a love story."

"Noted," Sarki repeated. "Now, who are these people who have such a bond?"

Lily began to touch her fingers as she counted. "First is Henry—Colonel Henry Walker, I should say. Retired military and a decorated World War II veteran. He's a widower and a handsome gentleman of a dying breed. And he just glides when he waltzes." Lily's upper body swayed as she talked, the sleeves of her kaftan floating.

Reba added, "And then there's Beatrice Caldwell. Bea, as we call her, until she puts on her tutu."

Sarki looked puzzled. "Tutu?"

"Just metaphorical, but you'll know when she becomes the prima ballerina, and then we must call her Beatrice. She won't answer to Bea. She'll look at you like she has no idea who Bea is."

Lily snickered. "Bea's an aging ballerina who has literally danced her way around the world in leading roles with major ballet companies. Fortunately for her, with the burial of every husband, her assets increased. Would that I could have been so fortunate, but that's another story. Bea's third husband and Henry were best friends. Served together for years in the military, and dear Henry made a deathbed promise to him that he would take care of Bea. And as a loyal soldier, he keeps that promise, always trying to keep Bea happy and entertained. She's quite a lovely little wisp of a thing who dances in and out of reality. I'll just say that when Bea connects the dots, her picture is a bit different than yours. I know, Reba, as a psychotherapist, you'd say this differently, but I'll just say it out straight: Bea's pirouetting on the edge of crazy."

Reba put her hand over Lily's on the table. "Lily. No. Bea is not even near crazy, just a diva with a bit of dementia."

An unusual grin seeped across Sarki's face. "Reba's probably right. I've seen crazy, and pardon my grammar, but that ain't it. Crazy is a . . . what should I say? A mature woman with long flaming-red curls who drinks pinot noir from a mug and wears a silk kaftan all day while she's painting abstract landscapes of some galactic place no one has ever seen but her. Now that's crazy."

Lily lifted her mug. "To friends who always tell you the truth. And, I might add to that, crazy is an art instructor who'd take a psychotherapist and a forensic psychologist on an artists' retreat."

A low chuckle escaped Sarki's mouth. "Noted. Move on. Who's next?"

Reba said, "Then there's Laura Sutton, pianist and former professor of music and wife of a pharmacist who works in research for a pharmaceutical company."

Lily added, "That's Reba's way of saying he's a real lab rat. But don't worry. We won't be bored with him. He's not making this trip. Laura came home from Grey Sage after Christmas, quit her job, and now spends her time baking, gardening, and doing volunteer work. That's the magical spell of Grey Sage. Laura is now the most contented and engaged I've ever seen her."

Reba agreed. "She truly is. Her baking skills are unbelievable—just a natural. I've told you about my daughter, Emily."

"Noted. The one who fell in love with Kent on the Christmas trip, and who just got married at Grey Sage a few weeks ago and moved to Albuquerque. More of Grey Sage's magic."

"Yes, and Laura went out a week before the ceremony to make the wedding cake. It was stunning. A replica of the inn. Truly stunning."

"It was all stunning," said Lily. "A moonlit ceremony on the bridge, and we had to sit there that evening until the moonflowers opened. But that's another story. I'd say the wedding was more like 'Grey Sage magical.' And you'll get to meet Kent and Emily, Sarki. They're driving over for the weekend."

"Noted. So, Henry is the only male on this trip?"

"Yes, but Maude informed me that a professor from Colorado who is on sabbatical and doing research in the area has been there for about three weeks. His wife is with him. And there's a younger guy—a novelist-screenwriter type—who is there as well. Writers in residence through October. Apparently they're busy during the day, but Maude promises they'll be interesting dinner companions."

Sarki nodded. "Understood."

Lily grimaced. "Why do you keep saying 'noted' or 'understood'? It sounds odd."

"Just my normal professional response. How would you like me to respond, Lily?"

"Unprofessionally, of course. Reba's the only one in this group of compadres who is still a professional. The rest of us are just retired, experienced, and free to go and do as we please. Speaking of going, ladies, it's time for you to go. I have some calls to make, and I need to start packing."

Sarki stood from the table. "Noted. Excuse me, I meant to say, 'Got it.' I may be experienced, but I am a novice in the apparel department. How are we to dress on this trip?"

"Comfortably. No need for dress clothes. Jeans, T-shirts, something that will tolerate paint and brambles, sweaters, comfortable hiking shoes, and by all means a jacket. We layer. Could be hot or could be cold. Oh, and cowboy boots if you have them. Just know that dressing up where we're going is a clean pair of creased jeans without patches and an ironed shirt."

"Got it. If I don't have what I need, I'm guessing you would take me shopping."

Lily led them toward the door. "Of course. We're planning an excursion into Santa Fe. You might need to forego the true dining experience, but I'll not have you miss Canyon Road and all its art."

Reba followed Sarki to the door. "We'll see you early Friday morning at the airport."

Lily laughed heartily. "Noted."

She closed the door and walked to the window. The last glow of golden orange bled across the sky, a color she couldn't replicate, not even with cadmium red light. Lightning in the distance. A storm approaching from across the lake.

Thursday morning
Grey Sage

Maude stood in front of the bathroom mirror brushing her wavy silver hair as Silas shaved. She plaited her hair in one long braid, coiled it into a bun, and secured it with two mother-of-pearl combs at the nape of her neck. Silas had bought them for her in Greece. She stepped into the closet for her clothes. "Will you be going into Santa Fe with Lita and me this morning?"

Silas rinsed his shaving brush. "If you don't mind, I think I'll stay here and enjoy the peace and quiet before Lily's storm arrives."

Maude, tall and slender, slipped into her favorite jeans, a red blouse, and a denim vest. "I know you enjoy your solitude, but you always seem to come alive when Lily brings a group. You'll enjoy seeing Henry and Bea again." She slid her feet into her favorite calfskin boots.

"Did I hear you tell Lita that Henry is now diabetic?"

"Seems he is."

"I guess he's returning to make certain Bea behaves. You must respect a man who lives up to the promise he made to his friend to watch after Bea. With her dips in and out of reality, Henry must be a patient man."

Maude fastened her silver concha belt. "It pays to be kinder to each other as we age." She adjusted the belt, tightening it one more notch. "Silas, I think I'm shrinking."

He turned to look at her. "We all shrink as we age, dear, and you'll be getting shorter too." He approached and wrapped his arms around her. "But we still fit. And you just had your annual physical, and your labs were those of a thirty-five-year-old."

"Is that my husband or the doctor speaking?"

"Both."

She kissed his cheek and backed away. "Dr. Thornhill, if you see my husband, will you tell him to hurry and get dressed. He needs to get the coffee started."

"I'll oblige, ma'am. What's for breakfast?"

"I think Lita said something about sweet-potato pancakes and bacon and eggs this morning. Seems that's Boots' favorite."

"Then I'll add a dash of cinnamon to the coffee. It's getting that time of the year with these cooler September mornings."

Maude left Silas to dress and walked down the long hallway to the kitchen. She was getting out coffee mugs and dishes when she heard the bells. Lita had crocheted a door hanger with jingle bells years ago, and they just left them hanging from the doorknob in the mudroom. That way, Lita, whose hands were usually full, didn't have to knock, and Maude knew she was entering.

Lita's early-morning voice squeaked, "Alo's getting a few pieces of firewood. It's forty-five degrees this morning. He thought Silas might enjoy a fire in the gathering room, and maybe the guests would like one in the library if they're staying in today."

"Sounds cozy. Let's serve our guests in the morning room, and the four of us will eat in here by the fire."

"I prefer it, especially if Double D didn't crawl out of bed in time to take a shower this morning."

For the next half hour, Maude and Lita worked in the kitchen doing their usual. Silas made the coffee. Alo built the fire. The last few years of practice had trained them to work together like a well-oiled machine. They ate their breakfasts and served the guests in the morning room. Then Maude and Lita cleaned up while Silas and Alo drank their third cup of coffee and read the newspaper.

Maude spoke to Lita. "I hope you don't mind that I invited Mrs. Boone to go to town with us. I figured I'd drop you off to get groceries, and I'd head over to get the art supplies Lily requested. Mrs. Boone can go with me. There's a yarn shop that I think she'll enjoy, and it's just a couple of blocks from the art store."

Lita rinsed out the sink. "More yarn? I don't even get close to her for fear that I'll wind up in the tangled thread of one of her blankets. That woman needs to get a life. I think she knits in her sleep."

Maude knew Lita would be chagrined when Mrs. Boone gifted her with a hand-knitted baby blanket for her new grandbaby scheduled to arrive around Christmas. When Mrs. Boone learned about the baby, she had asked Maude about a yarn shop. This morning seemed the perfect time to take her with them into Santa Fe.

They were finishing up when their quiet morning was shattered by a shriek echoing down the long hallway, a wail that sounded like a wounded animal. Maude turned from the counter and saw Alo jump up and run toward the sound. That was his nature. Alo had always been their protector. Lita was on his heels, and Maude and Silas followed more cautiously.

Drake stood in the hallway outside the library door, scowling, hands raised and clutching sheets of paper, and muttering. They could hear Boots inside the library. Alo bolted into the room with Lita right behind him while Maude tried to speak with Drake, but all he would say was, "What a mess," over and over. She and Silas left him standing in the hallway and entered the library.

Maude surveyed the room, listening to the conversation between Boots and Alo. Books and loose papers were scattered across the room—on the floor, on the pine table that took center stage in the room, and on the chairs. Everywhere lay papers. Maude watched as Alo closed the window and joined Mrs. Boone, who was gathering the sheets. Lita stood in dismay.

"Why would you leave the windows open?" Boots grumbled. "Look what happened. The wind blew our papers everywhere. It will take us hours, maybe days, to make sense of this mess. I had printed over two hundred pages of my manuscript, and Drake had his script and research papers too."

Alo attempted to appease him. "Sir, I am so sorry. We'll help you get everything back in order."

"You can't help with this. This is something only Drake and I can do. You could have helped by not opening the window."

Alo was calm. "Sir, we don't open the windows in the library, especially when it is forty-five degrees outside."

"Well, you can see it was open," Boots blared. "No screen to keep out the bugs, and big enough for a bear to crawl through. I went to my room before Drake did last night, and the window was closed. Let's see if Drake is calm enough to ask him." He walked to the doorway where Drake still stood. "Drake, look at me and listen."

Maude joined Boots. "Did you open the window last night before you left the library, Drake?"

Drake looked glassy eyed. "It was like a brick pizza oven in there while I was trying to work. I might have cracked the window just a bit for some fresh air."

Maude asked, "And you didn't close it before you went to bed?"

Drake stared at her, and then his eyes began shifting from side to side as he tried to recall. "Maybe. I don't remember. Maybe I didn't."

"I am so sorry. In this terrain, it can get dreadfully windy when the temperature cools in the evenings." Maude turned to Boots. "Were the pages numbered? Perhaps that's the best place to start. We'll just turn what looks like a catastrophe into a project this morning."

Boots relaxed. "Thank you, Mrs. Thornhill. Drake and I will handle this. It is not your responsibility."

"At least allow us to help gather your papers and leave

them in stacks for you on the table. Then the two of you can do the sorting."

Lita and Silas left the room without a word while Maude and Alo joined Boots and Drake in picking up the papers. Within fifteen minutes, the papers were stacked and the room was back in order.

"Now, gentlemen, we'll leave you to do the sorting." Maude turned to Mrs. Boone. "Lita and I'll be leaving at nine thirty if you'd still like to go into Santa Fe with us."

"Yes. I don't think I'd enjoy being here with these two this morning. I'll meet you at the front door." Mrs. Boone waddled down the hall to her suite.

Maude and Alo walked the long hallway back to the kitchen area. Alo was more than his usual calm and quiet, almost too quiet for Maude's liking. "What are you thinking, Alo?"

"I am thinking the window did not open itself. It was a cold but calm night. Wind did not scatter the papers, and it certainly did not scatter books."

Maude responded. "Yes, but they've had lots of stacks of books, and Drake is not known for neatness."

"Possible. But did he leave dusty tracks on the rug and some of the papers?"

Maude had seen the tracks too. She sensed an unsettledness in her stomach. They said no more.

Chapter Three

𝒪𝓂aude's favorite month of September washed the mountains with autumnal colors and brought cooler evening breezes. Standing on the portale that connected her studio to the main house, she pulled her shawl tighter, leaned against the smooth tree trunk that supported the roof, and watched as Alo and Lita walked the lane to their casita. The chimney of Jedediah's cabin was not visible, but smoke curled in the air above, and its soothing whiff floated across the creek. The last light of day was slipping away, and in only moments the sky would be star studded and the woods of Grey Sage would be dark.

Her day had been chock-full of shopping, helping Lita with last-minute menu options, and organizing the art supplies she had purchased. The guests were now occupied in their suites. Alo and Lita were gone, and Silas was making final preparation for the Bible class he taught on Sunday. The house was quiet. Finally, solitude.

With images of the open window and papers strewn across the library still in her mind's eye, Maude thought of the missing axe and the dabbles of red paint Lita had cleaned in her studio. Maude had perused the counters, the cabinets, and floor this afternoon as she put the supplies away. Nothing seemed missing or out of order.

Painting was inherently messy, and as of late, she was messier than usual. For the last few weeks and before Lily's arrival, she had been frenziedly trying to finish a panoramic landscape, a knife painting larger than most of her work and requiring more oils and medium. Her painting sessions had required more cleanup, but she was usually meticulous in washing brushes and wiping any large splatters of paint on the Saltillo tile floor. She even tidied her palette board before putting it in its plastic tray. It was kept in the refrigerator in the corner next to the door to keep the oils from drying until her next painting session.

The red paint in the studio, the axe, the library? Puzzling. Perhaps explainably coincidental, but she feared Alo would not agree. His demeanor had been different since the library incident. One did not have to dig deep to know Alo was bedrock solid, unmoved by surface activity. When others paced and wrung their hands, Alo became even more still and quiet. Since yesterday, he had been that kind of still and quiet, and that unsettled feeling niggled at her.

She checked all the glass sliding doors on both sides of the studio and locked them, which she rarely did, and walked from her studio through the portale to the gathering room.

Hearing a Schubert string quartet playing in the background, she knew before she entered the room that Silas was still studying. Alo had built a fire before dinner, and the embers were smoldering. She pulled her chair closer to the fireplace and removed her shoes, then sat quietly looking over her notes and lists. Thankfully, Lily was bringing only one new guest, and *Sarki* was not a name easily forgotten. Remembering names was another challenge lately.

Lily's gaggle, as Silas called them, would bring some activity and lightness to Grey Sage that would take her mind off these things.

She heard Silas close his book, her signal to close hers. She slid her chair back and put on her shoes. "All finished?"

"For now. With Lily's gaggle arriving tomorrow, I thought it best to get my preparation done tonight." He stacked his books and Bible on the bottom shelf of his chairside table, stretched his slender arms, and inched forward in his chair. "I may need a few minutes to brush away any cobwebs Sunday morning." He tapped his head as though knocking on a door and smiled at Maude. "A few more cobwebs these days."

She returned a forced smile. "Cobwebs I can tolerate, just not the spiders. Will we be hearing some deep and profound theological lesson or treatise on Sunday?"

"Not from me. I've chosen the shortest verse in the Bible as my subject."

Maude moved to the edge of her chair. "Even I know that one: 'Jesus wept.'"

Silas nodded. "Yes, you do, and yes, He did. But think about it, Maude. Jesus was God, and He wept, and why? For what reason?"

"Maybe it's the same reason we all weep—out of our hurt and sadness."

"Wise woman. And the Bible says Jesus cried two other times too. And there's a common thread in all three events, but you must wait until Sunday to hear about that." He stood. "What do you say we have a cup of chamomile and call it a day. I'm all tuckered out, and I can only imagine what tomorrow will bring."

Maude took his arm and walked with him into the kitchen.

What tomorrow will bring. Hopefully tomorrow will only bring good things.

Friday morning

Alo had no trouble persuading Lita to rise early and get to the inn before sunup. They used their key to enter the mudroom, Alo holding fast to the jingle bells so as not to disturb the silence. He helped Lita remove her jacket and hung it up but kept his on.

Lita went straight to the kitchen with Alo following. She stopped at the refrigerator to remove the pot of oats that had been soaking overnight. Alo headed to the coffee bar.

Lita joined him. "I'll make the coffee. You build a fire to chase away the chill."

"No fire this morning. I'll be headed into town to pick up our guests, and Silas may have plans for the morning, and his plans may not include fire tending." He grabbed a mug from the shelf above the coffee maker and set it next to the pot. "I heard you say Kyah is working almost every day lately, but will she have time to help you in the kitchen when Lily's entourage arrives?"

"No. Kyah's an energetic young girl. Excellent help with the cleaning and making things lovely, but she knows next to nothing about what goes on in a kitchen except turning on the dishwasher. I'll be tying an apron around her older sister Tanzi. She's married but doesn't want a full-time job because she's taking classes at the culinary school in Santa Fe. I interviewed her, and I think she'll be quite good in the kitchen. She's willing to work a few hours each day while Lily's group is here. Works great for me and for her. I get skilled help, and she gets practical experience. Besides, if push turns to shove, Laura Sutton is returning with Lily, and she's an easy kitchen mate."

A low growl escaped Alo's lips. "Hmmm."

Lita gyrated from the coffee bar with her hands on her hips. "Don't give me that 'hmmm.' I know that sound and exactly what it means. You think no one can work with me in the kitchen."

"Yes. You are right about what I am thinking, and am I right? Three women in a kitchen sounds worse than three women in a teepee."

"Tanzi will not be working with me. She will be working for me. My sous chef. And with Laura around, I'll be on my best behavior."

Lita turned back to the bar to pour Alo's coffee. She handed him the mug of steaming liquid, and he walked toward the mudroom.

"Where are you going?"

"I need to check on something in the barn, and I'll bring in another armload of wood for the great room. I make every trip count these days."

Alo took the large flashlight from the mudroom shelf and quietly closed the door. The sky was still dark with only a hint of gray on the eastern horizon. He drank his coffee, shining the flashlight on various objects along the path as he walked to the barn. Once there, he put the flashlight down, opened the barn door, and turned on the lights. He had overseen the building of this barn and workshop years ago, and his plan included flooding the barn with overhead light.

He scanned the structure before entering, then walked to the back entrance to look around. Nothing unusual. He returned to the front, turned out the lights, and closed the wooden door.

Alo continued his surveillance outside, walking the outer perimeter of the barn before doing the same for the inn. He looked for open windows or anything unusual in the landscape. This property was as familiar to him as the touch of Lita's hand. Every tree. Every boulder. Every rise and slope of the land all the way to the arroyo.

Finding nothing different, he was breathing easier until he reached the front porch. A configuration of fist-sized stones lay on the welcome mat. He pointed the flashlight to investigate the cluster of rocks. They were smooth like those in the creek bed, and they had been carefully laid out in a pattern. He put the flashlight down, pulled the paper from his hip pocket, unfolded it, and knelt to get a closer look at the stones. The gray morning light revealed the pattern was the same. He folded the paper, returned it to his jeans pocket, and reached for his phone in his jacket pocket.

For several years, he had resisted a cell phone, claiming he had no use for such technology. Finally, at the insistence of Catori and Doli, his two daughters who lived away, he had caved. He was grateful for his phone this morning as he spotlighted the stones with the flashlight and snapped a picture. He then moved the rocks, carefully sliding them with his boot into a small pile behind the sage bush next to the front door. His fingerprints would not be on these stones.

Alo continued his walk around the front of the inn and the path encircling the studio. He checked the glass doors. Locked. Maude kept the sliding doors open day and night during the summer for the air fresh to remove the scent of paint. Screens kept out varmints and insects and allowed the breezes to flow through the expansive workspace, but she had apparently closed and locked them. No doubt the library incident had sent her into alert mode.

Alo had asked Silas about the missing axe, and Maude and Lita had chimed in during that conversation. Later, when he told them he had found it and no one inquired further, he had chosen not to tell them about the tree or the graphic image on the paper.

He continued his walk. The light in Maude's bedroom window caught his eye. She and Silas were up, getting ready for breakfast and Lily's anticipated arrival. The window went dark as he passed.

He wrestled with his thoughts as he continued his investigative walk around the property. *How much and when should I tell them? And what would I tell them? I've seen this image, but I have no knowledge of what it means. But in my deep place, I know it means something. What I know would only cause them worry. Lily's coming. She'll be a distraction. With so much activity around Grey Sage, whoever is doing this might have second thoughts. The visit buys me some time. I need answers, and I know where to get them.*

He was about to open the mudroom door when he remembered he had told Lita he was getting firewood. He put his coffee mug and the flashlight down on the back porch and headed to the woodpile next to the barn. Moments later, with an armload of wood and a quick good morning to Maude and Silas, he passed hastily through the kitchen on his way to the great room. He was satisfied they had no reason to think he'd been surveilling the property since before sunup. The firewood dispelled any questions. Now, he only needed to conjure a believable reason for heading into town early.

"That woman has done it again." Lita cranked the sifter faster. Flour was flying. "Just like she always does. One surprise after another."

"I know, and I'm sorry." Maude set the milk carton on the counter. "But she had an explanation. Lily invited this gentleman weeks ago when she began to plan the trip, and he had declined because of other travel plans. But he surprised her when he returned early Wednesday and called her, insisting on making this trip."

"You're telling me the *gentleman* insisted? I believe that just like I believe Lily will ever let that red mop of hers go gray. Now, he might have given her a call, but I know who did the insisting, and it wasn't the gentleman."

Maude chuckled on the inside and attempted to be agreeable. "Probably so. I think you have Lily's number, Lita."

"I got her number all right. So now her six has becomes seven, and with Kent and Emily, it's nine." Lita huffed as she stirred the sourdough and melted butter into the bowl of flour. "Oh, let's not forget the cowboy and his yarn-twisting wife and Double D. So now it's twelve, and the four of us makes sixteen."

Maude began cracking the eggs into a bowl. "I suppose it's good that we have a table for twenty."

Lita's wooden spoon whirred in the pancake batter. "Sixteen is right. And I instructed Kyah to get out the fall linens, placemats, paper goods, and three sets of dishes for fifteen."

Silas poured himself a cup of coffee and stopped at the counter next to Maude. "You might want to go easy on the pancakes, Lita. You know they require a tender batter unless you want to feed them to the horses." Maude felt the slight nudge of his elbow in her ribs and grinned as he winked at her.

"Don't you start with me, Doctor. I've been flipping flapjacks as long as you've been removing tonsils. I know a thing or two about sourdough."

Maude agreed. "Yes, you do. Ready for me to turn on the griddle?" She almost bumped into Alo as he rounded the corner.

"Give me another minute." Lita poured more milk into the batter. "Okay, I've got Sarki Malarkey. What is this man's name?"

"Noble Sinclair the Third. A retired Chicago banker."

Maude knew Lita was grimacing without even looking at her.

"Poor fellow doesn't even have his own name. But I guess if he's a banker, he's rich. That's the kind Lily chases." Lita sighed. "I'll call him Global Noble unless I don't care for him. Then I won't call him at all."

"Lita, why would you grumble about one more guest?" Alo asked. "As I recall, you were the one years ago who wanted Grey Sage to become an inn. Inns house guests. At least successful ones do."

Maude noted the irritation in Alo's voice and his clenched jaw as he stood at the sink and glared out the window. She knew his face, every muscle and bone—the high, sloping forehead; the chiseled cheekbones; the dimple in his chin; and the leathery texture of his weathered skin. She had studied both their faces when she did a sculptured bust of them for their twenty-fifth wedding anniversary. Alo was tense and uneasy.

"Maude," Lita called. "Maude, didn't you hear me? Turn on the griddle."

Maude returned from her thoughts. "Certainly. Medium-high." She stepped to the griddle and turned the knob. "I'm scrambling eggs. Are the guests eating with us?"

"No. Continental breakfast at eight thirty. I'll serve them then. They'll be out for the day and back for dinner. Get the eggs scrambled and let's eat."

Maude heard Lita repeating to herself in a hushed voice, "Sarki Malarkey and Global Noble, Sarki Malarkey and Global Noble."

Kyah came in as they were finishing their pancakes and

eggs. Maude offered her breakfast, but she politely refused.

Lita started with instructions. "You know how you got everything out for fifteen yesterday. Well, today it's sixteen. I need you to get that taken care of before lunch." She paused. "Oh, just make it eighteen. Lily may pick up another one or two on the way."

Kyah dismissed herself, and Maude watched Alo stand from his chair holding his plate. Before he left the table, he spoke to Lita. "Lita, do you think that's enough grumbling? There are bigger problems than one more guest." He turned to Maude. "If she doesn't calm herself, let me know. I'll tie her by her apron strings to the inside of the pantry door until she changes her attitude."

Lita responded. "I'll check my attitude if you'll check yours. You've been grumpy for two days."

Alo took his plate to the sink. "I am sorry. We both will do better for the sake of our friends and our guests. Maude, I'll be leaving soon. Is there anything else I need to do?"

"No, but thank you. I think we're prepared to receive our guests. But their flight doesn't arrive until almost noon."

"I am aware. I have the flight number, but I want to get the van cleaned, and I have a couple of other errands before their arrival. This morning gives me time. I will keep checking with the airline for the exact arrival time. If they're on time, we should be back here by one o'clock."

With a playful grin on her face, Lita rose from her chair. "And I'll have a lovely lunch for this delightful group, including Global Noble."

Maude felt a slight reprieve when she saw Alo smile for the first time in two days and heard him say, "The old threat of tying her up with her apron strings works every time."

Chapter Four

*A*lo drove the van hurriedly down the lane from Grey Sage to the main road, careful to keep the tires in the well-worn ruts. The dirt-packed lane, now worn smooth with use, had been almost impassable forty years ago when Maude and Silas purchased this property. Mountains in the distance were vibrant with quaking aspen trees shimmering every shade of gold and yellow in the morning sun. The verdant ponderosa pines and crimson maples, equally as dazzling, dotted the panorama and provided a contrast, giving the aspens center stage only in autumn.

Alo and young Elan, Silas's son who'd died, had planted over eighty ponderosa seedlings at Grey Sage. The pines were nearly forty feet tall now, especially the ones along the creek bank. Alo wanted to be like those evergreen ponderosa pines—tall and strong, keeping down erosion and unshaken by the summer or winter storms.

Alo's family and Maude and Silas were like an ancient clone of aspens, trees forever entwined from the same root source. Grief and joy formed bonds that could not be broken. They had experienced the loss of Elan and the joys of watching Catori and Doli grow up at Grey Sage. They shared memories and stories and holidays and quiet evenings in the gathering room. They were family.

But by choice, Alo had walked alone with this heavy dread since Wednesday. Like ponderosa pines protected the soil in which they grew, he would protect Silas and Maude. He just needed to know from whom and how to protect them.

Lost in his thoughts, the half-hour drive to Santa Fe was but a blur until the traffic picked up and he realized he was on the edge of town. The car wash was his first stop to honor his concocted reason for coming into town so early. Normally, he would have done the job himself, but it was money well spent this morning to let someone else do it while he made a few calls.

Forty-five minutes, a spotless van, and two conversations later, Alo was driving into the parking lot of Museum Hill. He parked near the Wheelwright Museum of the American Indian. If this stop didn't produce answers, the Museum of Indian Arts & Culture was only steps away.

Alo entered the Wheelwright Museum and decided to check out the Case Trading Post shop. He might get a good start there. The perimeter walls were lined with shelves from floor to ceiling, populated with handmade pottery and other pieces of American Indian art. In the center of the spacious room sat glass cases of jewelry.

The image on the paper and the stone configuration had looked somewhat familiar to him, but he needed to know its significance. He perused the shelves for any sign of the image in the designs of the pottery, paintings, or woven goods. Nothing. He moved to the jewelry cases, quickly moving from the rings and earrings to the belt buckles. There, in the right-hand corner. A bolo tie with a black braided-leather rope and a sterling-silver bolo with inlaid turquoise. He had seen one similar before but could not recall where.

The young female store clerk approached Alo. "Could I

help you, sir?"

"Yes, please. I'd like to see that diamond-shaped bolo." He tapped the glass and pointed to the piece in the corner.

"Ah, sir, you have a very good eye." She opened a drawer underneath the glass case to retrieve a piece of black velvet. She spread it on the glass top, unlocked the case to get the bolo, and laid it on the velvet. "This is some of the finest craftsmanship we have. It is the artistry of a fourth-generation Navajo artist who does exquisite inlaid work."

"Navajo." Alo raised his head to look at the young woman, obviously a Native American. "I am Hopi. Are you Navajo?"

"Yes, I am." She pulled the long strands of her shiny, inky black hair and tucked them behind her right ear.

"I believe I have seen this design before. What is its significance?"

"That, sir, is the Eye of the Medicine Man. It is a powerful symbol for a shaman or a medicine man."

"What is the deep red stone in the center? It doesn't look like coral."

"As I said, sir, you have a good eye. This artist uses blood coral in many of his pieces, especially his belt buckles, but not in this piece." She ran her index finger over the raised red oval that appeared like stone. "This is not stone or coral. It comes from the rare spiny oyster shell. The colors of these shells range from orange to purple." She pointed to the scarlet center piece. "The color here is such a deep red that it is almost purple. Quite an unusual contrast to the silver and turquoise."

Alo's memory sharpened. *Now I know why this was familiar. It was Silas. Maude commissioned a native artist to make a bolo for him years ago for his birthday. Probably chose the design because Silas is a doctor. But I haven't seen it in years. I need to get my hands on it, but how without raising suspicion? This has to be a key to what's happening at Grey Sage.*

Alo picked up the piece, studied it, turned it over to see if the inlay went all the way through. He looked at the price tag. One thousand eight hundred seventy-five dollars. He laid it down.

"Sir, would you like to try it on? It's a stunning piece of art. With this bolo, you'd never need another silk tie. I think it would suit you."

"No, thank you. I have no silk ties to replace, and I have a turquoise, coral, and silver bolo my father wore. But I am grateful for your time. I really must go now."

Alo quickly turned and walked out of the Trading Post. He looked at his watch. Ten thirty. With only half an hour left before heading to the airport, he walked briskly to the Museum of Indian Arts and Culture. He entered and saw no one else in the museum except the elderly man behind the information desk. He inquired if there might be someone who could answer a few questions, someone knowledgeable about Native American symbols.

The elderly man had shoulder-length silver hair framing a face that looked as if it was carved from the Red Cliffs of Abiquiu—cliffs that had enchanted and inspired artists for generations. There was a striking resemblance to Alo's deceased grandfather on his father's side.

The elder rubbed his chin. "Well, my friend, that depends upon the symbol."

"I need to know more about the Eye of the Medicine Man symbol."

The old man reached for a pad of paper and a pencil. "I know this symbol." He quickly sketched the diamond shape inside a larger diamond shape with a circle in the middle. He picked up the drawing and handed it to Alo.

"Yes, that is the symbol. Do you know its significance

and what it means?"

"Only that it means one who wears it is a shaman or medicine man. It is a powerful symbol. With most of these symbols, each line means something. But for their meaning, my friend, I cannot help you." He paused. "We do have someone who would be able to assist you in acquiring this knowledge, but she is not here today. You could do some research here this morning if you like, or you could return on Monday to speak with her. She knows of such things and much more. Ask for Chooli."

Alo nodded. "I am grateful for your time, sir. I'll return on Monday to speak with Chooli." He turned and walked away.

The voice behind him cracked from too many years of smoking. "I will see you again on Monday, my Hopi friend."

Surprised and puzzled, Alo stopped and turned to look at the man. "How did you know I am Hopi?"

"You did not ask for a book. You asked for someone to tell you. We learn from talking and telling stories. That is our Hopi way."

Alo's large brown eyes met the smaller brown eyes of his elder, cradled in the folds of wrinkled skin. There was an unspoken understanding between them, as though they had known each other for a long time. "Yes. I will return on Monday to hear the story."

Maude sat at her desk. As she listened to Emily explain why she and Kent wouldn't be coming to Grey Sage for the weekend, she stared at the portrait of Elan above the fireplace—the one she had painted of him when he was only six. The portrait had been the painting she annually unveiled at Christmas as her gift to Grey Sage. She had captured Elan playing on the creek bank, his eyes full of wonder and a smile that rarely left his face. It seemed as if that boy had been born smiling and talking, mostly asking questions and listening intently. He had even smiled through adolescence when his friends seemed sulky and uncommunicative.

Sunday would have been Elan's fortieth birthday if he had lived. So many would-have-beens since his death. She wondered if he would still have blond curls or if he would have grayed prematurely as Silas did. And seeing a small child with a grandparent had often brought the question of what kind of woman he would have chosen for his wife and if his children would have resembled him.

Elan's death had left a hollow place deep inside Maude, a place that nothing else could fill, not even her deep love for Silas nor her love for Lita's family. Twenty-three years and she still felt the void of something that had been severed from her. She had accepted that this cavernous, painful lesion in her soul was not like a physical wound that would heal and leave only a scar. Silas had reminded her often through the years that grief was the price one paid for love. She was still paying and praying.

Maude finished her phone conversation with Emily, straightened the papers on her desk, and was headed to the kitchen when the phone rang again. Alo was on his way home.

Lita was standing on her tiptoes and stirring a large kettle of soup when Maude approached. "Let me stir the soup, Lita. If you get any shorter, Alo will need to build you a stool. You can hardly see the top of the pot. I hope you know what you put in there."

"Believe me, I know. The strangest soup I ever made.

The Grey Sage Gumbo is always rich with chicken, beans, peppers, and vegetables, but it won't be the same today."

"Smells good. Let me see."

Lita handed Maude the spoon and went to the island to prepare the fruit salad. "Never made soup without tomatoes or peppers or potatoes. I just doubled the corn and beans and cream cheese."

"If you made it, it will be satisfying. Alo just called, and they should be here in about half an hour. The travelers and their bags are loaded, and he was pulling away from the airport when he called." She lifted a spoon of the soup to her nose. "Smells rich, like maybe you doubled the cumin too."

"I had to double something when I couldn't use my ancho chili powder, so it was cumin with a dash of turmeric. But Maude, I am not doing this again, ruining my gumbo for everyone just because Sarki Malarkey can't have nightshades. Tanzi's coming to help with dinner, and I'll ask her to prepare a special dish for Sarki. Tanzi says she can work magic with sweet potatoes. The rest of our guests will have the usual. I'm not having them all turn orange from eating too many sweet potatoes this week."

"Maybe you could ask Sarki what she usually eats or what she likes to eat."

"I'm not sure I want to know what the woman eats. My plan is to let Tanzi cook for her."

"Sounds like a good plan. And speaking of plans, I just had a call from Emily. Can you believe they're not coming? And she was bringing the wedding pictures for all of us to see."

"I'm sorry not to see them, but I'm not getting my knickers in a twist about another change."

"Well, Emily's knickers are in a twist. Some high-ranking general flew in last night for a surprise visit to do some kind of inspection, and Kent can't leave the base. There's a slight possibility they might drive in for the day on Sunday, but they won't know until then. So we're back to fourteen." Maude paused. "I think it's fourteen."

"Won't matter. I've had my attitude check, and we will have plenty to eat. God provided, and I get to prepare and serve our guests." Lita went to the sink to rinse the strawberries. "I guess Reba will be disappointed to be so close and not get to see Kent and Emily."

"Oh no. Reba's not returning with the group to Chicago. She's going on to Albuquerque to spend several days with them."

Lita hooted. "That's Reba. Those kids have only been married a month. Just what newlyweds wish for: an uptight psychoanalyst mother who moves in for a week. She needs to give them a break and some privacy. Somebody should tell her, if her psychotherapist brain can't figure that one out. Add that other block of cream cheese to the soup, please."

Maude stirred the soup to melt the cream cheese. "I can assure you that I will not be the person to have that conversation."

"Get Lily to tell her. Lily could and would tell her straight without blinking an eye."

"Yes. Let's leave that to Lily. Right now, let's finish getting this lunch ready. I'll need to greet them when they get here, and we will keep them entertained until you're ready for us in the dining room. Just ring the bell."

"You mean before Lily blows her whistle, and I blow my last fuse?"

Maude put the lid on the soup pot. "Something like that. Soup's ready."

While lunch was served in the dining room, Kyah delivered the guests' luggage to their suites. Maude had given Kyah a list of the guests and suite assignments with some personal notes about each guest. Maude noted how Kyah prided herself in doing unusual things to make the guests feel pampered—things Lita and Maude had never had time nor the inclination to do. Maude's focus had always been the art or writing experience, and Lita lived for the final push-back from the table, the satisfied sighs, and the comments about their dining experience.

Silas and Maude were seated next to each other at one end of the table, and Alo and Lily were seated at the other end. Rarely did Lita dine with the guests. She was always too harried preparing the next course and clearing the table. On occasion she would join them for dessert and coffee.

Maude and Silas enjoyed familiar traditions handed down from their families, but over the years at Grey Sage, if something was done more than a couple of times, it became a tradition. If a meal was served at the dining table, there was always a blessing, and the official welcome to Grey Sage was customary around the table after their first meal together. When everyone was finished eating, and Lita and Tanzi had cleared the table, Lita joined the guests. Maude watched as Lita pulled an extra chair next to Alo and gave Silas the time-to-get-up nudge.

Silas stood from his seat to formally welcome the guests. "What a delight to see you enjoy your meal and to hear snippets of your conversations. Your presence graces us here at Grey Sage, and we look forward to the next few days with you. Now, most of you have been with us before—some of you about a month ago for Kent and Emily's wedding—and we welcome your return. And for you, Ms. Hanson and Mr. Sinclair, Maude and I want you to feel right at home here with us. You've all met Maude, the heartbeat of this place, and now I'd like to introduce you to Alo and Lita."

Maude watched the obligatory smile spread across Lita's broad face, her caramel-colored skin highlighting her perfectly white and straight teeth.

Silas continued. "I know you've already met Alo, but I want you to know Alo and Lita are family to us, and between the two of them, they run this place. Lita is the only one I know who can make a ham sandwich a culinary experience, and Alo keeps everything humming around here, from a chainsaw to his harmonica. If there is anything we can do to make your stay more pleasurable, please let us know. Now, I think Maude has a few things she'd like to say."

Silas sat as Maude stood and placed the wooden key box on the table. "Again, welcome to our home, to Grey Sage. Those of you who have been here know that each of our twelve suites is named after an artist. While we were having lunch, Kyah, our housekeeper, put your bags in your suite. You'll notice the extra little things that Kyah does to make your stay with us memorable."

Maude lifted the lid of the wooden box. "Silas has already told you that Alo is handy with a chainsaw, but he's a master with wood-carving tools and a soldering iron." She held up a room key attached to a one-by-four–inch strip of wood. "Thanks to Alo, your room key has your suite name attached, each a work of wooden art."

Beatrice interrupted. "Degas. That's my key." She quickly turned to the colonel next to her. "Henry, that is my key, isn't it? What is Maude doing with my key?"

The colonel patted her hand. "I think Maude is about to hand you your key."

"I knew it was my key. Degas painted all those pictures of me, and they're in my room. If any of you would like to see them, just knock lightly. You didn't sell those paintings of me, did you, Maude?"

"Never would I sell those, Bea." Maude observed the faces of the new guests. Their reserved smiles suggested that Lily had informed Ms. Hanson and Mr. Sinclair about Bea's entrances and exits from reality. "Yes, Degas did enjoy painting dancers, especially ballerinas."

Maude passed the key down to Bea, then continued handing out the others: Monet for Laura Sutton, Van Gogh for Reba Parker, Renoir for Sarki Hanson, Rembrandt for Noble Sinclair III. "And Colonel, we'd like you to stay in the Raphael Suite this visit. And of course, Lily, you'll be in the Pollock Suite."

"Of course I will," Lily retorted. "And I promise not to paint anything on the walls this time." A ripple of laughter broke out before she continued. "What about your other guests, and when will we see them?"

Maude closed the key box. "Thank you for reminding me, Lily. Yes, we have three other guests with us, writers-in-residence who are with us through October. You'll meet them this evening at dinner. Dr. and Mrs. Boone and Mr. Drake Dodson. Dr. Boone is a professor at Colorado State, and he's on sabbatical doing research here and writing, and Mr. Dodson is working on a film script. They are staying in the north wing in the Remington and Wyeth suites. Their schedules vary, but they are often away for the day and back in the evenings. You will see them around, but we will be spending most of our time in the art studio."

Lily, in black stretch pants, a black turtleneck, and a bright reddish-orange jacket almost the color of her shoulder-length, frizzy curls, interrupted. "Only the finest art studio this side of Chicago. But that will be only part of your art experience. We'll be making some day trips and going out to the mountains for plein-air painting. All of you will go home with a new work of art."

"Wait." Bea stood from her dining chair, barely five feet tall and a hundred pounds. "I'm not here to paint. I'm here to dance." She looked at the colonel, who was almost her height while seated, and lifted her arms gracefully as though she was about to take flight. "That is why I'm here, Henry. Is it not? I'm the prima ballerina for *Giselle*."

Colonel Walton took her hand, encouraging her to sit. "My dear, you can dance any role you like, and I'll be there to watch."

Maude marveled at how well the colonel had adapted to Bea's behavior since last Christmas. He knew how to keep her calm and maintain her integrity. Maude joined him in reassuring the aged ballerina. "You're our guest, Bea. You may paint or dance or both."

She looked at her watch and then her notebook. "It's one forty-five. Now that all of you have your keys and your rooms are ready, why don't you find your spaces and get settled or take a short siesta. We will meet back in the great room at two thirty for Alo's walking tour of the inn and the property, and he will give you a bit of its history. It is such a perfect afternoon to enjoy the views and the breezes." Maude pointed to Alo. "I will tell you that Alo is more than a little knowledgeable about the plant and animal life around here, and we count on him as our resident meteorologist. For those of you who were with us last Christmas, you know how quickly the weather can change in these mountains, and Alo is here to keep us informed."

Maude noticed the familiar heads nodding in agreement.

"Then, at three thirty, Alo will bring you into the studio, where we'll spend a couple of hours getting ready for our painting session in the morning." She acknowledged Lita. "And Lita, what time is dinner?"

Lita stood from her chair. "Our dinner will be served promptly at six thirty right here in the dining room, with dessert and coffee following in the great room."

Before Maude could continue, Lily stood, fumbling with the neck of her shirt, and pulled out the sterling-silver whistle. "Now those of you who've traveled with me before know what this is. It's a whistle to get your attention. It can be heard for miles, and believe me, it will echo for a while within these adobe walls and open portales. When you hear it, gather in the great room. That's the big room we entered upon our arrival."

Maude caught Lily's glance and wink at Silas, and she didn't miss Lita's blaring eyes. "Well, Lily, perhaps, since we'll all be together most of the time, Lita's antique school bell will work just as well. It did just fine for lunch." She motioned for everyone to rise as her uneasiness forced her to add, "Oh, one last thing. You and your belongings are safe here, but since the inn is almost full, and sometimes we do have curious folks who just drop by, we ask you to keep your rooms locked at all times."

She purposefully looked at Alo. Not one of his facial muscles moved.

Chapter Five

Friday afternoon

Alo stacked the last piece of wood in the fireplace, closed the metal curtain, and sat in the adjacent wing chair to wait for the guests.

Colonel Walton and Bea were the first to arrive. Bea said, "I saw you. What were you doing to that fireplace? You shouldn't be playing with matches."

"No matches, Miss Beatrice. Only loading it up with wood for a fire after dinner tonight. The speed of the clouds coming from the north tells me it will be a cooler evening, and if I remember, you love warming yourself in front of the fire."

Alo snickered under his breath as he heard Bea whisper to the colonel. "And they think I'm nuts. This guy talks to clouds. They shouldn't let him near matches."

As the others began to gather, Alo invited them to take a seat. Lily was the last to arrive and was pulling her whistle from beneath her jacket as she entered the room. Alo announced, "No need for the whistle, Ms. Mayfield. They are all here just waiting for you."

"No need to wait. I'm ready to go." Lily stepped to center stage in front of the fireplace, grabbed the mantle for balance, and lifted her right leg. "What are we waiting for? I have on my new water-repellant hiking boots. I hope you all have on good walking shoes. No ballet slippers, Bea. I learned my lesson the last time I took a walk with Alo. Let's go."

Alo calmly stood. "We'll start our walk in just a few minutes, but I thought you would be more comfortable sitting as I first tell you about Grey Sage."

He waited for Lily to take a seat before he told them how Maude and Silas had moved to Santa Fe and bought the acreage with a small cottage on it. He described how Maude had sketched her dreams for the house's expansion and how he had helped make her dreams a reality with each expansion over the years.

"Maude's desire was to stay true to the culture of the area and to be good stewards of this land, and that meant constructing an adobe-style home. The original inhabitants of this area have been building these kinds of structures for six hundred years. Perfect structures for this climate. The inn is flat roofed, and its walls are built out of natural materials: earth, straw, and water, giving the walls their natural color that blends with the landscape. The outside walls I'll show you are in some places twenty-two inches thick."

Bea interrupted. "Twenty-two inches? Why, my waist is smaller than that. Once, when I was in Berlin, the male principal dancer said I had the smallest waist he ever—"

The colonel patted her hand. "Let's allow Alo to finish his story, Bea."

Alo placated her. "I'm certain with a waist that small, his hands could encircle you." He saw her head lift and her eyes close as though she was waiting for the music.

He began again. "The earthen walls are thick to provide cooler temperatures in the summer and warmer temperatures in the winter. The walls actually store the temperature. Even the interior walls are fourteen inches thick."

Alo acknowledged Maude with the nod of his head as

she entered the room and sat in her cuddle chair centered in front of the box window. He continued, "You'll see, as we walk around the structure, it appears to have a flat roof, but it is actually slightly angled so that water does not collect. Where we are here is considered high desert, but semi-arid. We get on average about fourteen inches of rain a year, but at this elevation we can get up to twelve feet of snow in the winter here at Grey Sage. This structure is built to insulate us from the extreme temperatures."

Noble interjected. "That's why you have such gorgeous trees here in spite of it being high desert."

"Yes," Alo responded. "We'll be seeing those trees shortly, and we are fortunate to have a running creek on the property. We will walk down to it. Some of the boulders in the creek bed have become favorite spots for our guests to spend a few quiet moments. The creek swells with the first thaw of the spring but can be bone dry in August. We've had more rainfall than usual this summer, so you'll see running water today."

He paused to look at his watch. "One last thing to note before we begin our walk. You'll notice that the house is a maze of portales, which are covered porches that connect the wings of the house. You'll see the handmade Saltillo tile floors continue throughout the house and portales, and the posts that hold up the roofs of the portales are actually trunks of trees that were cut down to clear this property for the building of this home. We have tried to be kind to the earth as we have built. The portales are a way of inviting the outside in. With all that said, let me invite you to follow me outside."

For the next half hour, Alo led the group around the property and answered their questions about the wildlife and plants. He pointed to the sagebrush. "That, my friends, is where Grey Sage got its name. It's an herb that has been used in this area for thousands of years for many things: to make dyes, for cleansing and purification ceremonies, and for good medicine. To this day, my mother makes a tea from the sagebrush to treat colds and headaches. It works. You might ask Maude about making her own paint pigment from the sage. It's her signature color."

He led them down to the creek, showed them the bridge where Kent and Emily had had their wedding, and pointed out the boulders downstream. They then walked back up the hill to the inn and through the portales to the studio. He entered through the outside doors. "Maude, they're all yours now. I promised to tell them more about the pines and aspens when we take them out for their plein-air painting excursion. Thank you, my friends, and I will see you at dinner."

His duty done, Alo walked down to the creek, removed his shoes, and walked in ankle deep water over smooth stones to his favorite boulder. He needed the solitude. He belonged to this land. On his human journey, this land was his home away from heaven, where his soul felt at peace and where he could hear God whisper in the trees. The place he never wanted to leave and the place he longed for when he was away. His memories spoke to him here: Catori's laughter, Doli's singing, Elan's questions, Lita's hand comfortably in his, evenings with Maude and Silas in front of the fire. Retelling their story to the guests had reminded him that he belonged here. He would not allow anyone to disturb the serenity of the life they had built here. He perched himself comfortably on the boulder and pulled his harmonica from his pocket and began to play.

For the next half hour, Maude and Lily distributed easels and canvases and dispensed paints, brushes, and palettes. Maude made certain everyone was comfortable with a stool and their workspace. "It's Friday, and in less than a week, you'll have finished a landscape to take home with you."

"Where are the aprons, Maude?" Lily asked.

With a paint brush in her hand, Maude pointed to the closet in the corner. "They are folded on the bottom shelf. But I don't think we'll paint this afternoon. The light is fading, and there is so little time. Maybe we should talk about getting our palettes ready for tomorrow."

"Fine. But I'm going to work. Something about this place rouses my creative notions. You can do the talking." Lily pranced across the room with a stack of aprons, practically tossing them to the participants and keeping one for herself. "Let me show them how I get started."

Maude had some idea of how this would turn out; this wasn't her first time hosting one of Lily's groups. "At your pleasure, Lily." As Lily took over, Maude perched on her swivel stool, prepared only to make comments when Lily let her pencil breathe. In silence, all except Bea sat comfortably waiting for Lily's magic.

Lily was sketching from memory. The entrance to Grey Sage, its double wooden doors and the shutters on the adjacent windows, even the clay urns on the corners of the porch landing, began to appear on the canvas. In only minutes, the scene was recognizable. Maude had always known Lily's talent was remarkable.

Through the open doors Maude heard the faint wistful moan of Alo's harmonica. She became absorbed in watching Bea, who could not have shown any less interest in Lily's talent. Bea was putting on her pinafore apron, wrapping the ties in the back around her waist and tying them in the front. Then she assumed fourth position, feet and arms, with perfect posture and her nose held high as though she was centering herself. Maude knew this because her own mother had been determined that her West Texas children would be cultured. That meant ballet lessons for Maude. After two years, Maude had convinced her mother she was more comfortable in boots and jeans and on a horse. She was far too gangly for tutus. Her mother forgave her when she started painting.

Bea then moved with grace and intention into a new position. Her right leg was perfectly extended in front of her with her petite foot elegantly pointed and slightly touching the floor. Her chest expanded, as though she had taken a deep breath and held it, and her head was held high, tilted to the back. Her eyes were closed. Her lower arms disappeared behind her back.

Degas. Right before her eyes, Bea had become Degas's statue *Little Dancer, Aged Fourteen*. Maude had purchased a bronze replica at the Metropolitan Museum of Art, and it stood in Bea's suite.

No longer engrossed in Lily's sketching, Maude sat lost in thoughts about the world where Bea lived. Alo's harmonica in the far-off background accompanied her random thoughts and Bea's artistic movements. How real was this imaginary world to Bea? Was dance so much of who she was that it was all she had left? Wherever Bea was, she seemed happy there.

Maude heard Lily. "And into which painting did you wander off to, Maude? I called you three times."

Maude apologized. "Actually, I was in another world, thinking of a statue I once saw. All artists do that, you know—wander off into our own spaces. The ones who paint. The ones who dance. The ones who write. And the ones who make music. The right sides of our brains offer us an alternative world where time doesn't matter, and most of us wish we could live there."

"I don't need you getting all philosophical on me. I was only asking you to tell the group how you make your signature color—grey sage."

"Oh, so now you're asking me to be a chemist. Actually, I've tried a number of methods. I start by gathering the sage leaves when I think they're at their height of color before the winter sets in. I have been known to strip the bushes of their leaves before the first freeze. There are methods of making paint such as boiling the leaves to extract the color, and I often do this with other plant material. But I have found that drying the sage leaves and grinding them into powder works better to achieve the color I want."

Laura Sutton waved her hand.

"Yes, Laura?"

"How on earth do you dry that many leaves?"

"You need to know this because you have gardens of flowers and herbs, all good for pigment making. To answer your question, I use food dehydrators and dry them slowly. When all the moisture is extracted, then I grind the dried leaves in a food processor. And sometimes I actually use a mortar and pestle to get the finest powder. Then I add a binder to make the paint the consistency I prefer."

Laura nodded. "Thank you. I might try that."

"Grey sage is my signature color. We'll be painting with it tomorrow." She turned to Lily. "With your permission, we'll get started. I have a display of landscape photographs here on the table. Most of the photos were taken here at Grey Sage or just a few miles away, and they were taken at this time of year, when the fall colors are at their peak. I'd like each of you to choose the one you'd like to paint. And today, let's get some initial sketching done on the canvas, put some paint on our palettes, and tomorrow we start painting."

Lily announced, "Once we get an initial layer of paint on the canvas, then weather permitting, we'll do some detail and color correction when we do the plein-air painting. Nothing like painting outside in the natural sunlight, especially here in the high desert and the mountains where the air is so clear and we're closer to the sun."

"Lily's right. We will take you to a clone of aspens like you've never seen. And Alo says the weather will be kind to us: warm, sunny, breezy autumn days where the sun is slanting at a marvelous angle. You've come at a perfect time." Maude stood from the stool where she was sitting. "Choose your photos, and then Lily and I will be available to assist or answer any questions.

"One last thing, Maude. What's on the large easel in the corner draped in black velvet?"

"If I told you, it would spoil my surprise. It will be revealed a bit later. For now, let's get busy putting something on these canvases."

The studio buzzed with activity as the six chose their photos. Maude was observant of the way they selected their favorites. Laura picked up several photos and walked around holding three in front of her face as if pacing would make her decision. Reba picked up every photo, scrutinized each one, and then chose the first one she saw. Sarki stood, arms folded in front of her, scanned the entire table without touching one photo, and then reached for one of the red cliffs.

Maude knew Henry had never picked up a paintbrush, but as a colonel would be, he was thoughtful and decisive and chose one that he was likely to be successful at painting. Bea fretted like an overly stimulated child. She loudly announced her displeasure that none of the photos had pink flowers. Maude promised to find her a photo with pink milk glass and peonies.

Noble stood back like a gentleman and waited until the others had chosen, then he sorted and arranged the remaining photos in a fashion that only he understood. His calculated choice was one with a mature ponderosa pine as its focal point and a stream in the foreground.

The way her guests chose revealed something about each of them. Maude anticipated how each of them might approach the canvas.

In moments, pencils moved across canvases, and Maude flowed from one easel to another to assist. Another hour passed before she announced it was time to stop and get ready for dinner. She found something positive to say about each canvas as they put their pencils away.

"Casual dress for dinner at six thirty in the dining room. Lita will be serving our traditional welcome dinner this evening." She paused. "I can promise it will be something you will request again before you leave."

Maude refreshed herself before joining Lita in the kitchen. The Grey Sage casseroles were out of the oven, and Lita checked the buffalo chicken under the broiler. Maude walked over and introduced herself to Tanzi, who was just an older version of her sister Kyah. "We're so glad you could help us out. Having guests with special dietary needs means extra work for Lita."

Tanzi wiped her hands and extended one to Maude. "It is my pleasure, Mrs. Thornhill. I have a lovely dinner prepared for Ms. Hansen, and Mrs. Loloma has introduced me to her signature casserole. Quite a hearty and zesty dish."

Lita, wearing her striped apron in Southwest colors, spoke. "Tanzi, please call me Lita, and please get the salads on the plates. And Maude, go ring the bell before Lily uses the whistle and I have to hang her from the barn rafters."

"Yes, Lita. I think most of them have assembled in the great room and are ready to come and take their seats."

Maude stepped into the doorway between the dining room and great room and rang the bell gently. The guests filed passed her and took their seats, leaving the seats at the ends of the table empty.

Silas was last through the doorway. He handed Maude the name tags for the late guests and whispered to her, "Alo just spoke with our writers. The time got away from them, but they are back and getting ready for dinner."

Maude watched the guests, wearing the name tags Kyah had made, take their same seats as lunch. This was a phenomenon that never failed. They left empty seats at the opposite end of the table from Maude and Silas. Maude laid the name tags like place cards at the empty places and announced, "Our writer friends were out for the day, but they have returned and will be joining us momentarily. Tanzi, our chef in training, will take your drink orders while we wait."

In only moments, the other guests entered the dining room, and Alo directed them to their seats. Dr. Boone and his wife were smartly dressed for dinner, and Drake looked as though he'd been riding on the back of a garbage truck all day. With drinks, fresh bread, and salad delivered to the table, Silas stood and said his customary grace.

"Lord, we pause to give thanks as we sit at a bountiful table to enjoy what You have provided. And thank You for these friends who have come to Grey Sage. Now we ask that You nourish our bodies with the bounty and our souls with the beauty that surrounds us. Amen."

Hushed amens echoed around the table.

Silas sat. "It is always good to give thanks for such bounty, and bounty it is when Lita serves her Buffalo Chicken and Grey Sage Casserole. You'll know you're in Santa Fe when you taste her cooking."

As if on cue, Lita entered with Tanzi at her side. "Thank you, Silas. We prepare meals that you'll talk about once you leave Grey Sage. Tonight, we begin with a salad of romaine lettuce, avocado, pickled beets, and jicama, drizzled with homemade bleu cheese dressing with bleu cheese crumbles. And there are always baskets of freshly made bread and rolls on the table. The salad will be followed by Broiled Buffalo Chicken, Grey Sage Casserole, and steamed broccoli."

Lily mouthed off sarcastically. "You might as well tell everyone what's in the casserole, Lita, and we know you don't give out your secret ingredient."

Maude saw Lita's forced grin and watched Sarki to see if she turned green as Lita listed the ingredients. "That would be a mixture of summer squash and zucchini, onions, garlic, tomatoes, chili peppers, homemade and fried tortilla strips, a splash of homemade salsa, and a dash of my secret ingredient, all smothered in cheese and baked until the bubbles appear."

Noble was the first to speak and surprised Maude. "Then I'd say bring it on."

"Momentarily, sir. And for dessert, we'll be serving cinnamon coffee, an assortment of teas, and Butterscotch Icebox Cake to cool your palate. Alo will light the fire so that you can enjoy your dessert in the great room."

Forty-five minutes later, Boots announced that dinner had been lip-smacking good, and everyone moved to the great room, staking out their favorite seats. After dessert and coffee, Maude stood from her chair. "Since we'll be spending the next week together, sharing meals and this home, I'd like for us to get to know each other. So, I'm asking you to answer these three questions to help us learn something about you. Please tell us where you grew up, who or what influenced you most to enter your profession, and then name the person you'd most like to spend an evening with for quiet conversation. That person can be living or not. Colonel, would you go first?" Not knowing exactly what to expect, her hope was that Henry would be the best model and that these strangers just might share some experiences over the next few days that would encourage them to become friends.

The responses, questions, and more responses went on for almost an hour and a half. So many interesting answers—and possibly the most interesting was Bea's responses. Maude thought she was the most lucid she had ever seen her. And Drake's answers were surprising and helped Maude view him differently.

As the evening crept toward an end and the flames fell to embers, Boots, who had made sure everyone knew he preferred his nickname over being called Dr. Boone, spoke. "I'm sorry, I almost forgot to tell you, Maude. After yesterday morning's fiasco in the library, Drake and I finally got our papers back in order and our books stacked again. Nothing was missing, but I did find one paper that wasn't ours. It had a rather unusual drawing on it, a Native American symbol, I think. I assumed it was yours since you're the artist around here, so I left it on the table in the library. All our books and papers have been moved to our rooms, so your other guests have use of the library. Just watch out for the disgruntled spirit in there." Boots laughed heartily.

Maude wanted to stuff his mouth with the nasty hand-kerchief Drake had been using for days, but she said, "Thank you, Boots." She could remember no such drawing. But she saw Alo leave the group and walk down the hallway leading to the library.

Bea spoke loudly, "What fiasco in the library? What disgruntled spirit? Are we in danger?"

Maude quickly spoke to calm Bea. "Nothing for you to worry about, Bea. The window was left open in the library, and some of the professor's papers got blown around. But I can assure you all the windows are closed and latched."

Silas joined Maude. "I wish for all of you a good sleep. There will be fresh coffee and tea available at six-thirty. And Lita has said a hot breakfast will be served at seven-thirty. Sleep well, my new friends."

Maude heard the continuing conversations as they left the room. She knew there would be no sleep for her until she found Alo and saw the drawing.

Chapter Six

Saturday morning

Alo, even more watchful after picking up the drawing in the library last evening, came in from making his early-morning rounds to check the property. Nothing out of the ordinary. All was well. He heard chatter in the dining room. Early risers for coffee. Lily, Reba, and Sarki were standing in front of the urn and already gulping the morning elixir.

"Looks like you ladies are dressed for a hike. Weather's perfect. A breezy fifty-five degrees, and the sun is just above the horizon."

Lily, dressed in leopard-skin jogging pants and jacket, held her mug in both hands and sniffed the aromatic steam. "Finally, a hot cup of coffee, and it doesn't taste like a bakery chef baked it. I can't understand why anyone needs to adulterate good black coffee with cream and sweetener and cinnamon."

Sarki grinned. "There are some things that simply don't need your understanding, Lily, nor your opinion. Drink up, and let's go. I don't want to miss breakfast."

Alo added, "Lily, you know the hiking trails around here, but I might suggest the one that parallels the arroyo this morning. Foliage is at its peak. The trail is well-worn and clearly marked. Can't get lost. Just go to the wooden bridge down the hill and walk about three-quarters of a mile east. You'll see the sign where you'll cross the creek and hike back home on the other side. By the time you're crossing the bridge again, breakfast will be ready. Enjoy."

He returned to the kitchen as the ladies left through the front door. Maude and Lita were preparing breakfast, and Silas, drinking his second cup, was seated on the stool at the kitchen island.

Alo went to the coffee bar for his second cup. "Just saw Lita, Reba, and Sarki in the dining room having coffee. They're off for a morning hike."

Lita stood at the sink, looking out the large windows. "I see them. Lily looks like a malnourished cat, except for that orange, fleecy mane looking like a bramble bush aflame. That hair is as untamed as she is." She laughed loudly. "Would you look at that? Sarki Malarkey and Reba are pointing east and Lily's pointing west."

Alo joined her to look. "I told them to go east. Surely one of the three will look for the sunrise." He put his mug on the counter. "Maybe I should go and give them better directions."

"Drink your coffee," Maude answered as she cut up the fresh pineapple. "They'll figure it out."

Lita laughed again. "I'm not so sure. Lily's headed across the bridge by herself."

Silas looked over the newspaper. "What's new? Lily has never been one to take directions or do the conventional."

Alo picked up his mug and stood at the window, watching as Lily turned around and almost sprinted across the bridge and up the trail to catch up with Sarki and Reba. "I'd give a good cigar to hear that conversation."

He heard the bells on the mudroom door and turned to see who was entering so early. Kyah walked through the mudroom into the kitchen, holding long-stemmed pink roses wrapped in paper. "Good morning, everyone. I came a little early."

Maude replied. "And good morning to you, Kyah. I hope you'll join us for breakfast. We have plenty, and I'll fix you a plate."

"I will, and thank you, ma'am. I hope you don't mind that I brought roses for Miss Bea. You said she loved flowers. I went down to the fence row to look for some sweet briar roses, but no blooms."

Lita nodded. "Even if they're wild, it's too late for rose blooms in these mountains. They need lots of sunlight and warmth."

"Yes, ma'am, but the leaves were red and burgundy, almost as pretty as the roses in the spring." Kyah hesitated. "Miss Maude, I know you said you have a budget for flowers and special things we do for our guests. I hope it's okay that I bought these. They're sure to put a smile on Miss Bea's face. I'll leave them as a surprise for her when I clean her room this morning. I'll go and get a vase from the closet."

Maude sliced the bananas over the crystal bowl of fresh pineapple as Kyah left the kitchen. "That is one sweet girl. She will make some man a happy husband one of these days."

Alo grinned. "Just like you and me, Silas. Happy husbands. Don't you agree?"

"Why, we'd tie for first prize in the Satisfied Husband contest."

Kyah returned to the kitchen with the vase and picked up the flowers from the counter. "I'll arrange these in the butler's pantry." She started to walk away and then turned. "Miss Maude, I almost forgot again. Things have been so busy around here, and I keep forgetting. Did a Mr. Taylor call you about booking the inn for a retreat?"

Maude paused. "No, I don't recall anyone by that name calling to book a retreat. I've had no calls this week. What makes you think he would ring?"

Alo looked at Kyah. She lifted her head and squinted her eyes as if trying to remember. "I think it was Tuesday. You had gone to town to mail some packages, and I was here alone, getting things ready for the retreat. I didn't hear the bell, but there he was, standing in the great room when I walked through. When I asked if I could help him, he told me his name and said he had just dropped by to take a look. At first I thought he wanted a room for the night, but I told him that the inn was not really like a hotel, that it was only for special groups who were here for planned retreats. He said he was looking for a place to host a retreat and asked if he could look around."

Alo frowned. "What do you mean 'look around'?

"He wanted to see the rooms. So, I showed him a couple of the suites and the library and the dining room. He asked about the retreats, and I told him about the writers who are here and the artist retreats Miss Maude has. He had seen Dr. Boone and Mr. Drakeford working in the library. He wanted to see the studio, so I showed him that. Then he left and said he would be in touch. I gave him a brochure. I guess he wasn't so interested after all."

Maude answered, "Maybe he prefers something a bit more modern with better meeting facilities with all the latest technology."

"He did ask about Internet and security. I told him that he would need to speak with you or Alo about that."

Alo's curiosity was rising. "Did this Mr. Taylor leave a card?"

"No, sir. He just said he would be in touch."

"If he's interested, he'll give us a call," Maude said. "You did the right thing."

"Yes, ma'am." Kyah left the kitchen.

"Do you think we need a fire in the great room this morning?" Alo asked.

Maude shook her head. "I don't think so. It's not that chilly. And besides, Lily's group will be in the studio all morning, and our writers will either be gone for the day or in their suites. And if they're staying in for the day, I invited Mrs. Boone to the studio if she would like to join us. No sense in building a fire if there's no one to enjoy it."

Alo took the last swallow of his coffee. "Then I'll just go and clean out the fireplace and get it ready for this evening."

He went straightway to the butler's pantry to grill Kyah. "Kyah, tell me what this Mr. Taylor looked like. I think I might have run into him."

"He was Native American, maybe about thirty-five. He wasn't dressed like a businessman. Jeans with a silver and turquoise belt buckle. I remember that belt buckle. Unusually large."

"Size?"

Kyah held up both hands, touching thumbs and forefingers to form a circle.

"Not the belt buckle. The man."

Kyah glanced at Alo. "A little larger than you. Maybe six feet, but really slim. Short dark hair."

"No. I don't think I've seen this man." Alo wasn't lying, but he wasn't entirely truthful about his questions. He disliked this feeling.

As he walked away, Kyah spoke up again. "Oh, he was carrying this leather pouch or a wallet, like something a lady would carry. I thought it odd since he was so manly."

Alo found that unusual as well but kept walking. "Could have been his phone or a calendar."

In the great room, Alo opened the fireplace chain curtain and shoveled the ashes from last night's fire into the tin bucket. A few minutes into his task, Henry and Bea walked arm in arm into the room as if they were entering a ballroom and about to dance the first waltz. "Good morning, Sir and Miss Bea. I hope you had a good rest."

"Indeed, I did," the colonel replied. He looked down at Bea. "And what about you, Bea? Did you sleep well?"

"Like a princess on a silk pillow."

Alo stood with the bucket and closed the fireplace curtain. "Glad to hear it. Coffee's ready in the dining room, and breakfast will be served shortly. I'll leave you. I must get a load of wood for this evening. Cooler weather later today as a front moves in. Maybe even a shower."

Alo walked through the kitchen on his way to empty the bucket and get wood.

"Alo," Maude said. "I looked in the library last night for the drawing Boots mentioned. I didn't see it. By chance, did you pick it up?"

Alo had always been as straight as an arrow with Maude, always truthful, never hedging or hiding anything. He knew she was on high alert, just as he was, but neither had confessed it to the other. "I did. It didn't look like anything of importance or value, so I just picked it up."

"Oh. Was it something I sketched?"

He headed toward the mudroom. "No, it was nothing like your penciled drawings. Just trash. Probably was just mixed in with all the writers' papers, maybe some of Drake's doodling. Looked like stick figures."

Alo was out the door before she could ask him any more questions. Although he'd had a soul-struggle in deciding, he had chosen not to tell Maude that the sketch was in his back pocket, neatly folded and next to the paper he had found with the axe. When he knew more and could offer a solution, he would tell Lita, Maude, and Silas the truth—the whole truth. But for now, he had no truth to tell. Their quartet had always operated in harmony, but with these suspicious secrets, he'd chosen to go solo.

The sliding glass doors of the studio were open on both sides, and the autumn aromas drifted through, mixing with the smells of paint and turpentine and drifting out again. Maude passed over the opera recordings and chose a recording of her favorite Native American flute player to fill the hollow space while they painted. The flute's warbling sounds resonated throughout the studio. These enchanting sounds were another way to introduce the retreatants to the culture of the high desert and its people.

The artists filed in and went to their stations, which had been left clean and ready from their work yesterday. After a few moments of instruction and encouragement from Maude, they became quiet and absorbed, seemingly mesmerized by the music, the refreshing breeze, and the act of creating.

Lily had positioned a large canvas on a standing easel in the corner away from the others who were working with smaller canvases on tabletop easels. Maude watched as Lily painted copious swaths of bold colors with a broad brush. She remembered watching Lily for the first time when they were in college. Her friend still painted with the same abandon and passion, but now with a noticeable tremor. She would ask her about that later when the time was right. Lily's reactions through the years had taught her the importance of timing.

Some of the artists held their chosen photograph in one hand and sketched with charcoal pencils. Some of them had already begun to block in the painting with color. Maude wandered around the studio observing what each was doing and disturbing the silence only with a low whisper when one needed a bit of direction. To Reba, she said, "Remember, start with the darkest color when you begin blocking in the painting. The dark shades will create the shadows." And to Henry, "Dark colors for shadow, but not black. Try the dark green."

Maude drifted around the room like the breeze. After observing the way each had chosen their photos, Maude had concluded accurately how they might approach the canvas. She pointed to the trunk of the ponderosa pine on Noble's canvas. "Try softening the edges. Not such harsh, hard lines. The eye will do what it needs to do." She was not surprised at Sarki's ease with the process. She watched Laura struggle as she drew, erased, and drew again.

For Bea, Maude had set up a still life of pale pink peonies and silvery green foliage in a pink milk glass vase on a draped piece of dark-blue velvet. She had sketched it quickly and prepared a palette with the colors Bea needed. She watched Bea examine the silk petals.

"With that weird music, and the birds, and the wind blowing, I feel like I'm in a teepee on the Indian Reservation," Bea exclaimed loudly. "And pray tell, how am I supposed to paint these? They're not even real flowers. Just look at them."

Maude tried to dissuade her. "Well, Bea. Use your imagination and your brush and those beautiful paints to make them look real. I even gave you some of my grey sage paint." She pointed to the glob of green paint on Bea's palette. "See, it's there. It will make the Dusty Miller look so real."

Bea looked puzzled. "Who is this Dusty Miller? And why does he need to look real?"

"Dusty Miller is the name of this plant. Oh, I think it's also called Silver Dust." Maude took a stem of it from the vase. "But this is real. I cut it fresh from my garden this morning. I plant it because it's so beautiful with the sage bushes, and the feathery nature of this will give a contrasting texture next to the peonies."

Bea put down her paint brush. "I cannot paint those peonies. I told you, they are not real. I might as well be painting the white towels on the bed in my room. I've never seen towels and washcloths folded into flowers. And why would they not be in the bathroom where towels are supposed to be?"

"Oh, Kyah does that. She folds them into flowers and sometimes animals. Isn't she so talented?"

"Talented? And I suppose that's why my toilet paper looked like a leaf."

Maude patted Bea's hand. "Yes. She folds the toilet tissue into all kinds of interesting designs too."

"Well, you should warn your guests. I dried myself off with the shower curtain, and I'm just thankful that girl didn't do something weird with the box of tissues." Bea swiveled slightly on her stool in Maude's direction. "And maybe you should just give her some more work to do if she has time to do such strange things with towels and toilet paper."

Maude suppressed her giggle. "You know, Bea. You're right. But Kyah is young, and she takes pride in making our guests feel special." Maude pointed to the canvas. "Why don't you start with the blue velvet cloth? I wish I had a ballet slipper with pink ribbons. Don't you think a ballet slipper would be so interesting right there underneath the peonies?"

Bea hopped down from her stool. "Ballet slipper? You want a ballet slipper? I'm sure I have my ballet slippers in my suite. I'll go and get them."

Before Maude could stop her, Bea was off, almost floating in the air to the hypnotic Indian flute melody, her graceful arms looking as though she was about to take flight and her petite body gliding to the flute's rhythms. She looked twelve, and she looked eighty-five, all at the same time.

Maude looked at her watch. "Where has the morning gone? I suppose it has blown southward with the breezes. Time to clean up a bit and get ready for lunch. This afternoon, we will move from the walls of this studio to the outside and do some plein-air painting. Alo says we may get showers late this afternoon, so let's get started at two o'clock."

As Alo predicted, the temperature dropped, and the clouds became heavy and dark around four o'clock, meaning the plein-air painting experience was curtailed early. The painters rallied quickly to get everything inside before the rains came.

Maude did not mind the change, for serendipitous plans had developed for the evening. An earlier dinner and unexpected entertainment. Alo had told her days ago that Kyah was a gifted singer. When she asked Kyah to stay after dinner and play her guitar and sing, she also learned from Kyah that Clara Boone was an award-winning storyteller. She was impressed that Kyah was so congenial with their guests.

After lunch, Maude had privately invited Clara to share a story with all the guests after dinner, and Clara had agreed. Singing and storytelling around the fire on a raining Saturday evening would make up their program for the evening. Maude was more tired than usual and looked forward to sitting next to Silas in the cuddle chair and listening from the back of the room.

After a dinner of green enchiladas, rice with onions and

chiles, and jicama salad with fresh mango drizzled with a lime dressing, Maude whetted their appetite for the evening's entertainment and Lita's signature dessert of flan served cold with fresh blackberries and whipped cream.

The group was unusually chatty as they left their familiar seats around the table to take their familiar seats in the great room. Seating was an unspoken rule at Grey Sage. If you sat in a seat once, it was yours for the duration, and they all knew that the cuddle chair in the back next to the box window was off limits.

When everyone was comfortable, Maude formally introduced Kyah to the group. "Not only does Kyah use her creative abilities to keep your rooms lovely and refreshed, she plays the guitar and sings. I've asked her to sing for us tonight."

Bea interrupted. "That girl brought me roses today." Bea stood and looked around the room. "Did anyone else get roses?" When no one spoke, Bea sat down.

Maude watched the flush rise on Kyah's cheeks and rescued her. "No, Bea. Only you received roses this morning, but who knows about tomorrow?" She turned to Kyah and pulled the stool in front of the fireplace. "Now, Kyah, you're our songbird this evening."

Kyah sang a couple of familiar tunes and then led them for a sing-along of campfire tunes reminiscent of their childhoods. After the guests applauded, Kyah announced, "One more. This is one you've not heard before." She strummed the guitar, moving fluidly through minor chord progressions and plucking the E string as the constant and steady beat. She then closed her eyes and hummed a mournful sound similar to the warble in the flute recording Maude had played in the studio. When she opened her eyes, she began the ballad, a storytelling song about a river's journey.

Maude watched as Alo came to the edge of his chair and pulled his harmonica from his pocket. He joined Kyah with a spontaneous, haunting countermelody. She was watching creativity in its purest form, and for a few moments it was magical as these two seemed lost in the music. Kyah intoned the story as the harmonica, infused with acoustic guitar, reverberated through the room.

When they finished, the room was silent. No one moved and hardly breathed. Even Kyah's hands remained still on the guitar until the sound faded. She opened her eyes and looked at Alo. No smile. No nod. But there was communication, an indescribable knowing that these few moments they had created together had taken wing, never to return.

More applause. Maude knew Kyah had just achieved a new respect from their guests.

Kyah moved from the stool to the back of the room as Maude stood again. "What an incredible story we've just heard sung, and from such a beautiful voice." Already knowing the answer, she looked at Alo. "Have you been rehearsing with Kyah?"

Alo shrugged. "No. I've never heard the song, and I am supposing that it is original to Kyah. But it moved me, and we found a harmony, like the river and forest whose story she sang."

Maude was captivated. "It moved us all as we watched and listened. And we have another surprise this evening. It has come to my attention that Clara is a master storyteller—award-winning, I might add. We know that Boots is a distinguished professor doing research here for a new book, but it was a surprise to learn that Clara has national recognition for her storytelling. She has accepted my invitation to tell us a story this evening."

Alo stoked the fire as Clara joined Maude in front of the fireplace, which over the years had become center stage for such performances. As Maude moved back to her seat, Clara slid the stool to the side and came back to the center, standing with her head bowed and hands folded. When the room was as quiet as a secret, Clara raised her head, took two steps, and leaned forward as though trying to get nearer to the audience. She put her finger to her lips.

"Shhhhhh."

Silence. She looked around as though searching the room.

Again, "Shhhhh." Then softly, "Do you hear it? Do you hear the river? Do you hear the cooing dove? Listen. They are telling us their story."

For the next twenty minutes, Clara narrated through words and vocal expression her story of the river, an Indian mother and her daughter, and a rare white dove. Maude surveyed the room as Clara brought the story to a close. In the intimacy of this room, for more than twenty minutes, Clara had, like Kyah, held her listeners in the palm of her hand, engaging their senses, tugging at their emotions, and stirring their souls and their imaginations with her vivid descriptions and vocal expressions. Maude had heard the river, felt the whir of the dove's wings, smelled the porridge cooking on the Indian woman's open fire, and sensed the young girl's longing to fly away with the mysterious white dove.

Maude had been deeply moved by this evening's events—Kyah's singing and Clara's storytelling. This morning had given no notion of what a remarkable experience the evening would bring. Her heart smiled in thinking of the unexpected changes that had blown in, as if the rain knew what was to be.

She and Silas had always considered themselves stewards of this land, this inn, and the experiences people could have here. Not for the first time, Maude knew she had encountered the mystical and transcendent this evening. She would sleep and dream of the river, and the wind through the willows, and the white dove that fluttered its wings, leaving behind the gift of iridescent feathers, and then flew so high it was seen no more.

Chapter Seven

Sunday

Sunday was a different day at Grey Sage, and Maude offered no apology to their guests for that fact. Sunday had been a day of church-going since they were children, and she and Silas never let a retreat keep them from attending church, where Silas taught an early-morning Bible class. They always welcomed their guests to attend with them and yet made them feel comfortable to stay at the inn if they preferred.

Their Protestant church met in a historic mission a few miles away, with a congregation that welcomed members from miles around and travelers from all over the world. Silas taught in the chapel immediately following the early-morning worship service. Attending were the faithful members and, on most Sundays, an eclectic group of curious visitors and tourists filled the pews.

With the colonel and Bea, Lily, Laura, Reba, and Clara accompanying the Thornhills and the Lolomas to church, the van was nearly full. When Sarki and Noble announced they were staying behind to paint, Maude noticed that Lily's head spun, and her hair took on a certain bounce. She imagined Lily had some design on the retired banker and was therefore surprised when Lily didn't change her mind about going to church.

Boots and Drake planned to take a hike with their cameras. With some direction from Lita, Tanzi was left alone in the kitchen preparing brunch.

Maude regretted that Lita and Alo worked on Sundays during retreats, but she never asked Kyah to work and always explained to their guests that housekeeping would resume on Monday morning. She and Lita made it light on themselves by offering an early, self-serve continental breakfast and a buffet brunch at one o'clock. The evening meal was more like snack time with finger foods and always ended with a delectable sweet.

The morning drive was spectacular with color as they rode through the mountains to the church, nestled among the pines and cottonwood trees. Conversation affirmed that Maude was not the only one to recognize the rare gift of last evening's singing and storytelling. Clara told them how she'd gotten into storytelling years ago. Reba informed them that Emily had called with the news she and Kent were still in Albuquerque and would not be able to drive up for the day after all.

"You all seem to know Emily and Kent, but who are they?" Clara inquired.

Reba answered. "Oh, Emily is my daughter. She and Kent met here last Christmas when we were on another trip with Lily. Emily was with me, and Kent had returned from Afghanistan after being wounded and was traveling with his parents. Seems all of us for one reason or another were avoiding Christmas at home. Being stranded at Grey Sage during a snowstorm gave those two time to fall in love."

Clara smiled. "I can certainly understand how that happened."

"It did, and I couldn't be happier. About a month ago, they were married at Grey Sage in a picturesque ceremony on the bridge crossing the creek. And then Kent was transferred with the military down to Albuquerque. I do miss Emily. They were hoping to drive over today and show us all the wedding pictures, but his duty calls."

"I am so sorry that you won't get to see them," Clara responded. "It is a shame to be so close and miss the opportunity."

"Oh, I'm not missing that chance. I'll be going down to spend a few days with them when the group returns to Chicago."

Maude knew without looking that Lita's eyes were rolling and that she was likely itching to say something about newlyweds not needing a guest. She was grateful for Lita's silence.

Two hours later, after worship and Bible study, Alo drove them back to the inn. They rolled out of the van with Maude's instructions to get comfortable and ready for brunch, which would be set up on the portale outside the great room.

Even with serving themselves at the buffet table on the portale, the gang returned to their same places at the dining table. When everyone was seated, Silas asked them to bow their heads while he gave thanks.

As soon as the amen was pronounced, Reba spoke. "Silas, let me say again how much I was inspired by your lesson this morning. I never knew two words could stir so much thought and discussion."

Silas, about to take his first bite, held his fork above the pasta salad on his plate. "I suppose it depends on the two words," he replied thoughtfully.

Unlike her usual buttoned-up behavior, Reba leaned forward and propped her elbows on the table. "As a counselor, I deal with people's emotions all day long. That's why they come to see me. But somehow, I was moved by the fact that Jesus wept. I've read that scripture many times, but today it seemed to jump off the page."

"It's amazing how scripture does that sometimes," Maude added, "almost becoming three-dimensional as we view the scene."

Reba, who rarely showed any excitement, was more animated than usual. "I suppose it's reasonable that the human part of Jesus grieved the death of his friend, Lazarus. But I recall that you said the Bible mentioned two other times when Jesus wept. You didn't elaborate then. Would you care to now? I'm interested to know more about Jesus's emotions."

Silas put his fork down beside his plate. "First, let me ask our other guests if they mind if we continue our morning's discourse at the table. Anyone prefer that we continue this discussion after lunch?"

Only Boots spoke. "I'd be most interested to hear it myself, but could you speak a little louder?"

Before Silas could begin, Boots continued. "I know the story about Lazarus. Now, I don't claim to have any theological knowledge, but before you tell us about the other two times, I find it most interesting that Jesus knew He had the power to raise Lazarus from the dead and that Lazarus would live again. So why would He cry?"

Clara turned to Boots. "If you had been with us this morning, you wouldn't be asking that question."

Silas patiently answered. "That is a good question, Boots. I do notice in this story, when Jesus arrives to find Mary and Martha—Lazarus's grieving sisters—and all their grieving friends who had gathered, He didn't tell them not to cry. He didn't tell them not to be sad. Instead, He was moved in His spirit and cried with them. Perhaps Jesus's tears say something to us about the heart of God. The Bible doesn't tell us specifically what caused Jesus to weep, but He saw their sorrow and heard their sobs. If God is a compassionate God—and I believe Him to be—then would He not be moved by the tears of those He loves?"

"But that was just Jesus in this story," Boots stated emphatically. "Now, you're talking about God."

Maude watched a knowing smile ease across Silas's face. "Boots, where I come from there is no 'just Jesus.' There is only one God, and I can't explain the mystery, but Jesus was God, fully divine and fully human. And therein, my friend, is where rational explanations end, and our faith begins."

Maude observed the difference in Silas's peaceful demeanor and the bewildered look on Boots's face. Their visages pictured the difference between faith and unbelief.

Reba spoke again. "Back to my question, what other times did Jesus weep?"

Silas turned to her. "Well, Reba, that's my lesson for next Sunday. Since you won't be here, I'll tell you. It's interesting that all three of these events were near the end of Jesus's life, a time, perhaps, during which He would do and say what was most important to Him. He compassionately wept over His personal friend Lazarus. And then you may recall Palm Sunday, when He entered Jerusalem knowing He was moving toward His death. He stopped to look out over the city, and He mourned for the people of Jerusalem. And then there was His cry of anguish in the Garden of Gethsemane as He prayed before He was taken away by the guards to jail." Silas paused. "But there was another time. When Jesus learned that His cousin, John the Baptist, had been killed, He left His disciples and He went alone to grieve. I have to believe that He shed tears in His grief then too."

"Thank you. I may want to get those scripture references from you later. To know that God grieves, whether it's for one or for many, says so much." Reba began to eat.

"Yes, it does," Silas responded. "Grief is not something distinctive to humans. We are created in God's image. For me that means we love, we create, we reason, and we grieve. I know when Maude and I lost our only son twenty-three years ago, our grief journey began, and it has not ended. Grieving is the price God pays for loving us, and it is the price we pay for loving too."

Silas looked at Maude. "Forgive me. I didn't mean to dispel the joy at this table. And forgive me for slipping into my teaching mode."

Drake, who rarely spoke, asked, "But you're a medical doctor. How do you reconcile this whole faith and science problem?"

Maude waited, knowing what was coming. This was not the first time Silas had been asked this question. She knew Drake was about to hear something to ponder over the afternoon.

"Well, my friend, for me there is no problem, nothing to reconcile. I learned enough in my first anatomy class to know we weren't blown here with stardust. The complexity and detail of the human body alone tells me there is a Master Designer. If science could explain, or even if it ever gets to the point it can explain everything physical in this world as we know it, we might know what and how. But wouldn't there still be questions?"

Drake spoke again, but not as loudly. "There'd be nothing left to question."

Wise Silas answered. "So, what you're saying is there'd be no 'why' questions like, 'Why am I here? Why will I only live a short time on this planet, and then what happens to me when I die? Why is it that good people suffer? Why did everything come into existence as it did?'" Silas waited, but Drake had no response. "Drake, science will never be able to answer those questions. I wish I had some profound words for you. I don't, but I will quote Albert Einstein, perhaps the most brilliant and famous scientist the world has ever known, who said, 'Science without religion is lame, religion without science is blind.' I don't know about you, but I don't really want to stumble around on this planet lame or blind."

Started by Lily, a light laughter rippled around the table before Bea spoke. "I'm with you, Silas." Then she turned and pointed her fork at Drake. "And to you, young man. I'm certain your mother taught you to shampoo and comb your hair better. And about your question, forget the *why* and the *how*. When you get down to it, there is really only one question." Silence reigned as everyone waited. Bea quipped, "Whodunnit?"

Even Drake laughed heartily. Maude breathed relief with the lightened moment. *Thank you, Bea. You got us out of this one.* She wondered if the diva really understood the profundity of what she had just said.

Maude and Silas rose from their nap and freshened up for the afternoon. It was understood that Silas always napped on Sunday after brunch, and lately Maude had begun to join him. As they walked from their wing, Maude could hear the chatter of conversations echoing through the open doors.

She saw Drake and Boots in the library and could hear Drake quizzing Boots about Indian burial grounds. Maude waved as they walked past the open door.

Silas took a left in the great room and headed toward the kitchen. "I need a cup of coffee, then I'm settling in for a while with the paper. If I'm needed, I'll be in my chair."

Maude walked down the hall. "I'm headed to the studio to see what's happening out there. Lita will be back in about a half an hour to make sure Tanzi's getting everything done for our supper. Tanzi's had a long day, so let her know I'll be back to help."

On the portale, she passed the colonel and Bea sitting with Clara, who was knitting with the baby yarn she'd purchased just days ago. Maude noted the progress and was certain Clara would be finished long before they left Grey Sage and would be handing this to Lita for her new grandbaby.

Maude stepped into the studio. The spinto soprano voice of Leontyne Price reverberated around the room. Lily, in the corner with her smock on and an orange bandana taming her hair, was painting to the rhythm of "Habanera" from the opera *Carmen*. Her painting was blocked out, and details were emerging.

Maude stopped and made quiet comments to Laura about her progress. Henry's and Bea's seats were empty. The colonel's painting indicated that he might not leave Grey Sage with a finished work of art, and Bea's still life of peonies was bare of color except for the blob of midnight blue underneath the vase. Her palette and brushes lay next to the painting. Maude picked them up and started to paint. Maybe Bea would just keep going in the next session, assuming she had painted the peonies.

Maude painted for a few minutes and then cleaned the brushes. She noticed Sarki and Noble had pulled their chairs a bit closer together and were conversing as they painted. Noble had made more progress than any of the others. His ponderosa pine now had distinguishable bark. She found a small brush for him and showed him how to use it to make individual pine needles. He was a quick study and talented with an artist's eye.

Sarki was having a more difficult time with the red cliffs in her photo. The blocking was done, but the colors were wrong. Maude advised, "Let's do the blocking of the cliffs over, and try starting with a dark, dark burgundy."

Sarki handed her the palette. "Burgundy? But the cliffs are more orange, like clay."

Maude mixed a bit of red, blue, and brown and returned the palette to Sarki. "True." She picked up the photograph and pointed. "Look at the crevices. What color are they?"

The look on Sarki's face was like a switch had been flipped. "Ah. I see now. Do I need to remove this orange and rust paint?"

"Not necessarily. Just layer it and paint over it with the darker color. This will be stunning if you get it right, and to help you get it right, we'll take you to see those cliffs tomorrow when they're reflecting the afternoon sun."

"Painting's like life, I've discovered," Noble noted. "It can be wonderful if you just get it right."

Sarki laughed. "Spoken like a banker who lives and breathes numbers. But there again, numbers are perfect. Unfortunately, in my experience, there are more shades of gray when dealing with human behavior. Life with good humans can be beautiful, and there's nothing uglier than life with humans that aren't so good."

Maude found her statement interesting. "And your line of work, Sarki?"

"Crime. Solving crimes and teaching others investigative techniques. That means studying deviants, psychopaths, and criminals too. As a former FBI agent, I've seen ugly."

"But surely sometimes crimes are committed by people who are basically good, and they just make a mistake."

"Crimes of passion or desperation, maybe," answered Sarki. "Like someone who steals money from one of Noble's banks to pay for his child's medical care because wealthy bankers have little concern for the needs of the poor."

Maude noticed that Noble never stopped painting when

he replied in a matter-of-fact tone. "Now, Sarki, that sounds a bit like an indictment, and an unfair one. Even so, I won't take offense. I know you've seen the darker side of life, but don't assume all wealthy people live on the dark side."

"You're right, Noble. I've seen the dark and ugly, and I've seen the better side, too, my friend. You helped me see that this morning."

Maude was curious. "And how did he do that?"

"Noble and I were the only ones here except for the girl in the kitchen preparing brunch. It was as quiet as a tomb in here, and we were painting when a young woman wandered into the studio. Looked surprised to find us, but Noble spoke with her. She was looking for help, said her car broke down on the highway and she needed to make a call. Noble found a phone, and the woman placed a call. She told Noble she didn't know how she would pay for repairs, and that she had to get back because she'd left her son in the car out on the highway where the car broke down. We didn't have a vehicle to help her, but I watched Noble pull three hundred-dollar bills from his wallet and give to the woman and send her on her way."

"That was generous of you," Maude responded, looking to Noble.

Sarki playfully bumped his arm. "So, forgive me, Noble, who was generous and noble after all. Your heart doesn't bleed green like most bankers."

Maude grinned. "We all bleed the same color when we're wounded, don't we?"

Noble nodded. "Well said, Maude."

"You two keep at it with your painting and make us see how beautiful the world can be."

In the late afternoon, Maude strolled quietly through the inn as the guests, usually in pairs, relaxed in the cozy chairs on the portales to enjoy the changing colors of the late-afternoon skies. She did not intrude on their conversations as she was quite at home with her own thoughts. The day had been an enjoyable one, with stimulating conversation and studio work. Except for church, the schedule had been more casual and less structured. Maude had found herself enjoying those days more and more in the last few months, and today gave her opportunity to observe her guests, one of her preferred pastimes.

Maude had welcomed hundreds of guests to Grey Sage over the last decades. Maybe a thousand, but she didn't keep those kinds of records. She had always believed that every visitor was supposed to be there at the time of their visit for a particular reason, and her assignment was to provide a space and time for the guest to discover that reason. She had seen lives changed after a visit to Grey Sage. Lives like Laura Sutton's, and Kent's and Emily's. She wondered which of her present guests' lives would be changed with this visit.

There was no official gathering after the light supper they all enjoyed. All guests were on their own to create their own entertainment. Maude assisted Lita and Alo with the cleanup. They'd sent Tanzi home with their compliments for her creations.

Night drew its curtains on the deep golds and corals of a spectacular sunset. The kitchen was clean and ready for breakfast, the house was quiet, and she and Silas now walked hand in hand to their private wing. She stopped and stood at the wall of windows in their bedroom, gazing at the night sky and listening to the last nocturne of the crickets. With cooler evening temperatures and their waning chirps, she knew winter would soon be knocking on their front door.

She felt the familiar weight of Silas's arm draped around

and over her shoulder. She turned to look at him. "Do you know what today is?"

"Our boy's birthday. Forty years ago today, in my excitement, I almost forgot everything I knew about delivering babies when Elan decided to come a week early. I held him when he entered this world and took his first breath, and desperate to find a pulse, I held his broken body when he left us. It was almost too much, Maude, but we've survived these twenty-three years."

"I wasn't sure you'd remember." Maude heard the melancholy in his voice.

"Even if I hadn't remembered, your face would have told me. Your face has always mirrored your heart, Maude."

"That obvious?"

"Yes. Reading your face is as revealing as using a stethoscope."

She shifted her weight a bit but continued to look into the opaque heavens. "So much was buried when we buried our boy. So many hopes and dreams. I wonder what he'd be doing now if he were still with us."

"He would be a doctor like his father. No question. He had the brains, the compassion, and the drive."

"Or maybe a medicine man. That boy lived so close to the earth. He knew every square inch of this land, treated his own bumps and scrapes with herbs and plants, and could have lived for days off the land just eating nuts and berries."

"Alo taught him all those things like he was passing that knowledge down to his own son. Our boy couldn't get enough information. We can be so proud of him. Elan risked his own life trying to save another. That's who he was. Fearless when someone else was in danger."

Maude slid from Silas's arm. "'A friend to many.' That's what his name meant." She walked toward the dressing area and pulled her nightgown from the drawer.

Moments later Silas stood beside her at the hammered copper sink and washed his face as she pulled the pins from the braided bun at the nape of her neck and began to brush her hair. "Quite timely, your lesson this morning, Silas. I think it was just for me."

He pulled the towel from its holder to dry his face. "And it was for me. I've been thinking about Elan and heaven all week while I studied. There's something comforting just knowing that God doesn't ask us to dry our tears and get on with it. This lesson reminds us we don't hurt and cry alone."

"That's why I thought the lesson was for me—to remind me that God sees my tears." She stopped brushing her long silver hair and looked at Silas. "Do you think when we see Elan again he will still be our sweet boy?"

"I don't have an answer for that one. We will know him, and he will know us. But I think it will be a different kind of knowing. In heaven, perhaps Elan is all that God ever intended him to be, and so we will be, and age won't matter."

"Something to ponder." Maude draped her long hair over her shoulder and braided it again. Her voice was almost a whisper. "Do you still cry?"

Silas's warm brown eyes became glassy. "Yes, I do. I miss him, Maude. I miss everything about him still. His infant cries, his little boyness, his sweaty blond curls, his delight with the electric train, the way his eyes fluttered when he was going to sleep... The conversations, teaching him to shave, that impish grin of his—that grin that looked just like you. I miss it all. I still miss our boy, and I know I always will."

"Would that grief were a disease that could be treated and cured." She walked to the bed and pulled back the covers.

Silas joined her, pulled back the comforter on his side of the bed, crawled in, and snuggled up next to her. "There's just no expiration date on grief, Maude. As long as there is love, there will always be grief. But what I hold onto, besides you, is that God is love, and He is eternal. That means love is eternal, but the best part is there'll be no tears in heaven."

"Yes. And really, Silas, we have grieved over many things, and we still do. Mostly the people we have loved who died, and especially our Elan. But we have experienced more than our share of love and beautiful moments of joy." She rolled over to kiss his cheek. "Good night, my love." Silence, and then under her breath, "Happy birthday, my sweet boy."

Chapter Eight

Monday morning
Santa Fe

After a breakfast of sweet-potato pancakes with sour cream and agave syrup, country ham, scrambled eggs, and fresh fruit, everyone was off to their scheduled activities. Maude and Lily and her group to the studio. Drake and Boots off to the university in Albuquerque for research. Clara to her knitting. The colonel and Bea to the library for reading. Silas to his morning walk. Kyah to the cleaning.

Lita was loading the dishwasher when Alo returned from the barn with an armload of wood. "More firewood?"

"It's a full day, and Maude said Clara had promised another story for the evening. I need to get the fireplace ready for tonight before I leave this morning."

"Leave for where?"

"Hardware store for more plastic tarp for the firewood that's coming later this week." Alo hated the ambiguity, but he was determined to keep things to himself until he had more information. After his morning trip to town, he hoped to have some answers. But more than his hoping to solve the mystery, he hoped that the reasons for his suspicions would not return. Last Wednesday, a missing axe. Thursday, the library in shambles. Friday, a configured pile of rocks at the front door. And two pieces of paper with cryptic symbols in his wallet. These occurrences had meaning. He just didn't know what they meant. Things had been quiet since Friday morning, maybe because of all the people and activity. But he feared this wasn't the end of it.

Alo headed to the great room, loaded the fireplace, and closed the screen. He walked hurriedly back through the kitchen and stopped long enough to kiss Lita's smooth cheek. "See you."

"Try to be back by lunchtime. Maude's counting on you to drive the group over to the cliffs this afternoon. They want to see the aspens, and they're planning to do some outside painting." Lita closed the dishwasher and dried her hands.

"Maude told me. I won't be long. Anything you need in town?"

"A bushel of sweet potatoes, a cow, and someone to churn the butter," she teased. "But Tanzi's picking up what we need on her way out here this morning. Better to leave the grocery shopping to her."

"That'll save me some time. I'm off." Alo walked out the mudroom door and headed to his truck. He saw Silas in the distance, walking up the hill to the barn and waving. He pretended not to notice, but before he could get into the truck, he heard Silas behind him.

"Where you headed this morning?"

Alo knew Silas never turned down a trip to the hardware store, so he skirted the issue. "Checking on some more firewood. Early winter on its way, and we're going through wood like Lita goes through butter. I'll be back before lunch." He quickly got in and cranked up the truck, backed out, and waved goodbye.

Twenty minutes later, Alo was at the hardware store for the tarp. He had purposefully not purchased the material to build the additional wood rack in case he needed another excuse to leave Grey Sage without suspicion.

When he had the tarp and was back in the truck, he pulled out his phone and called the Museum of Indian Arts and Culture to make certain Chooli was there today. He would not waste the drive across town if she wasn't. She answered his call and agreed to see him.

Alo drove to the museum, parked, and looked at his watch. He had no more than an hour. He entered the front door and was met by the same white-haired elder who had sat at the front desk on Friday. "Good Monday morning to you, my Hopi friend. You're getting to be a patron here at the museum. I knew you would return."

Alo approached the desk. "Yes, sir. I came to hear the story. I have spoken with Chooli."

Before he could say more, the elder nodded. "Yes, and she is expecting you. Follow me."

Alo followed the man, who shuffled down a short hallway to a meeting room.

"Take a seat unless you'd care to look at some of the artifacts. I'll let Chooli know you are here."

"Thank you."

The elder left, and Alo perused the room, its walls lined with shelves of books and photographs of indigenous people. That done, he sat down at the conference table and removed the two pieces of paper from his wallet. He unfolded the items and pressed the wrinkles and creases with the palm of his hand, trying to smooth the ragged edges made by the axe. This conversation had rumbled through his thoughts all weekend, and he was still uncertain as to how much he should reveal to Chooli in this visit. With only the symbol of the medicine man, he possibly could have escaped telling her the details. But with the new drawing, he wasn't so sure.

He turned both drawings over, facing the table. He would hold back and see how the conversation progressed.

Phyllis Clark Nichols

A few minutes later, Chooli, a short, heavy-set young woman obviously of Native American descent, entered the room and walked toward the table. "Mr. Loloma, I am Chooli." She extended her hand.

Alo shook her hand and nodded his head.

"Please, sit down. How can I help you?"

Alo sat on the edge of the seat. "First, thank you for seeing me on such short notice."

She settled back in her chair, her feet barely touching the floor. "Honovi told me when I arrived this morning that you would be calling today. He's usually right, so I wasn't surprised when you called."

"Yes, I spoke with him on Friday. He was helpful to me and suggested I return to speak with you." Alo paused. "Honovi? That means 'deer,' if I remember."

"Yes, 'strong deer.'"

"Let me say before I get started that I will gladly pay you for your time."

The shake of her head showed resistance. "I am here to help, Mr. Loloma. I am paid by the museum. But thank you."

"Please call me Alo. I understand, but perhaps I could make a contribution to the museum."

"Donations are always appreciated, but again not necessary. So how may I help you?"

Alo turned over the first drawing. "I am hoping you can explain the significance of this figure." He slid the paper toward her.

After an initial glance, she said, "Ah, the Eye of the Medicine Man." Alo noticed the immediate scowl.

"Yes, I know that, but I need to know more."

She picked up the paper and studied it in silence before she spoke. "This is a powerful symbol." She traced the outer lines and pointed with her index finger. "This outer diamond represents the universe, and these four corners are like North, South, East and West in the physical world. The inner diamond represents the Spirit world. Only the medicine man or shaman has knowledge of both worlds. And this center circle represents the eye of the shaman and his ability to see into both worlds, but especially the spirit world. The Shaman is believed to have unusual powers—powers to heal and even to see into the future."

"I understand."

She turned the paper over. "How did it come to be torn like this?"

He hesitated but sensed he needed to answer. "I found this held to an ancient oak by the blade of an axe. The axe cut deep into the trunk. It saddened my spirit to see the bleeding tree."

Her squinted eyes and drawn brow indicated that his decision to tell her was the right one. Alo cleared his throat and continued. "I am assuming this axe, the tree, and the drawing have some significance."

"I would agree. The tree could be significant, maybe a marker tree, but I would need to do further research."

"Yes, I know about message trees."

"Could only be symbolic, but then there's the color red. Many of the Native American geometric symbols are most often seen in black or in black or silver if used in jewelry." She handed him the paper.

"If you think the red is significant, what does it mean?"

"Red often means the life force or blood. Even power. Young warriors would paint their faces and their horses red before going into battle."

"Red for blood."

"Historically. But today, red is used to call attention to the missing or the murdered, those who are no longer seen."

Alo leaned over the table and rubbed his chin. "Is there

any way to know for certain what this means?"

Her face was still. "No. There is too little information."

He turned over the other drawing and slid it toward her. "Would this help?"

He did not miss her immediate withdrawal—almost repulsion, as though she did not want to take it.

She slowly moved the drawing closer, studied it, and began to explain. "This is another piece of your puzzle. The circle represents family, and inside the circle these stick figures represent the family members. Look, if I hold the drawing like this, the two larger stick figures seem to be standing. They would represent the mother and father. The smaller stick figure is turned upside down, a crude drawing of one lying down. It would be the child. But the head-down position of the child figure would indicate that the child was dead."

Alo took the paper and turned it around. "But if you look at the drawing like this, it could indicate the parents are dead, and only the child is left."

"Correct. It is not possible to determine from this drawing alone. Where did you find it, and how was it positioned?"

He told her about it being found in some disheveled papers.

"No true way to tell, then. Drawn in red, again. The life force of the missing, or in this case the dead." She pushed the paper back across the table to Alo. "Where again was it left?"

Alo decided to tell her everything he knew: Grey Sage, Dr. Thornhill, the missing axe, the disheveled library, and this drawing. She sat like a statue as he explained, with no movement and no comment.

"And there is one last thing," he finished. He pulled his phone from his pocket and searched for the photograph, handing her the phone. "I found this configuration of stones at the front door early Friday morning. It had to have been placed there overnight."

She scanned the photo. "Clearly the Eye of the Medicine Man, and again the red. Seems to be paint."

"I suppose, but I touched nothing. I only moved the stones with my foot. Slid them over into a pile behind the shrub. I did not want my fingerprints on the stones."

"That shows wisdom."

"You have heard my story. You have seen the images. What can you tell me?" Alo felt his hope turning into desperation.

"I can tell you no more about the images, but I do not believe these events to be coincidental. They have some connection. Someone is sending a message. A strong message." She looked away and paused and then looked back at Alo. "I sense that the message might be meant for Dr. Thornhill. The ancient oak could be a symbol for him." She came forward in her chair. "He should be careful."

Alo had been suspicious since he pulled the axe from the tree. "Since no law has been broken, there is nothing else I can do at this point except to be vigilant."

"Yes. I believe these messages are not meant for good. Be watchful, especially of Dr. Thornhill. I am sorry I could be of no further help." She stood from her chair. "I am available to you if there are other messages." She took a card from her pocket and scribbled something on the back. "Here. This is my cell number. You may call me at any time." For the first time since meeting her, he saw a slight smile. "I want to help. Dr. Thornhill delivered me twenty-seven years ago. It was a difficult birth, and my mother told me from an early age we owed my life to him. I will help if I can."

Alo stood and took the card. "Thank you, Chooli. I will

let you know if there are further developments. Right now, we have several guests at Grey Sage, and there is much activity. Maybe that will deter things for a few days. But I will be cautious and watchful. Again, thank you so much for your time. You've been most helpful."

They shook hands again and walked the hallway together to the front desk before Chooli turned toward her office.

The elder spoke as Alo moved toward the front door. "You came to hear the story. Did you hear it?"

"Yes, but I heard only part of it." He waved at the elder as he opened the door and departed. The part of the story he had heard was worrisome and confirmed his suspicions. Dread gripped him.

Monday afternoon

Maude pulled a light jacket from her closet. "Silas, are you going with us?"

"I suppose I am. You may need a bit of help entertaining Henry and Bea while the others are painting."

"And Clara. She's coming with us too. Lily will take care of Sarki, Noble, and Laura, and I've asked Alo to guide us through the aspens and do what he loves to do—talk about trees and wildlife."

"Then for certain I'm going. I'll get my camera. With Drake and Boots in Albuquerque for the day, the inn might get lonely."

"Grey Sage just might enjoy the peace and quiet with everyone gone. Kyah's finished for the day, but Tanzi and Lita will be in the kitchen preparing dinner. It's the heartbeat of this house, and it's rarely silent. Even when we're all asleep, there's usually something happening in that kitchen—like Lita's bread or rolls rising or the vegetables fermenting." Maude stepped out of the closet. "Here's your jacket. It's breezy, and you know how it gets cooler at the higher elevation later in the afternoon these September days."

Maude and Silas gathered with the others in the great room. Before they could join a conversation, Lily whizzed through the front door and was pulling her whistle to her mouth when Maude grabbed her hand to stop her. "No need for that. Look around. We're all here and ready to go."

Lily gave Maude the squint eye. "You're such a pleasure spoiler, Maude. You know how it amuses me to see these people react when I blow the whistle."

"True on both accounts, but I don't think you'd like to see how Silas or Lita might react." Maude loosened her grip on Lily's hand and patted it. "Maybe you should wait until you're on your way out of town to spit in your whistle."

Lily stepped forward. "Okay, you people. Those of you who have a light jacket may load into the van. For those of you who don't, go get one. Alo says you'll need it. And sunglasses. You need sunglasses." Nobody moved. "So, somebody do something."

Maude's head waggled. "They all have jackets and hats and sunglasses, Lily. Why don't you just lead us to the van before sundown?"

Lily turned swiftly. "Let's go, people."

They all climbed in and took a seat, except for Bea and Lily. Bea stood staunchly at the passenger-side front door. Lily approached her.

"Bea, Henry's already on the van, and he's saving you a seat in the back. Why don't you join him?"

As she had on a thousand stages, Bea stood statue still, as though she was waiting for the curtain to open. She didn't even turn her head. "Why don't you join him yourself, Lily?"

"Because it's the best seat in the van, and he's holding it for you."

Bea's body was rigid, but her head swiveled to look at Lily. "Do you think I'm senile or just plain senseless? I know where the best seat is, and I'm riding in it."

"But that seat's for Silas," Lily argued.

"I've already straightened that out with Silas, and he's sitting with Henry, and you can stay here or sit with Maude." Bea faced the van. "Aren't you going to open the door for me?"

"Bea, you're going on a beautiful drive. Think of this as a limousine and you're in the back being chauffeured in comfort to your destination."

"That's fine. I'll open my own door." Bea opened the door and proceeded to get in, hiking one leg up and pulling herself into the van, holding on to the seat as though it was her dancing partner. "I have ridden in limousines around the world, and I always sit in the front with the driver."

She slammed the door, leaving Lily standing in the breeze.

Lily was the last one in and took her seat next to Maude. "That woman. I must be getting far too soft allowing her to still travel with this group. Any group really. I'm the leader, and she's no longer a diva."

Maude snickered. "You're wrong about that. Once a diva, always a diva."

"Her size probably qualifies her for a child's safety seat. Her mind certainly does. Look at her. She's so short she can't even see above the dashboard."

"Not the point, Lily."

The pitch and volume of Lily's voice rose. "But who? Who sits in the passenger's seat in a chauffeured limousine?"

"A diva who wants to sit there." Maude was near exasperation. "Does it really matter, Lily? We're all arriving at the same time. Bea's happy. Silas and Henry are in the back enjoying their conversation. You're the only one with her knickers in a twist. Sit back and enjoy the drive. You don't get to see the changing leaves like this in Chicago, and I only get to see them a few days in a year myself." She pointed to the aspens.

Lily gave in, and the ride passed with intermittent conversation and enjoyment of the scenery. In a half hour, Sarki, Noble, and Laura were standing in front of their easels, attempting to match the color on the canvases with the natural colors in afternoon light. Alo had chosen a location where Sarki could view red cliffs and Noble and Laura could see and touch the aspen trees, their bark, and their leaves. Lily stayed behind with those painting while Alo led the others on a walk.

Alo guided them into the clone of aspens and paused. "We walk into the quiet peace of these aspens that have seen many walk among them for over a century, or maybe two." He spoke in whisper-like tones as though not to disturb them. "Look at them quaking in the breeze. These trees were likely here during the Civil War. You may think they're individual trees, and in a way, they are. But if you could see underneath into the soil, you would see each one comes from the same root system—a root system that lies dormant, possibly for years, even decades, until the conditions are just right for their growth. Then they begin to break the soil and populate the area. Their home is in the high desert, and they can survive with little water, but they cannot survive without sunlight."

Maude held Silas's arm and thought that they and Alo and Lita were much like a clone of aspens, their family ties like these unseen roots seeming to appear from the same stock when the time and conditions were right. She knew that without Alo and Lita her vision of Grey Sage would likely not have been realized. Together, they all had been stewards of the land and of the inn.

Alo continued. "Aspens grow well in this environment, but I advise against planting one in your yard. They're better left where they naturally grow and survive. Nature has its way, and aspens are its way of creating a mature forest."

"How so?" the colonel asked.

"All part of a cycle designed by our Creator. Let's say there is a forest fire or an entire forest is lost because of logging or disease. The aspens are the first to appear on the stripped land. They are fast growing because they only need sunshine to survive, so they establish quickly and keep the soil from eroding until the trees of the forest appear again. And when the trees return and grow to maturity and shade the aspens, the aspens die back from lack of sun. Their roots lie dormant until they are needed again."

"God thought of everything, didn't He?" Bea supposed. "Like I said yesterday to that young writer, you can ask what and how and why, but the most important question is who."

Maude chuckled, amazed at Bea's insight, and more amazed that she could even remember yesterday's conversation at the lunch table.

Alo nodded in agreement. "Yes, Miss Bea. The Great Creator even thought of a way for this tree to provide sustenance for the wildlife in the winter." He led them closer to one of the larger trees. "Look at this bark. If I took my pocketknife and scraped and peeled away the white layer, there would be a layer of green that is like sugar. The elk and the deer know this, and even with three feet of snow on the ground, they can find food in the bark of the aspens. And this green substance is like the chlorophyl in green leaves, producing sugar that keeps the tree alive and growing even in the dead of winter."

Bea was more curious. "Do it. Scrape it away. I'd like to see."

Alo looked at her with gentle resolve. "I'll not do that. I am glad you are so interested, but these trees are like elders. They have fought hard to live, struggling through drought and harsh winters. I will not be the one who wounds this tree and causes it to labor to heal its own injury. We will just appreciate its beauty and its determination. Let us walk deeper into the forest now."

For the next half hour, Alo guided them through the aspens and into a grove of towering pine trees, the forest floor carpeted with pine needles. He stopped. "Now we are truly in the forest, and you are surrounded by ponderosa pines, probably eighty to ninety feet tall. They grow differently than the aspens that all come from one root system. If you could see underneath this stand of trees, you'd see that their root systems are entangled, but each tree has an individual tap root that may grow as deeply into the earth as the tree grows above the soil. The tap root is always in search of water."

Silas spoke up. "Don't forget about their medicinal benefits."

Alo nodded. "Yes, Silas, but I'll add that I don't recall ever seeing you use the bark, the sap, or the needles like the indigenous people did. They used them for everything from fevers and coughs to skin issues." He picked up a pinecone from the forest floor and pressed it with his finger until a seed popped out. "The birds and the wild turkeys feed on these seeds. That is, if they get to them before the squirrels, chipmunks, and mice."

Bea let out a war whoop that sent the birds fluttering. "Mice. I don't like mice. Let's get out of here."

Maude wondered if Lily and her group had heard the

scream and would come running to find them. She had a sense that Sarki was trained to run toward danger.

"You won't see the mice. I'll make sure of that. But let me take you to a most beautiful spot. It will be worth your walk. Get your cameras or phones ready."

Alo stepped to Bea's side and took her hand as they walked noiselessly through the pines. He led them into an emerald-green meadow bordering a quiet stream, its mercury-like water trickling gently over smooth rocks into a glassy pool of silver. No one spoke as they stood in wonder.

Maude looked at the group. They had the same look on their faces that she must have had the first time she came here, stepping out of the deep forest into this clearing. She felt she had walked into the Shepherd's Psalm, a lush carpet of verdant grass and crystal-clear water touched only by God's hands. She breathed in its beauty once again and thought how like the aspens and the pines they all were, bound together in some inexplicable way, each made by the same Creator, each with a unique purpose, and yet experiencing this sacred space together. For a few moments, Maude's heart was at peace.

Chapter Nine

Monday evening

*L*ita walked around the spacious kitchen island as Tanzi stood at the end with her arms folded in front of her. As Lita inspected the plates the young chef had prepared, Lita was aware of Tanzi's nervous breathing.

"Colorful and eye-pleasing, nutritious plates of goodness from soup to dessert." Elated with what she saw and tasted, Lita raised her hands. "Tanzi, I am more than pleased to serve your dinner to our guests tonight. Each evening, after our dinner guests are seated at the table, I customarily announce to them what I'll be serving and take their drink orders. Tonight, I'd like you to do that. This is your creation, and you deserve the satisfaction of seeing their delight."

She noted the look of surprise on Tanzi's face.

"But Lita, I'm a mess. I've been standing over the outside grill for the last hour, and I smell like a fishmonger that someone set on fire. And my hair? It has been under this net all day. Are you certain you want me to present?"

"Yes, but certainly not looking and smelling like that. You can freshen up in the butler's pantry as I do every evening. I've learned that a splash of water on our faces, a spritz of lemon spray, a quick brush of the hair, a fresh apron and chef's hat, and we're top of the town. That routine has worked for years." Lita smiled.

In a few moments, Tanzi returned from the butler's pantry and spun in front of Lita. "You're right. Much better, I think. My plates passed your inspection, now do I?"

Lita smiled as she looked at the slim young woman, her light-brown face with shiny peach cheeks, and her thick, almost black hair tucked neatly under a clean chef's hat. Her fresh apron sat loosely around her coke-bottle waist. "Amazing what a trip to the butler's pantry can do. You look perfect, like someone equal to the food you prepared."

Tanzi's abilities and her commitment to excellence gave Lita hope that Grey Sage's culinary traditions and excellence might have a chance of continuing when she chose to give up her duties. "Let's go, girl. Our guests are beginning to gather, and nobody likes cold fish."

At six thirty, Lita rang the dinner bell, and the guests took their customary seats. Lita and Tanzi entered the dining room, stood side by side, and Lita squeezed Tanzi's hand.

"Good evening, friends. You are in for a culinary treat this evening. I'm here only to take drink orders for those of you who prefer a glass of white wine rather than our white sangria." She picked up a crystal pitcher from the sideboard. "The sangria is made with the last of the fresh fruits of the season—peaches and strawberries—white wine with a splash of peach schnapps, and a double splash of apricot liqueur. I must say it is a perfect pairing with what Tanzi has prepared. But if anyone prefers a glass of white wine to the sangria, please let me know, and I'll get the chardonnay." Lita waited, but no one lifted a hand.

"Tonight is a first for us at Grey Sage. For nearly thirty years, I have prepared dinner for our guests. But this evening, Tanzi has prepared your meal, and I have been her sous chef. Tanzi, would you please tell our guests what you have prepared for them?" Lita stepped back slightly behind

Tanzi.

"Thank you, Lita, for the opportunity of creating this meal and presenting it." Tanzi rubbed her palms together. "You are here at this welcoming inn in the Sangre de Cristo mountains in the autumn, my favorite time of the year. But this evening, we have the gift of the last of the summer fruits and fresh fish. I will begin by serving you a Greek-style lemony fish soup much like a chowder, only with Greek spices, followed by a frisee salad with oranges, shallots, slivered almonds, and Manchego cheese drizzled with lemony vinaigrette. Of course, there are always baskets of Lita's fresh, warm, crusty bread on the table at Grey Sage with a titillating spread of orange marmalade butter. Your entrée is a filet of grilled, just shy of blackened, orange roughy topped with a zesty mango-lime salsa and served over a bed of quinoa with steamed broccoli. And for dessert, although I'm not a pastry chef, I'm pleased to serve you a slice of delicate pistachio-cream crumb cake."

Tanzi stepped back to Lita's side.

Lily abruptly spoke before Lita could respond. "Are we on a five-star Mediterranean cruise ship? That sounds absolutely delectable. Pour the sangria, and let the party begin."

Lita was almost forgiving of Lily when she followed her outburst with a round of clapping. The other guests joined Lily and agreed.

Tanzi took Lita's hand again, acknowledged Lily and the guests with a gentle nod, and continued. "Thank you. We will cool your palates with citrus this evening, and Lita will warm them again before bedtime. I've enjoyed the aroma of Lita's autumn-spiced chocolate-chip cookies baking this afternoon. They'll be on a platter in the great room served with a cup of warm cinnamon milk for your bedtime snack."

Lita smiled at Tanzi. "Not only is Tanzi an incredible young chef, but I do believe she is a poet. Such enticing words to describe the food she has prepared for you. Let us dine."

An hour later, with the last course served, Lita and the guests deemed Tanzi's dinner gastronomically successful. Lita sensed the pride in Tanzi's face when the guests applauded her once again after dessert and coffee. Lita nodded to Maude—their familiar code to move the guests out of the dining room so that the cleaning could be completed.

Maude stood. "Again, Tanzi, we thank you. And Lily, our maiden voyage with Tanzi will keep us returning, won't it? And to think that after such a delightful meal, we have evening entertainment. Clara will return to the stage, backlit by a luminous fire to chase away the evening chill."

She turned to Clara. "I've looked forward to this all afternoon. This art of storytelling is extremely interesting. I wasn't so much aware at the time when I was growing up in West Texas, but much of what I learned about life was sitting in the lap of my Memaw and listening to her stories. My, how she connected me to the past and the present with her tales. I much preferred them over her reading me a fairytale, and I still remember many of her stories." She turned back to their guests. "And tonight, Clara has graciously agreed to spin a yarn for us. So, take a few moments to get yourselves comfortably seated in the great room, and Clara's tale-telling will begin at eight fifteen."

Lita and Tanzi, with Alo's help, cleared the table and began the kitchen cleanup. Lita commented, "Tanzi, your meal was absolutely perfect. I enjoyed every bite. I don't normally eat all four courses at dinner, but tonight I did, and with great pleasure."

"Thank you. To know you're pleased makes me so

happy." Tanzi paused. "And you know what else makes me happy? Look at all these plates. They're almost clean."

"I see that. Even Bea's plate is clean, and she normally eats like a little bird, just a little peck at a time."

Alo walked into the kitchen with more plates. "I heard that. I eat a peck at a time too. In my case, a peck is more like a quarter of a bushel. Your meal was outstanding, Tanzi."

"Thank you, Alo. I have something else in mind for tomorrow evening…with your permission, Lita."

"Permission? Girl, you just got yourself hired. I know you're in culinary school and you can't work full time right now, but you can work here anytime you have a few hours or a day or even a weekend. And when you finish school, I just might retire and hand you my apron. But until then, I'll be your sous chef anytime. You proved tonight that you can pull it off from start to finish."

"Thank you, ma'am. I love it here. Small crowds, the most beautiful and functional kitchen and pantry in Santa Fe, and such wonderful people. The freedom to create and use the finest ingredients. It's a dream job. I'll be back tomorrow to prepare dinner, but I have class in the morning."

"I can handle breakfast and lunch, and Maude is helpful. And one of our guests, Laura Sutton, is dying to get into the kitchen and make a cake for us. Should I let her do so tomorrow night?"

"Perfect. That will give me more time to prepare the meal."

They continued working until the kitchen was clean and everything was put away. Lita got out the tray for the cookies and started to mix the cinnamon milk.

Tanzi joined her at the island. "Here, let me help. I'll put the cookies on the tray since I've never made cinnamon milk. I'm interested to see how you make it."

"Easy. The hardest part is to get the cinnamon combined. That's why I scalded some milk before dinner, and a dozen cinnamon sticks have been steeping in it for the last hour. Next, I'll heat milk with powdered cinnamon and brown sugar on the stove. This becomes the concentrate. Then it all goes into the big urn over there, and I add enough milk to serve the guests."

"That seems easy enough. Should we put the urn in the great room now before the guests get seated?"

"We'll serve the cookies and milk on the table in the hallway outside the library. It's the perfect spot so we don't disturb what's going on in the great room. Alo will take the urn and plug it in for us. When he's done that, you can put in the milk, and I'll bring the other ingredients when I'm finished. You can plate the cookies for now."

"Yes, ma'am. And I might just take a couple of these cookies home to my husband."

"You're always welcome to take home whatever we have to him, be it a meal or a treat. We'd like to get to know him. Maybe you could invite him to come out and share a meal with us. We're family here, you know."

Tanzi stopped plating cookies. "Do you mean it?"

Lita stirred the brown sugar and cinnamon together before adding the mixture to the pot of milk on the stove. "Yes, I mean it. Kyah works here. Now you're working here. We would like to meet him. Invite him out."

"Chepi would really like that. Kyah and I have told him so much about the inn. I know he would like to meet all of you, especially Dr. Thornhill."

Alo was getting the urn from the butler's pantry. "Is Chepi Hopi?"

"Yes, sir. We all are."

"What does Chepi do?" Alo asked.

"He is a paramedic. It's a long story. Three years ago, he graduated at the top of his class at the Law Enforcement Academy. But after a year as a policeman, he learned that he was not suited for a job that could require him to take a life. He preferred saving lives. His supervisor recommended that he become a paramedic. It was the best advice Chepi ever got. He loves what he's doing now."

Alo responded. "And you must not worry so much about him."

Tanzi sighed. "Yes. Now I can sleep through the night. I worked as a waitress to help put him through his training, and we waited until he had full-time work so that I could attend the culinary institute. We are both happy. So happy."

"Sounds like you're both doing exactly what you should be doing," Lita said. "Every day's a good day when you enjoy what you're doing. Why don't you ask Chepi to join us tomorrow evening? We'll set another place at the table."

"Tell him to come early, and I'll give him a tour of the grounds," Alo added.

"That is so kind of you. I will ask him, and I know if he's not pulling an extra shift, he will gladly accept your invitation."

Tanzi left, and Lita looked at her checklist. All done. The urn of cinnamon milk was simmering on the table in the hallway alongside the cookies. She removed her apron and turned to Alo. "I think Tanzi is one pleased young chef and an excited wife. I'd wager my favorite gingham apron that she's on the phone with Chepi right now." She took Alo's hand and walked down the hallway to join their guests for Clara's storytelling. "I like that girl. There just might be a future for her here."

Before Kyah left for the day, she had told Maude that she'd been over some details for Clara's performance this evening. Kyah gave Maude instructions to light the candles she had placed around the great room, especially the pillar candles in the windows and on the mantle. She also left a recording of trickling water in the CD player. Maude was to turn it on when Clara began her story. Kyah told her the candlelight and the sound of water would create an intimate ambiance for Clara's storytelling.

Maude was growing more impressed and appreciative of Tanzi and Kyah, their attention to detail, and their interest in making the Grey Sage experience a memorable one for the guests. With Elan gone, she had hoped that Doli and Catori, Lita's daughters, might be captured by the spirit of Grey Sage and would be the next generation to carry on, but they had moved away and now had careers and families. With each passing year, her dream for Lita's daughters to return was fading. For now, she was glad that Tanzi and Kyah seemed to be filling that void.

The candles were lit, and the fragrance of vanilla candles and cinnamon milk competed with the smell of the ponderosa pine in the fireplace. Alo always threw a couple of pine logs on the fire for the aroma and for a quick start before adding the aged hardwood. He knew how to build a fire that would last the evening.

Maude stood in front of the fireplace while the guests took their seats. Lily joined her, yanking up her tunic top and backing closer to the fire. "I'd forgotten how cool it gets after sunset this time of the year. I'll get myself all warm before I take my seat next to Noble." She winked at Maude.

Maude looked behind Lily and raised her eyebrows. "Lily, not so close. Setting yourself on fire is not what I had planned for tonight's entertainment."

Lily moved forward. "I might make a spectacle of myself, but not like that. The fire just feels so good, but you're right—some of these synthetic fabrics catch fire easily and melt, and I don't think I want a paisley imprint on my butt until Christmas."

Maude laughed. "You'd better sit down. I see Reba eyeing the seat and the gentleman who seems to have seized your attention."

Lily flipped her red curls over her right shoulder. "Honestly, Maude, do you think I, the shameless hussy that I am, would be concerned about Reba? She's milk toast. I am burgundy bourguignon. Just watch."

Lily walked over to the sofa where Reba was about to take a seat and squeezed in next to Noble. "Excuse me, Reba, but Noble and I would like to finish our conversation."

Lily had never failed to amuse Maude. She was shameless, as she described herself, and fearless, and insensitive at times, but there was a goodness down deep and a rare understanding in her unique way of looking at the world. Lily had been novel when they met in college, but Maude had grown to see and love Lily for who she was—another choice person who took root in her life like a ponderosa pine, stalwart and distinct, with entangled roots that kept them both strong and standing after decades of friendship.

The room naturally became tranquil when everyone was seated. Even Lily and Bea were quiet. Maude addressed the room. "On evenings like this, I wish for an extended, raised hearth that was more stage-like. Wouldn't that be just perfect for Clara's storytelling?" She looked at Alo. "One of these days, Alo, let us make that happen. But for tonight, this whole room is Clara's stage as she tells us one of her enchanting stories." Maude went to the CD player and awaited Clara's signal.

Clara, dressed in dark-brown pants and top underneath

a flowing sheer tunic the color of loamy earth, stepped in front of the fireplace. As she opened her arms wide, the firelight shimmered through the flowing sleeves. She thanked Maude, recognized the audience, and said, "Maude, I cherish what you said tonight about your memaw and her storytelling, and you are so right about stories connecting us to the past and often to the future. Tonight, I will continue the story that I told you on Saturday, attempting to reconnect you to that time and place when the mysterious white dove appeared." She bowed her head and clasped her hands together.

That was Maude's cue. She turned on the CD player and took her seat next to Silas.

Silence, except for the relaxing sound of a trickling stream. Clara gradually raised her head with eyes closed and put her finger to her lips.

"Shhhhh."

Silence. She opened her eyes. Again, "Shhhhh." Then, almost in a whisper, "Do you hear it? Do you hear the river flowing like molten silver over the stones worn smooth by the centuries?" She made the soft, mournful sound of a cooing dove. "Do you hear the dove in the distance, the dove with incandescent wings that flew so high into the heavens that it was thought to be gone forever? Listen. The river and the dove are telling us their story."

For the next half hour, Clara mesmerized the group with her story, the swooshing sounds of the river, the moaning sounds of the dove, and the voice of delight with the Indian girl's conversations with her mother and with the dove. Her pauses, like the music made in the silence between the notes, gave the listeners time to engage and to anticipate what would come next. The moments of her storytelling were mystical, captivating the listeners and transporting them to another place and time. The brief shadow passing the moonlit window caught Maude's eye. Then the scraping noise. A pine limb she thought.

With a last hushed, moaning sound of the dove again, Clara ended her story. "The white-washed dove flew high into the azure sky of the heavens. The girl with long braids held tightly to the one white feather it left and gazed long until she could see the dove no more. And the molten-silver river kept on flowing. Shhhhh. Listen to the river. It knows all."

Clara stepped back, clasped her hands in front of her and bowed her head. "Shhhhh."

Silence.

A startling scream shattered the silence and the moment. Maude quickly surveyed the darkened room. Her eyes met Alo's.

Where was Lita?

Chapter Ten

Monday evening

Alo almost leapt from his chair and ran toward the hallway. Sarki shot from her seat to follow him, as if by instinct. Stunned, Maude and Silas stood from their cuddle chair in the back, Maude moving to turn off the CD player.

"Who's screaming?" Bea squealed. "Why is someone screaming?" With no answer, Bea shrieked louder. "Who's screaming?"

Lily went to Bea. "You're screaming! Shush, Bea. Everything's fine. No one is screaming."

As Lily calmed Bea, Maude moved to the front of the room. She passed the entrance to the hallway leading to the library and glanced to see Alo with Lita standing at the library door. Alo held Lita by her shoulders as she covered her face with her hands.

Maude spoke as she neared the fireplace where Clara stood alone. "Everything's fine. Alo is with Lita. Probably something happened with the urn on the table outside the library. That's where she's serving our bedtime snacks."

Maude heard the ripples of relief resonate around the room. Silas joined her.

Bea whimpered. "Maybe she saw a mouse."

Silas calmed her. "More likely she dropped a cookie. Lita doesn't like to waste cookies. There's nothing you should worry about, Bea. Alo has it under control."

"But that Sarki woman . . . She- She's FBI, and she was running."

"Just her reflex," Silas answered. "I can imagine she was trained to do that. But she's never been to Grey Sage when Lita gets excited about something. I'm certain she's having a good laugh at herself by now. An FBI agent to the rescue of a cookie."

Maude forced a smile. "Let's just give them a minute to clean up whatever was spilled. I'll make certain they're ready to serve the warm milk and cookies. But more important, we did not have an opportunity to thank Clara for the incredible story she told us tonight."

Everyone applauded.

"I am certain with Clara's beautiful story and Lita's warm cinnamon milk and cookies, we'll all have a sweet sleep. I think I'll be dreaming of gentle rivers and fluttering doves. Let me see if Lita's ready to serve."

Maude stepped away and walked down the hall. Alo still held Lita, who was crying. Sarki's stance at the library doorway was as stern as the expression on her face.

"What happened?" Maude asked.

Sarki took control. "Let's just close the library door for now, feed the guests their bedtime snacks, and then we'll talk about it. I'll handle this. Nobody goes into this room. Do you understand? Nobody."

Silas had joined them. They all nodded in agreement.

"Start filling those mugs, Silas. Lita, take that tray of cookies out now. Maude, can you carry the tray of mugs?"

"Certainly." Maude knew something was terribly wrong. Her gut felt like the spin cycle on the washing machine. She felt lightheaded, and her breath was shallow. She handed Lita a napkin. "Here, Lita, wipe your face. Let's do as Sarki said."

"Alo, with me." She opened the door to the library and

turned back before going in. "No one else in this room until I say so."

Silas answered, "We understand." As Sarki closed the door, he began filling the mugs with warm milk and putting them on Maude's tray.

Lita, followed by Maude, took the tray of cookies and napkins into the great room and began serving the guests. She feigned a chuckle. "Oh, please forgive me, especially you, Clara. I should never have screamed like that. How thoughtless of me. And over just a little accident in the library. But maybe I can make up for it with these cookies and warm milk."

As they snacked, the guests gathered around Clara, asking how she'd gotten into storytelling and if she wrote her stories. But within half an hour, all the guests had retired to their suites. Maude, Silas, and Lita picked up the mugs and napkins and went to the kitchen for cleanup. As soon as no one else could hear, Maude was insistent. "Lita, what on earth?"

Lita looked ready to cry again. "Oh, Maude. I don't want to say. Let's go see what Alo and Sarki are doing." She started to walk away.

Maude confronted her, putting her hands on Lita's shoulders. "No, Lita. Tell me now. What happened in the library?"

Lita whimpered. "Oh, Maude, it's the painting."

"What painting?" Maude's pulse was racing.

"Your painting of Elan. It's . . . it's . . ."

Maude, with Silas and Lita following, rushed down the hallway and opened the door to the library. A sudden chill. The window was open, the evening breezes blowing the sheer curtains. Sarki stood above Alo as he knelt in front of the bookshelves, looking at the painting. The painting of Elan when he was six. The painting Maude treasured more than any of her other works.

Maude stepped closer, unable to speak. A blood-red circle with stick figures in the middle covered the blond curls and the bright face of her precious boy's image. The thought of someone doing that gripped her and grew tight around her chest. Her painting was ruined. She could paint over the red smears, but would she ever be able to recapture the wonder in her little boy's eyes?

Alo stood and stepped to her. "Oh, Maude, I'm so sorry you have to see this. We'll get to the bottom of it. I know this window has been shut since last Wednesday. Someone came through sometime earlier and removed the painting from the wall. Looks like they did their work on the table there. Puddles of red something."

Lita shook her head. "It wasn't sometime earlier. It was while we were in the great room for Clara's story. When Tanzi and I put out the cookies and filled the urn an hour ago, the library didn't look at all like this. This has been done in the last hour."

Sarki went to the window. "How can you be certain?"

"Because I came in and put the tray of cookies right there on the library table while we arranged the mugs and napkins on the table in the hallway. Then I came back for the cookies." Lita pointed to the painting on the floor. "I am positive the painting wasn't here, but that door to Maude's office was open. And . . ."

Before Lita could finish, Sarki began her interrogation. "So what made you scream?"

Lita sniveled. "I . . . I saw someone."

"What do you mean?" Sarki snapped.

"I . . . I could tell that Clara was almost finished with her story, and I came to make certain the milk was warm and everything was ready. I went to the library to turn on a light in case someone wanted to grab a book before bedtime,

and when I did I saw someone crawling out the window."
She sobbed. "And then I saw Maude's beautiful painting on
the floor there."

"Could you tell who it was?" Sarki asked.

"No. Only that it was a small man, dressed in dark
clothing. He moved quickly and was gone in seconds. I
think he was young."

"What made you think he was young?" Sarki probed.

"The way he moved. Like it was easy for him to get out
the window."

"Understood." Sarki paused. "Look, we're not going to
solve this tonight. I looked around outside, but there was no
sign of a man, or anyone, for that matter. Even if we called
the police, there's nothing they can do tonight that cannot
be done in the morning."

She turned to Maude. "Maude, I'll get to the bottom of
whatever happened here. That's what I do. There is no use
in bringing the group into this. Your job is to get everyone
out of here in the morning, maybe take them into Santa Fe.
I think Lily might have been planning a trip to Canyon
Road sometime anyway. Encourage her to do that tomorrow. I'll feign some excuse not to go. And Silas, I need you
and Alo to stay here. Maude, can you drive the van and the
group into town?"

"Certainly." Maude's heart ached for the loss of her
beloved painting. But although she preferred not to deal
with planning an outing, she realized it was her job.

"Good. But for tonight, Alo, I need you to close and
lock the window. And can we lock the library door?"

"Yes, I have the key right here." Alo patted the keys
hanging from his belt.

Before he went to the window, he turned to Maude.
"Lita and I will stay here tonight. We'll take the empty
suite."

"Thank you, Alo. I prefer knowing the two of you are here with us." Maude's voice quivered. "And thank you, Sarki. I'm glad you're here. I'm not certain I'm the best one to be making decisions right now. Come on, Lita, let's get the kitchen in order for breakfast, and we'll all go to bed and try to get some sleep."

Alo stayed behind to speak with Sarki. "I agree with Maude. I'm glad you're here. I'd prefer not to be handling this alone."

Sarki took two tissues from her pocket to avoid putting her fingerprints on the canvas or frame, picked up the painting, and placed it on the library table, careful not to disturb what looked like puddles of paint and the smears left behind. She studied the painting and the image now scarring it.

"Forgive me for starting to pass out the orders tonight. It's my nature, my training, and my experience. I'll try to be more subtle around the others, but I can tell you straightway: this is no random act of vandalism. It was carefully planned and executed by someone who either knows what's going on around here or is stalking Grey Sage to look for an opportune time. The big question is why."

Alo's fists were clenched so tight his knuckles went white. "I wish I could disagree or question you, but I cannot. This is not the first incident." He continued, telling her about the axe, and the break-in in the library last week and the stones. Then he removed the papers from his wallet and pressed them flat on the table.

"I spent time this morning at the Museum of Indian Arts and Culture with an expert in these matters. Chooli explained the symbol's meaning and the red signifying either power or blood. But she also said that in these modern times red, is symbolic of the dead or missing." Alo described the meaning and significance of the eye of the medicine man and showed her the photograph of the stone configuration left at the front door. Sarki fired questions and Alo answered as best he could.

"Chooli thought it significant that the axe was hurled into the heart of the tallest chinquapin oak next to the barn. The axe impaled this image there." He pointed to the Eye of the Medicine Man. "She thinks it's a message for Silas, being the elder like the tree and being a doctor—a medicine man, so to speak."

"A message for sure."

"Silas was the doctor who delivered Chooli in a difficult birth, and she stands ready to help if we need her." He hesitated. "And it's my belief this image on this paper was created in Maude's studio using her paints and in daylight hours when we were all here."

"Why would you think that?"

"You've been in the studio. You know that Maude, unlike most artists, is a stickler for neatness and cleanliness. She never leaves that studio without cleaning up after herself, especially her brushes, but just before you all arrived, I heard Lita talking to her about a mess of red paint left in the studio. Maude seemed puzzled. She was about to go and do the cleaning, but Lita assured her it had been cleaned and was ready for the arrival of our guests. I haven't pressed Lita for details because I've tried to be on the quiet side of this issue."

Sarki scowled. "If that's true, that is brazen. Either crazy brazen or coldly calculated brazen, sending even another message. It's like this person is moving around silently and invisibly and wants you to know it." She looked back at the papers on the table. "And what about this one? It appears to be the same image painted on this portrait."

"Yes. Chooli explained that one to me too. The circle symbolizes the family unit, the stick figures being the individual family members." He pointed to the smaller stick figure. "This one represents a child between the two larger figures who appear to be the parents. Notice they're not all the same. The upside-down figure or figures, depending on how you look at it, represent the deceased."

Sarki frowned. "What do you mean 'depending on how you look at it'?"

"The paper was found crumpled in the library, and there was no way to determine which was the top or bottom. So, if you put it like this, the child is deceased." He turned the paper one-hundred-eighty degrees. "But turned like this, the parents are deceased."

"The painting answered that question," Sarki retorted. "We now know the child is the deceased, and more significant that it is painted on the portrait of this child." She paused. "Who is this boy? I am assuming someone close to Silas and Maude."

Alo could feel his eyes growing glassy. "This was Elan, their only son. He died at age seventeen in a rock-climbing accident trying to save another climber. But Maude painted this portrait when he was only about six. It's always been her favorite." He pointed to the open door next to the bookshelves. "That's Maude's office. It's been hanging above the fireplace in there for more than thirty years. Yesterday would have been Elan's fortieth birthday."

He watched Sarki's eyes shift from side to side as though calculating. "You need to understand that for Maude, Grey Sage is more than just where she lives. Grey Sage is in her DNA. She believes it's her soul's home until she gets to heaven. And every Christmas, Maude has created a painting or purchased a work of art as a Christmas gift to Grey Sage. After all these years, I could walk around and show you each one of those works. The Christmas morning unveiling has always been special for her and the whole family. This was the piece closest to her heart. Much more so since Elan's death. And now it's possibly ruined unless Maude can restore it."

"I'm so sorry. The loss of a child is unnatural, and it's the kind of grief that never goes away. Expect her grief to return for the next few days until we get to the bottom of this. I've seen it when we've solved cold cases years later. We present answers thinking it will bring closure for the family, and it does. But closure also comes with fresh grief." She hesitated. "I want to go back to something you said earlier. Am I to understand that you're the only one who knows about all these incidents?"

"That is true. I mentioned the missing axe last Wednesday, mainly asking Silas if he had seen it, but then I told them I'd found it, just not where and how. And the disarray we found in the library and the paint Lita cleaned in the studio were somewhat explainable. But no one knows about the rocks at the front door or either of these." He pointed to the papers on the table. "I'm fairly certain Maude knows, or at least she suspects, something isn't right." He rubbed his forehead. "Oh, she doesn't have knowledge of what you and I have talked about, but she knows. Maude's just that way."

Sarki leaned closer to look at the painting. "I can't tell how this paint was put on here. It doesn't look brushed. It looks more like it was put on with someone's finger. Maybe Maude could tell us in the morning." She looked closer. Then, without another word, she went to the window. "Turn on a brighter light, please. I need to check something."

Alo brought her a flashlight from the closet. "Use this.

We keep flashlights in every room. Power goes out frequently when the weather's bad out here."

Sarki took the light and directed its beam to the window casing. "Look, smears, probably from what was on his hands when he fled through the window. But it already looks dry."

Alo felt her questioning stare and watched as she went back to the table. She leaned over the table and shone the light into the splattered drops. Then, dabbing her finger into one of the drops, she rubbed her finger with her thumb, brought it to her face and sniffed. "This isn't paint. This is blood."

Alo's own blood curdled at the thought. "Are you sure?"

"No doubt whatsoever." She searched her pocket for another tissue. Nothing. "Can you get me a tissue?"

Alo went into Maude's office to her desk. No tissues. He opened the door to half bath and got a piece of toilet tissue and handed it to Sarki. "Here. What are you doing?"

"Plenty of DNA to be gotten here and probably finger-prints. The blood will likely be dry in the morning, but I'm collecting it on this tissue. Now I only need an airtight plastic bag. I can give this to the police in the morning."

"I'll get one from the kitchen." He paused. "Although, if I go now, it will only cause questions."

"Understood. I'll wait until I'm certain Silas and Maude are in bed. Where could I find a storage bag in the kitchen?"

Alo explained where she would find one in the pantry. "I'll come back here to let you know the kitchen is clear. I'll leave the pantry light on."

"Understood. I need time tonight to process my thoughts. I'll meet the four of you in the kitchen in the morning at six o'clock. I've noticed we don't have early risers among this group, so we should be safe to have a conversation." She paused meaningfully but did not stammer. "Alo, the day has passed for keeping secrets from

Maude and Silas. I believe Silas is in danger. To keep him safe, he must know."

Alo left for the kitchen, his shoulders sinking under the weight of such knowledge.

While Sarki waited in the library for Alo's cue, she surveyed the room and went through the French doors into Maude's office. She looked above the fireplace where Elan's portrait had hung. She scanned the mantle for any scuffs or more prints.

Her thoughts rumbled and rambled. After a moment, she took a piece of paper from Maude's desk and a pen to make notes.

Why did the perpetrator take the portrait into the library? Convenience of the table for his handiwork? But Maude's desk was a flat surface. Was his plan to leave it in the library for everyone to see, or did he intend to rehang the painting when he finished? Maybe Lita surprised him, and he didn't finish. But what didn't he finish?

She was still making notes when Alo returned. "Maude and Silas have gone to bed, and Lita's in the suite we're taking for the night. We're two doors down from you in the O'Keefe Suite. I'm a light sleeper. Just knock if you need me."

"Understood. I won't be needing you tonight. I don't think our unwelcome visitor will return. I'm thinking he was startled before he finished what he came to do. But he knows that we know now." She clicked the pen in her hand. "I'll see you at six o'clock. You get Maude and Silas there."

She turned to go but stopped at a thought. "I'm assuming it would the police in Santa Fe who have jurisdiction here. Do you or the Thornhills have any connections with the local police?"

"Yes, ma'am. It would be law enforcement from Santa Fe, but to my knowledge, none of us have any connections. Never have had a need."

She nodded. "Get some rest. We'll get back at this tomorrow. I'll be up for a while longer. I'll take the papers with the diagrams with me when I go to bed."

"Please do. Just know I don't have copies. Good night now." Alo walked out.

Sarki was drawn back to the table. She pulled up a chair and sat near the painting and stared. The diagrams lay next to the painting.

Two times leaving the Eye of the Medicine Man. First with the axe in the tree. Second with the stones at the door. Two times leaving the family image. First on the paper left in the library. Second on the portrait. And twice entering the window in the library.

Sarki began quickly jotting her thoughts:

With it being blood, painting can be cleaned. Not ruined. Previous intruder or suspicious guest? Any unfamiliar person seen on the property in the last few days? Any previous threats or messages? Who has keys and what doors and windows are normally left open? Has a child died in Silas's care, especially to parents who were distraught? Or has a young child lost both his parents under Silas's care? Probably Native American, someone who knew the significance of the images. Any strangers in the last few days? Escalating threats. Possibility of hiring security for a few days?

Sarki folded her note and the other two papers with the images, stood from the desk, turned out the lights, and left the library. She stopped in the great room, now lit with the embers from the evening's fire and the two candles on the mantle, probably forgotten when the others were extinguished. She walked to the fireplace and blew out the candles, then turned slowly in a circle, surveying the room and remembering the beautiful evening they'd been having until the unwelcome guest made his presence known.

Chapter Eleven

Tuesday morning

*W*ith breakfast preparation to be made, Maude and Lily were in the kitchen at five thirty, thirty minutes before they expected Sarki. Lita browned the sausage while Maude peeled and diced the sweet potatoes.

"A good morning for sweet potato hash, sour dough biscuits, and a fruit compote," Lita commented. "Make sure you cube those sweet potatoes all the same, Maude. Otherwise, well, you know."

"Yes, I know, Lita. I have been told that before." Maude forced a grin. "Did you think of calling Tanzi to come in this morning to do breakfast since we need to have our talk with Sarki?"

Lita shook her head. "Tanzi has class this morning, but she'll be here after lunch to cook dinner, and Laura's making a special cake this evening. So, I have a light day—and I need a light day."

"Sounds good. Most of the group will be with me in Santa Fe this morning. We'll have lunch in town. Take it easy on yourself since you'll only have Sarki, Silas, and Alo for lunch."

Maude finished the potatoes and started preparing the fruit. She knew Alo and Silas were talking in the gathering room while they drank their coffee, but she couldn't hear their conversation. Silas had been obviously quiet last night—the kind of quiet that usually came with a heavy caseload of patients. Before going to sleep, Maude had brought up the painting. Silas had told her to go to sleep and dream sweet dreams of flowing rivers and cooing doves. She'd tried, but neither sleep nor sweet dreams ever came.

This morning there would be no escaping the conversation. She looked at the clock over the stove. Five fifty-five. "How are you coming, Lita? We have about thirty-five minutes, and Sarki leaves no impression that she would be two seconds late."

"Sausage is browned, and potatoes are almost done. I'll leave them to simmer. Sarki also leaves no impression that she'll take very long to say what she needs to say. As long as she doesn't take more than forty-five minutes, breakfast for our guests will be on time."

With two minutes to spare, Sarki walked into the kitchen and stopped midway between the kitchen and gathering room, her countenance dour and her gait appearing as if every step was intentional. "Good morning, and I hope each of you was able to sleep last night. Seems the inn was secure. I have been over the details, and I have a plan. Let's talk."

Sarki sounded different. Maude could not tell if her voice was professorial or more like the FBI chief that she had been before her teaching career began. "Could I get you a cup of coffee?"

"Yes. Black," Sarki barked. "Where would you like to sit?"

Silas and Alo had entered from the gathering room when Sarki arrived. Alo now followed Silas to the breakfast table, and Silas invited Sarki to join them. "Come and take a seat. Lots of conversations have been had around this table."

Maude doubted they'd ever had a conversation like this one would be. She and Lita came with their coffee and a mug for Sarki. They were about to take a seat when Sarki spoke. "Lovely view, Silas, and I apologize, but I need your seat, please. I never sit with my back to the window or to the main entrance to the room."

Maude watched Silas agreeably move from his seat at the end of the table.

Once seated, Sarki pulled out her notebook, opened it, took a sip of coffee, and began. "I have been over all the details, some of which will come as a surprise to you. First let me make it clear that this was not some random act of vandalism. It was planned and executed with a purpose." Without any movement of her head, she paused and shifted her eyes to Silas. "And Silas, I believe these acts were aimed at you, and they indicate you could be in danger."

Maude could feel her face growing pale and her pulse increasing. "You said acts. What other acts?"

Sarki looked at Alo. "Alo, would you like to answer that question, or would you like me to carry on?"

Alo responded without moving or blinking his eyes. "I think it best if you continue."

"Understood."

Sarki recounted the events of the missing axe, the disheveled library, and the red paint dabs left in the studio. She then pulled the two pieces of paper from her notebook, unfolded them, and placed them on the table. After explaining where they were found, she asked Alo to tell them about his visit with Chooli.

Alo explained the symbolism of the two images and then pulled his phone from his pocket to show them the photo of the rock configuration left on the front porch.

By the time Alo finished, the gentle river of Maude's life had turned into white-water rapids of information that left her grappling for anything to hang on to and too breathless to even ask a question. She had sensed a menacing specter in the shadows of the past few days. The puzzle of the red paint

Lita had found in the studio had caused her to question. The man who'd appeared and spoken to Kyah about a retreat and never called back. The library scene. And Alo. She had read the lines on his face and had sensed in his demeanor that something was akilter.

Sarki's voice seemed a distant mumble as Maude floundered down river with her thoughts of the symbols. Eventually she heard her name.

"Maude," said Sarki.

Then Silas's voice, louder. "Maude."

She returned to the reality of the moment. "Yes. I'm sorry."

Sarki continued. "Those are the facts, and here's the plan. We will call the police this morning and have them come out. Alo, I'd like you to make the call."

Alo nodded in agreement.

"Wait." Sarki looked to Silas. "Alo says that you have no inside contact in the police department in Santa Fe. Is he right?"

"Y-yes, Alo is correct. Oh, I know—or at least I used to know—some of the officers. As a doctor, occasionally I had to interact with the police force. But no, I have no special contact there."

"Then Alo, you make the call. Use my name and my FBI background if you think it will help."

She turned her attention to Maude. "I know all of this is upsetting to you, Maude, and I hate that this threat has entered the peaceful halls of Grey Sage. But I need your help. Do you still think you can get the group out of here this morning? Are you up to it?"

Maude nodded. "Yes. Of course, I'd prefer being here, but I agree that it would be best not to pull our guests into this. We don't even know what *this* is right now. I'll talk to Lily. We can take them to Canyon Road and lunch, and I'll have them back by midafternoon. Will that give you enough time?"

"Yes." Sarki looked at her notes. "I think you need to hire private security for the next few days. Do you know of someone or a company that provides that service? Preferably someone who would fit in and not be flipping his badge around. It would be best that no one knows."

Maude looked at Silas. "Do you have contacts? I don't have any ideas. We've never felt the need for security. Alo has always been our protector."

Alo responded quickly. "But that was from the four-legged creatures."

Lita broke her silence. "I know someone."

Maude noted Alo's surprise. "You do? Who is it you think you know?"

"I don't exactly know him, but yesterday Tanzi told me that her husband was a police officer for three years. Graduated at the top of his class from the police academy. But he was more interested in saving lives and became a paramedic. Maybe we could hire him for a few days. He'd certainly fit in, and with Tanzi and Kyah both working out here, it would look natural."

Sarki nodded. "Silas, do you want to make the call, or do you prefer that Alo make it?"

Alo answered before Silas could respond. "Let me make the call. He's Hopi like I am. First of all, we don't even know if he would be available. If he is, I'll check him out and make certain he's ready and willing for the task."

"And if he's not," said Sarki, "he could know some of the officers who might be available and equipped for the job. We need constant eyes on the property." She shifted to Silas. "And we do not need Silas alone at any time, not until we get this solved. As I told you last night, I will get to the bottom of this."

Silas blustered. "I don't need protection. I can take care of myself."

Sarki quibbled. "It's true you could probably take care of yourself in most situations, but my goal is to keep you from getting in that situation." She paused. "Now, for the last assignment. Silas, I don't know if you kept your medical records when you retired, but I need you to think about any young couple who lost a child who was in your care. Anyone who loses a child is naturally going to go through the grief process, the anger, denial, and depression before they get to acceptance. And you know these stages are not linear. They zig and zag, and anger can return years later. But I'm talking about someone whose behavior in their grief might have been over the top or different than what you might have expected. That information could be helpful."

"Unfortunately, I left all my medical records to the young doctors who took over my practice," Silas responded. "But let me think through this and see if anyone comes to mind. I am on friendly terms with the doctors, and I'm certain they would allow me access to the records."

"Understood. It might narrow the field if you think only about Native Americans. This perpetrator has understanding of these symbols."

Silas tapped his finger on the table. "That doesn't narrow the field by much. The majority of my patients were Native Americans."

Sarki turned to Maude. "Maude, there is a bit of good news. Your painting of Elan will be easily cleaned. It was not paint after all. It was blood. Probably animal blood, but I took a sample. I'll give it to law enforcement this morning. The crime lab should be able to give us a quick determination. If it is human, then we will have DNA."

Maude felt the first relief she'd experienced in the last ten hours. "Thank you for telling me. I will get the portrait cleaned and rehung."

"Yes, but not today. Not until the police have completed their work. We may need it for evidence. I'll put it back in your hands just as quickly as I can. Now, let's have some breakfast, and everyone to your assignments. Lita, your assignment is to keep everything as normal as possible at the inn."

When Maude suggested at breakfast that the weather would be perfect for a visit to Canyon Road today, everyone agreed. Knowing she needed to get them out of the inn as soon as possible, she announced they'd be leaving at eight o'clock sharp.

Of course Lily complained. "And why would we leave at such an hour? The galleries and shops don't open until ten o'clock, and if my memory has not escaped to the same place as your good sense, Maude, I recall that it only takes about half an hour to get there."

Maude restrained herself from speaking more sharply than usual. "Your memory and my good sense are still with us, Lily. It is a perfect autumn day. Yesterday you saw the red cliffs in the afternoon sun. We'll be driving in another direction today, and you don't want to miss the sun on these mountains this morning. Take your cameras or your phones for the scenic outlooks where we'll be stopping along the way."

As planned, Sarki bowed out, saying that she'd been called in on a case and would be on the phone for a while this morning. Sarki did not lie. She just did not tell the whole truth. To cover her story, Alo offered to take her into Santa Fe to join the group later if she finished her work and wanted to go.

"I'm sorry you'll miss the drive, Sarki. Maybe you can join the group later. We'll be eating lunch at the historic Plaza Café, and they serve dishes I'm certain you would enjoy. And Clara, you're always invited to join us." Maude turned to Boots and Drake. "What about our two writers? Nothing like a walk down Canyon Road with an artist like Lily."

Boots replied. "Clara and I are game."

Drake agreed to join them as well.

"So, eight o'clock it is. And you might want your first stop on Canyon Road to be the Teahouse. World-class offerings of coffees and teas. That should hold you until lunch time."

Laura apologetically asked, "Do you know what time we will return? I promised Lita that I would bake a cake for our dinner tonight. It will take about three to four hours."

"Oh, Lita told me. We'll make certain that you're back by three o'clock, maybe even earlier. That will give our artists two or three hours of painting time this afternoon. The art you see on Canyon Road just may inspire you."

"Thank you," Laura murmured.

At eight o'clock, with no threat from Lily to blow her whistle, the group gathered to load the van. Because Maude sensed a grilling coming from Lily, she was relieved that Bea took the front passenger's seat again. No sooner than they were on the highway, Bea spoke up.

"I remember Santa Fe and going to a tea shop and a candy shop where I bought bags of candy for everyone at Christmas. It was candy that made everyone happy. I do remember that. I'd like to go there again, please."

Maude hedged. "I too remember what lovely gifts you bought for everyone. Those shops are not on Canyon Road, and I'm not certain we'll have time to take you over to the

Railyard District to those shops today."

Bea countered. "Well, just drop all these people off, and you take me to the chocolate shop."

Maude's mind was in none of this. Her thoughts were twisted and taut, wanting to keep Silas safe and wanting to keep the guests out of the fray, but her hospitality had limits. "Bea, all of these people are my guests, and I'll be leading them all down Canyon Road. So that won't work."

"Well, then, you should have gotten your Indian to drive me this morning. He would take me to the candy shop."

Maude's reply was abrupt and terse. "First of all, Alo is not *my* Indian. He and Lita are family. Maybe you could take off your tiara and not be so demanding. Maybe you could just be a part of the group this morning. No one else asks for special treatment."

Bea wrapped her arms around her bag in her lap and attempted to stomp her feet on the floorboard, except they didn't reach. "Stop this van, right now. I'm getting out. I will not be treated like this."

Maude, whose heart normally pumped graciousness, was immediately remorseful. "You're right, Bea. I am sorry that I was so harsh with you."

Although clearly surprised at Maude's outburst, Lily attempted a rescue before there was an explosion in the front seat of the van. "Not to worry, Bea. We'll get you to the candy shop, but let's enjoy the drive and the tea shop first. You love tea, remember?"

With little hesitation, Bea followed Lily's rhythm. "Oh yes, I love tea. Take me to the tea shop please. I'll get out there."

The chokehold on Maude's neck and chest loosened. She owed Lily.

Driven by Maude, the van made two stops to take photos and to enjoy the long-range views from the scenic outlooks. She then dropped the entire group off at the entrance to Canyon Road and went to park. She told Lily she would call and find out where they were and catch up with them. As soon as she parked, she called Silas.

Silas gave her a full report. The police had come and gathered what they needed, including the painting. They had gotten a detailed account from Sarki and promised to give high priority to the fingerprints found on the window casing and the picture frame and the blood samples. They would run the fingerprints through their system within a few hours and hope to find a match. The DNA would take longer. They'd also taken the stones that had been left at the front door and the two papers with the images.

"But what about security?" she asked.

"Alo has spoken with Tanzi's husband, Chepi. He's coming out this afternoon with Tanzi to take a look at things and come up with a schedule for security. He has limited time, but he has two friends in the police department who do private security on their time off. He thinks he can work out a schedule."

"That sounds good. Is Alo bringing Sarki to join us after all?"

"No. That was a ruse. Sarki just wanted everyone gone so that she could surveille the property. And as you know, she is insistent that I am not left alone."

"Of course, how thoughtless of me. You, my love, are my only concern. This intrusion in our otherwise peaceful lives has me just a bit rattled. I'll check in again around noon."

When she finished her conversation, Maude connected with Lily by phone and walked briskly to meet her at the tea shop. She next spied Laura, Noble, and Reba looking at kinetic art in one of the gardens, but they did not see her.

Apparently Lily had turned everyone loose to tour the galleries and shops on their own, and Lily had taken an outside table at the tea shop with Henry and Bea.

At the sight of Maude, Lily bounded down the steps of the shop and grabbed Maude's arm. "What is going on with you this morning?"

"What do you mean? Just because I snapped at Bea, I'm getting grilled by you?"

"Maude, I know you. So, get rid of the smoke screen. Don't echo my questions with yours. I know something's going on. I could smell it at breakfast with you and Silas and Alo. And Lita . . . Well, she's always spinning like a top about something. Then Sarki, working on a case? Do you think I'm numb and dumb or as out of touch as Bea? You might as well tell me, because I'll stand here squeezing your arm until you do. Don't make me wait, Maude. I best tell you that I sent Noble off with Reba and Laura, and I'm not happy about that."

"I know. I saw them in the garden down the way."

"And I'd like to join them. Maude, this is the last time I'm asking. If you don't say something, then I'm calling Silas."

The dam that had held back Maude's tears since last night broke, and she began to crumple. Lily led her to an inside table in the corner, and they sat together while Maude told her the whole story.

"Should we order something since we took the table?" Maude asked before she began.

"No need. Bea and Henry are at an outside table. We all ordered tea and cookies."

The chain of events poured out of Maude like Lita's warm agave syrup. In her flummoxed state, she was amazed that she was able to explain the sequence coherently.

"But Lily," she finished. "You mustn't tell anyone in the

group. The police are there this morning to gather the evidence, and we're bringing in extra security. We don't want our guests to be worried or afraid. Sarki promised to get to the bottom of this quickly, and until then, we'd like to keep things as normal as possible."

"How's Silas handling this?" Lily inquired.

"The way you'd expect. He's calm. Probably a bit of denial, but most assuredly he's working to keep me from worrying. Sarki instructed him to think back through his patients who were children who died. Children whose parents might have been more upset than usual or who reacted badly to him because he was the doctor."

Lily rubbed her temples. "This is a bottomless bucket of devilment. Who, just who, would ever want to hurt Silas? I know of no other man who is so gentle and caring. Maude, this is high drama, like we've stepped into the middle of a crime novel—veiled threats, break-ins, blood, a portrait, and those images." Lily's eyes grew large as she stared at Maude only to see Maude staring back. "Maude, you don't suppose it's . . .?"

"Our writer Drake. I have questions about Boots too. Do you think he could do something like that?"

"That's exactly what I mean. But isn't Drake writing a novel? This would be firsthand research for him. An intruder. All the subterfuge. He could observe everyone's reaction."

Maude's spirits lifted momentarily only to sink again. "He's writing a screenplay, but both of them were in the great room last night when the incident with the painting happened. And . . ." She hesitated. "Everything else could be considered harmless, but the painting incident takes things to another level. I just don't think Drake would deliberately ruin my painting that way."

"Well, whoever this unwelcome guest is will be staring

Sarki in the face in a matter of time. She clearly has a mind and a will like a steel trap that won't let go. This lawless felon is already caught. He just doesn't know it."

"Looking at the positives makes this bearable. Our first FBI agent at Grey Sage exactly when we need her."

"Yes, what are the random chances of that?" Lily reached in her bag for a tissue and handed it to Maude. "Now dry your eyes, and let's get Henry and Bea. They're sitting outside sipping tea. She's still talking about chocolate."

"You go and join Noble. I'll get Bea and Henry, and we'll take a short walk over to the candy shop near the plaza. Maybe she won't remember it's not the Railyard chocolate shop. We'll meet you and the group at eleven thirty at the entrance to Canyon Road. Maybe I can make amends. By the way, I saw Reba, Laura, and Noble near the entrance looking at kinetic art, but I didn't see Drake or the Boones on my way to you."

"They were headed to the Morning Star Gallery to look at antique Native American art and some artifacts. More research, I suppose." Lily stood and grabbed her bag. "I'm headed to find Noble. You get Bea and Henry, and I'll see you with the group at the entrance at eleven thirty. And stop worrying. Sarki's on it." Lily cocked her head. "Have any idea what her name means?"

Maude stood slowly and continued to wipe her face with the tissue. "No. I've never heard that name before."

"Well, Sarki will proudly tell you about her name if you ask. Her ancestors came from West Africa, and her name means 'chief, the one in charge.' You remember that." Lily winked and walked briskly away.

Maude found Bea and Henry sipping their tea. With just a teaspoon of enticement, she convinced them to join her at the chocolate shop. "We have a whole hour before we meet the group for lunch," she encouraged. "That'll give you plenty of time to buy chocolate, Bea."

"Maude, you get the hospitality prize. You are just the finest host." Bea wobbled from her chair and took Maude's arm. "And for being so nice, you get your choice of chocolates."

Maude smiled, grateful to be back in Bea's good graces, grateful that Bea's memory was no longer than she was tall.

The rest of the morning passed quickly. A pleasant walk. Gallery hopping. Bea's eleven-pound bag of assorted chocolates. Cool breezes. A spicy lunch, and a nap-inducing drive back to Grey Sage.

Alo and Silas met them at the front door to assist with unloading the van. The grip on Maude's chest loosened when she saw no darting eyes, wary glances, or deep lines on their faces. But where was Sarki?

Chapter Twelve

Tuesday afternoon

As Lita sashayed around the kitchen with her apron strings flying, she saw Laura entering the kitchen. "How did I get so lucky? Tanzi's making dinner, and you're about to make dessert. Let me introduce you two. Laura, you're already aware that Tanzi is a chef-in-training at the culinary school in Santa Fe. She's a lovely local blossom and just happens to be Kyah's sister. And Tanzi, this is Laura Sutton, all the way from Ann Arbor, Michigan."

Tanzi wiped her fingers on a kitchen towel and approached Laura to shake her hand. "I am so pleased to meet you. Lita has told me about your baking skills. I did the shopping earlier today before driving out, and I have all your ingredients. I cannot wait to see and taste this cake."

Laura's shyness warred with her newly found confidence. "Oh, thank you. But you are formally trained. I'm only self-taught."

Lita popped Laura on her back side with the kitchen towel. "I beg your pardon. It was I who needed help with the baking last December when your group was stranded here in the snowstorm. You were the one to volunteer after a severe twist of your arm, and I had teach you what flour was." Lita draped the towel over her shoulder as she walked to the pantry for another apron. "Laura baked Christmas cookies and gingerbread for a gingerbread house," she explained to Tanzi as she returned. "Her first attempt was a masterpiece—a replica of Grey Sage. She was a natural and didn't know it." She handed Laura the fresh apron.

Laura smiled sheepishly. "I am sorry, Lita. I was your chief baker-in-training. I got my start here with the best. You were a great instructor and a better motivator. My life had been as though someone had hit the Pause button for the last several years. I was going through the daily motions and required activities as a professor of music theory. But being in the kitchen with you, Lita, I learned quickly that baking was my passion. I went home after Christmas and taught only one more semester before resigning my job." She tied the sashes on her apron. "I've taken some local classes, and now I spend my time baking and gardening."

Tanzi was butterflying the pork tenderloins. "Have you thought of opening a bakery?"

"Oh, heavens, no. I enjoy baking too much to do that. I bake birthday cakes for our friends and their children and some of my husband's colleagues. And I take cookies to rehab centers and nursing homes. But I have no desire to run a business. I just enjoy everything about baking, and I'm always experimenting."

Lita stood with her hands on her hips. "Here's the real scoop, Tanzi. Laura's far too humble, if one can be too humble. She and her husband live in a lakefront mansion that's been in their family for generations. They're financially independent, and Laura doesn't need to work. Her husband is a scientist who spends his time in a lab trying to find a cure for diseases." She smiled at Laura. "And to think, this wealthy, gifted musician bakes birthday cakes that look like clowns and sunflowers and gives them away just to make other people happy. And she visits the nursing homes to play the piano for the residents and takes them cookies. I am proud to call her my friend, and if she weren't in the room, I'd call her my protégé."

Laura lowered her head in seeming embarrassment and looked inside the bags of groceries on the kitchen island. "Yes, Lita allowed me to get my hands dirty. As the only child of two scholars, I was never allowed much adventure, and I was certainly never allowed in the kitchen. I grew up with books and music, but Lita taught me that making a mess can be wonderful fun. I guess you could say she set me free. And now, our kitchen has been remodeled for my baking, and I spend my days making up for the lost time when I never made a mess. And believe me." She smiled. "I've made my fair share in the last few months."

She took the box of cocoa powder from the grocery bag and held it up. "Speaking of mess, this really makes a good one."

Lita was pleased with the changes she saw in Laura. When she'd met her last December, she'd seen a woman who had settled—settled for a career decided for her by her parents, settled for the dust and prints left by previous generations in the mansion she called home, and settled for a childless life. Laura had been so withdrawn that she barely communicated. And when she did, almost everything she said sounded like her apology for being alive. But hours and days in the kitchen with Lita had made a difference. Laura had found her passion and her freedom in the kitchen.

Lita understood that. Normally the kitchen was her happy place where she was free and full of joy. There was nothing about cooking that she did not enjoy. She didn't even mind the clean-up, knowing that everything was in its place and ready for the next meal. Standing at the kitchen sink and washing vegetables, mindful of all the colors and textures of squash, potatoes, carrots, asparagus, beans, beets, greens, peppers, broccoli, and heirloom tomatoes was her time to pray. Her ritual was to thank God for providing such a variety, naming each one as she washed it. She thanked Him that she had resources to pay for the food and the opportunity to prepare it and enjoy it with the people she loved.

But today she was Tanzi's sous chef, and as she cleaned and chopped the vegetables, she found herself on automatic pilot with the prep work. But instead of giving thanks, she was praying for protection for them all, especially Silas. Fear had become her unfamiliar and uninvited companion overnight.

Her marriage to Alo and their life at Grey Sage had been more than she dared dream of as a young girl. Grey Sage and Silas and Maude were home, truly home to her. With Alo and them, she always felt safe.

The only other unwelcome caller to Grey Sage had been the day grief took up residence after Elan's death. She had grieved with Maude and Silas. She had grieved with Alo as he felt he had lost a son. And she'd grieved with Doli and Catori, who had lost a friend and brother. And now that familiar specter of sadness wrapped around her again—sadness that the peace and tranquility of Grey Sage had been disturbed by this intruder who meant harm.

She heard Laura's voice. "Lita, where are you?"

"I'm at the sink scraping carrots."

"I know that, but where are you really?"

Lita had been caught. "Oh, I was just remembering how much joy I get out of being in this kitchen, knowing people will enjoy our creation."

"If you don't answer my question, they might not enjoy my cake so much."

"Sorry, what were you asking?"

"I was asking if there's a splash of Kahlúa in the house. I didn't put it on the grocery list thinking you might already have some."

"Oh, yes. An ample reserve. We still serve it in the after-dinner coffee on occasion. It's in the special cabinet in the pantry. You know the *special* cabinet." She paused. "You're making me think it might be the night to add Kahlúa to our coffee to go with your dessert. Hope you have enough whipped cream left over for a dollop on top."

"Sounds like a fair trade. Your Kahlúa for my whipped cream." She tried to pop Lita with her towel on her way to the pantry.

Lita laughed. "Girl, you need some practice. Something else I need to teach you." The lighthearted moment was what Lita needed to pull her away from the gray shadows of grief.

Laura returned from the pantry. "I'd be grateful if you'd spend the next couple of days teaching me something that doesn't include a brush or paint. I am done with painting. I attempted it. I worked to enjoy it. But painting is not something I should be doing. So, I told Lily on the ride back from Santa Fe that I'd be spending the rest of my retreat time in the kitchen with you, if you'll have me. I'll be at your service for making bread, biscuits, cookies, and desserts, but I'm not keen on chopping vegetables."

"Tanzi, did you hear that? We'll look at the meal plan for the rest of the week, talk about some pairings, and give Laura some assignments."

Tanzi was putting dry rub on the pork loins. "What a team we'll be! I hope you'll consider a caramel cake. It's my husband's favorite, and I have yet to master it."

Laura opened the bottle of Kahlúa and inhaled. "Ah! Perfect. Caramel it is. It's a bit finicky, but so am I. Butter, sugar, cream, and patience."

Lita slid the colander across the counter. "Here are your Scarlet Nantes carrots when you're ready for them."

She looked at the clock. Two hours before dinner.

She heard Alo come in through the mudroom door. He walked to Lita, kissed her cheek, and whispered in her ear. "Sarki has news. Wants to meet with us after dinner."

She felt a sudden chill and quivered like the aspen trees out the kitchen window. But she nodded and raised her eyebrows as if to ask the question.

Alo shook his head slightly and joined Silas in the gathering room.

Maybe Alo knows nothing. Maybe it's not good news. Either way, I'll know in a few hours whether or not I will have another sleepless night.

All sixteen chairs were occupied at the dinner table, and Sarki, bored with the drivel of conversation, observed Chepi, Tanzi's husband. Alo had met with him earlier and reported to her that Chepi was certainly capable and willing to provide security, although his time was limited. She trusted Alo, but if she had the opportunity, she would quiz Chepi before her meeting with the Thornhills and Lolomas after dinner and make her own determination.

While they were waiting on dessert to be served, Maude announced, "Tonight after dessert, you're on your own to enjoy each other. We've had a full day, and you deserve some free time. We have a variety of games, including chess and checkers, and there is always a good conversation to be had in front of the fireplace. Wednesday will be a full day in the studio. Alo's observation of the clouds and the birds today indicates rain tomorrow, and Alo's always right. A perfect day to spend at the inn. Laura's decided to spend her last couple of days with Lita in the kitchen, and perhaps we can persuade her to make cookies for snacks. And I am told that we are about to be served a slice of her sensational Black and White Cake. I'm assuming she named the cake for the black and white pianos keys that are like home to her."

More random conversation. Sarki scratched her palms, something she always did when her patience was wearing thin. She was more than ready to push back from the table and to meet Chepi and see what his plan was for overnight. With all the activity around the inn tomorrow, Silas would likely be safe. The intruder was brazen but not fatuous. Even so, she would not let her guard down and expose Silas to potential danger.

Her palms were as red as the beets on her salad as she waited for dessert. She practiced her breathing, trying to calm herself. Because Lita and Tanzi had graciously catered to her peculiar dietary needs, she never wanted to appear ungracious. Nevertheless, she was eager for dinner to be over so she could check her email for the latest reports before meeting with the group.

Finally, Lita and Laura entered the dining room, Lita with the coffee pot and Laura with a large cake on a platter. She carried it as if she might be put before a firing squad if she dropped it.

Before Lita started pouring coffee, she said, "Normally, we would slice the cake in the kitchen and serve it, but this cake is a work of art. You all enjoyed the art on Canyon Road today, but you've seen nothing like this. Tell them about your cake, Laura."

Laura painstakingly placed the cake on the sideboard in the bay window of the dining room and took a deep breath. "We will be serving you Black and White Cake this evening. And Maude, I adore your suggestion about how maybe the cake got its name from my piano keys, but my reason for naming it is obvious and not nearly so romantic as yours. Four delicate chocolate layers with a dark-chocolate mousse filling and a white cream-cheese icing, all generously drizzled with a Kahlúa chocolate ganache and garnished with a bouquet of fresh strawberry fans. And Lita will be offering you a splash of Kahlúa for your coffee, topped with a dollop of Kahlúa-laced whipped cream. Enjoy."

Dessert was served, and Sarki managed to keep her patience while everyone ate. Finally, she took her last bite, rose from her chair, and said, "Laura, next to my grand-mother's West African Lime Cake, I think you have just served me the best dessert I've ever tasted. Thank you, and please pardon me. I need to excuse myself."

Laura lowered her head. "Thank you, Sarki. I'll speak with you later about your grandmother's cake. It sounds most interesting."

Sarki had been excusing herself all day for one reason or another. She hoped the others assumed she had an upset stomach, but her phone in her pocket had been vibrating for the last ten minutes. Something was up. She walked hastily to her suite, took the call, and began making notes. She waited until she heard activity in the great room, then she walked through the portales to avoid anyone seeing her on her way to the private quarters and kitchen.

Those she needed to see were all there, plus Laura, who had stayed to help with the clean-up. She walked straight-way to Alo, Silas, and Chepi in the gathering room adjacent to the kitchen and quietly told Alo to get rid of Laura and that she and Chepi would return in ten minutes to join them around the table. "I need to speak with Chepi outside."

Alo pointed to the entrance to the mudroom. She took his cue and left through the mudroom door with Chepi following.

Outside, Sarki stared into the night sky, watching the fast-floating clouds in the dim moonlight. She could feel the damp chill. Alo was right. Rain coming in. The only place she had ever seen such darkness was in West Africa when she'd returned with her grandmother.

Earlier, when she had asked Alo about outside lights, he'd told her there were plenty of lights on the inn and the barn and around the pavilion down near the stream, but they rarely used them. They preferred not to pollute the ever-changing night skies with light. Now she understood why.

She quickly asked Chepi a series of questions about his plan for the night. It was too dark for her to read his face, but she was satisfied with his answers. She looked at her watch and led Chepi back inside.

In exactly ten minutes they were gathered. Again, Sarki took Silas's seat at the end of the table, and Alo pulled up an extra chair for Tanzi. Sarki opened her notebook and perused the faces around the table. Everyone looked calm except for Maude. Her face was drained of color and had the weary look that Sarki had seen too often in the faces of victims or family members of victims.

Sarki broke the silence. "I'll begin by saying that we've made progress today. With a bit of encouragement, local law enforcement is making this a priority. We're no closer to finding the perpetrator, but I have two reports. First, none of the fingerprints that were lifted from the scene are in the system. I know that the intruder is not the only person to have touched the painting or the window frame or table, and I'm assuming that none of you have ever been finger-printed." She noted the nods of their heads. "It means the intruder is either not in the system or wore gloves. Oddly enough, the fingerprints identified were most likely female. Probably yours, Maude."

Silas interrupted. "You can tell the difference in gender with a fingerprint?"

"Not conclusively, but there are indications. Has something to do with ridge density. Too complicated to go into now, but I can explain later if you like. But we need to get on with this." She looked at her notes. "The good news is that the blood we found was not human. More likely from a bird than from a mammal. So, we know that the perpetrator hurt no human or himself or herself to extract the blood. The bad news is there's no DNA."

"But he did kill a bird?" Alo asked.

"Yes. Most likely."

Lita grappled with this information. "I do not like this. Who would kill a bird for something so mean?"

Sarki responded. "You'd be surprised. Someone you might pass in the grocery store. Someone who appears normal but inside is desperate for revenge. Someone who's hurting and wants someone else to hurt. A criminal. As I said, you'd be surprised."

Maude asked about the papers.

"The police have them. But I'm almost certain the paints from your studio were used to create them. The officer lifted some prints from a couple of tubes of your paint that matched. Again, no matching prints in the system. Probably yours, Maude."

Maude squirmed. "Would it help if I were to be fingerprinted for comparison? I'd be willing."

"Understood. I'll think on it, but my first thought is that it would be of little help." Sarki paused. "We have evidence, but no identification. We have reason to believe that there are likely to be other attempts. Which leads me to you, Chepi. You've been in law enforcement. I'd like to hear your assessment."

Chepi sat up straight in his chair. "Every one of these acts has significance, probably more than we understand right now. From the symbols on the papers to the vandalism, especially the vandalism of the painting. My gut says whoever the perpetrator is, he's doing this for the scare factor and to send a message that we don't yet understand. He wants to frighten you, to let you know that he is present without your knowledge. If he wanted to inflict harm, he's had opportunity. With that said, I am not willing to move forward on that basis, as there has been an escalation in activity, and this person is bold. So, without any possibility of identification through DNA or printing, we have to catch this person in the act. That requires round-the-clock surveillance and security. I'm available some of that time, and I have lined up two other officers who will work shifts as well."

"Understood. Thank you for that, Chepi. Almost a perfect summation, meaning that it's how I'm evaluating and making decisions. But I take one exception with you. I'm not certain the perpetrator is a male. I have my reasons, but right now those reasons don't matter. What matters is that we keep everyone not only safe but also feeling safe."

"Yes, Chief. You can count on me and my buddies to do that."

Sarki acknowledged him with a nod. "This inn and the property have more nooks and crannies than Lita's sourdough bread. Lots of places to hide, and more doors to enter than I can count."

"Eleven to be exact, Chief. I've been all over the inn with Alo this afternoon, and around the property, the barn, the trails. And you're right. With the portales and open doors, lots of ways to enter day or night. But we'll lock this place down like Fort Knox when the guests retire, and Alo has agreed to allow us to turn on the outside lights. Everyone will be safe under our watch. You can count on it."

Sarki was impressed. "You called me Chief. Why?"

"Ma'am, that's what I've always called my commanding officer, and with your credentials, I'm looking to you as my chief."

Maude interjected. "That's what her name means. Her name means 'chief.' Appropriate, I think."

Sarki quickly glanced at Maude. "How'd you know that?"

"Lily told me."

Sarki smirked. "Loose-lipped Lily. Not surprised."

"And I must confess that I told Lily what is going on," Maude added. "She knew something was wrong, and I sensed it best to explain. She's been my best friend for nearly fifty years, and she will not break my confidence."

"If she does, I'll have her arrested for conspiracy."

"Chief," Chepi said, "if you have a few minutes, I'd be most interested in learning about your name and why you got into the FBI and law enforcement."

Sarki tapped her pen on her notebook and stared at the ceiling. "Understood. Condensed version. My ancestors were slaves from West Africa and were brought to the coastal regions of Georgia, but when my great-grandparents married, they moved to Chicago. Wanted to live where it snowed. My mother was one of three children, and she was murdered on the streets, shot while walking home from work. Eight months pregnant with me at the time. I survived, but she did not. My grandmother says that when she saw me for the first time, I had my fist raised in the air and was pointing with my finger. She asked my father about naming me Sarki, a name she remembered from the stories her grandparents had told her. The name means 'chief,' and she said the name suited me."

She looked straight at Chepi. "I never saw my mother's face, and they never found her murderer. I grew up determined to keep this from happening to another little girl. I planned to be a street cop, but one of my officers in the academy put me on a different course with the FBI. I was an agent for twenty-seven years until I was injured and became a liability. I wasn't able to do the job and ensure the safety of my partner and myself. That's when I became an educator teaching criminology. I still get called in on some cases, and looks like I've been called in on this one right here at Grey Sage."

Chepi leaned forward. "Yes, Chief, you have. And again, you can count on me. I'll be here for the night, and I'll give you a schedule before I leave in the morning."

"Just call me Sarki."

"Ma'am, if you don't mind, I much prefer calling you Chief."

Sarki nodded in consent and turned to Silas. "Silas, I'm going through the list of names you gave me this afternoon. I've called in some favors with local FBI, and we'll be going through those names one by one doing background checks. I may have more questions of you tomorrow."

She stood from her chair. "What do you say we all get some sleep? I'll meet you here at six-thirty in the morning, Chepi. Again, I will get to the bottom of this. I always do."

Chapter Thirteen

Tuesday evening late

𝒜aude stood alone on the portale outside their bedroom suite. There was enough moonlight to catch glimpses of the fast-moving clouds coming in and bringing moisture. The night was unseasonably cool in spite of the southern winds. She pulled her shawl tighter around her shoulders and stared into the darkness, wondering if there was someone out there who could be watching her. In all her years of looking at the night sky from this spot, that question had never entered her mind.

She looked across the grounds to the guest wing. No light coming from any window. All the guests were safely and ignorantly asleep. Sarki, and now Lily, were the only ones who might have cause to leave on a light or still be awake.

Maude came in and locked the double French doors securely, something she had rarely done in all her years at Grey Sage. She warmed herself in front of the kiva. Kyah had readied the fireplace before she went home for the day and had left a note on the bed with a half dozen aspen leaves secured with raffia. Maude had smiled at such thoughtfulness and had lit the fire earlier.

She put on her nightgown, sat at her dressing table, and brushed her long silver hair and braided it for the night. The day had been long with the trip to Canyon Road, pacifying

Bea, worrying about Silas, and smiling when she felt like crying. Tomorrow's weather prediction meant she could stay home and out of the public eye at least some of the time. She found herself only wanting Silas's company.

She secured her braid, turned off the lamp, rose from her stool, and went to the kiva to warm herself before getting under the covers. She gazed at Silas stretched out on his back with the covers pulled up and his arms folded his underneath his head. She recognized his position as the one he took when he was ruminating over something. Grateful he was still awake, she slipped into bed beside him and turned out the lamp. The last embers of the fire gave the room a golden glow. She spoke softly because she was tired and because she hated to disturb the quiet peace. "I know you're thinking about something. I'd like to know what it is."

He moved his arm and put it around Maude. "Just thinking that we've enjoyed so many peaceful years here. We've had a predictable schedule since I retired a couple of years ago. We're here together every day in this spectacular place you've built for us. We're still in good health. Alo and Lita are always around, and we have such interesting guests with the occasional retreats you host. Life is good. No major crisis in our comfortable bubble."

"Until now, and someone has popped our bubble."

"I wouldn't necessarily say that. No one's been hurt. And what are the odds of having our own private FBI agent in charge? And then Tanzi's husband . . . What a fine young couple. And these good folks show up just when we need them. We must be grateful, Maude."

"I'm not ungrateful. I just wish I didn't need to be grateful for police officers with guns around our home." She snuggled nearer.

"I don't think it will be for long if Sarki's theory is right.

While you were out today, I combed and sifted through my memories of my patients, and I was able to come up with a short list of names for Sarki. That ledger I kept all these years came in handy."

"What ledger? The one in your locked desk drawer?"

"The very one. The list of names of every patient I lost in my care. Name, age, and date. Every now and then I get it out and look over the list, remembering the patients, their families, and their stories. That list always kept me mindful of things when I was still practicing medicine. Things I needed to remember: the brevity of life, the limitations of my work, and that I was not always the one in charge."

"All these years, and I never knew you kept such a record."

"Guess I am blessed that I only had one ledger for those names, and it still has blank pages."

Maude rolled to her back. "Well, you should have kept a record of all those patients you were able to help. Those ledgers would have filled up a whole bookcase. Those are the ones you need to remember."

Silas quietly chuckled. "I had filing drawers of patients' records for that, Maude. But that ledger reminded me that I couldn't stop death, and I couldn't prevent the grief that comes with it."

After moments of silence, Maude asked, "Did you put Elan's name in the book?"

She sensed his hesitation.

"No. I never did. As I told you many times, Maude, Elan was already in the arms of Jesus before I ever reached him. I've wondered so many times if it would have made a difference if I could have gotten to him a few minutes before. But I wasn't given that opportunity."

Maude did not want to add more to the heaviness of his thoughts, but she could never keep her feelings from him.

He was her rock, her safe place. "I've never believed it was God's will that Elan died, especially the way he died. I remember I heard that phrase too many times during those days after his death, like those words were supposed to be comforting. It used to make me so angry."

"People meant well, Maude. They just didn't know what to say."

"Then, why not stay quiet? Or just say 'I'm so sorry'?"

"Like I said, they meant well. We know bad things happen to good people, and Elan was good. Our boy was truly good."

"But why do such terrible things happen, Silas, especially to good people? Tell me again."

"Maude, we've talked about this so many times."

"I know, but I need to hear it again."

"Well, we have to accept that sometimes God does cause bad things to happen. He did it in Bible times and probably still does. Sometimes those bad things were for punishment. Other times for instruction. More often than not though, bad things happen as normal consequences of our own bad choices. I don't need tell you about those. And there are the times that God allows the bad thing to happen so that He can make something good of it. Remember the story of Joseph and even Jesus. Then honestly, there are times when bad things just happen and we'll never know."

"And now this bad thing that happened to someone is possibly bringing something bad into our lives."

"That seems to be Sarki's opinion. We'll know soon enough. I was able to give her a few names, and Dr. Harris will provide the medical files to give her more information. The fact that I was the doctor of record and I still technically own part of the practice made it easier to obtain the records. I think this will all be over very soon."

Maude sniffled. "I know that should make me feel better, but I don't. With Elan's birthday last Sunday, and then with what happened to his portrait, my grief seems as fresh as ever, even after twenty-three years."

There was another long silence before Silas spoke again. "I understand. I'm having some of those same thoughts and feelings. Sorry to say there are just no term or time limits on grief. It's not like grief time's up. You paid your dues. You've grieved enough. Now move on. We just move forward each day even when we don't think we can."

"But, Silas, someone hasn't moved forward. Someone is stuck in the grief and sadness, and that person wants you to pay."

"Maybe so. Even then, that someone is in pain, Maude. We know that pain. After Elan died, we wanted someone to blame too—the climber who took a dangerous risk, the paramedics who couldn't get to Elan in time. I even blamed myself for letting Elan go climbing that day. But we learned that blaming brings no relief from the sadness. We thought if we could just understand, that understanding might help. But Maude, we've lived long enough to know that some things are just beyond understanding. That's the mystery of God. Our job is not to understand, just to trust." He paused. "This is a storm, and like all storms, it may wreak a little damage, but it eventually blows over. What do you say? Let's pray and get some sleep. We're here together and we're safe."

Silas was asleep only moments after whispering an amen to their prayers. Maude thought of his words about good things and bad things, and grief, and gratitude. She thought of how she had loved him since she was a gangly ten-year-old, trying to impress him with her horseback-riding skills. They had come a long winding way from growing up on neighboring West Texas ranches, through her schooling in Chicago and his Boston medical training, to make a home at

Grey Sage. Grey Sage and Silas were her home. She couldn't remember a time she didn't love him, and she'd never loved him more than in this moment. Neither could she imagine anyone wanting to hurt Silas, her Silas. Unspoken tears left damp traces down her wrinkled cheeks.

Alo and Chepi had been walking for over an hour, checking outside entrances to the inn and looking for any sign of the perpetrator's activity. All was quiet, and all inside windows were dark. They stepped out of the blackness into the outside light at the barn entrance. Alo opened the barn door, returned with a thermos and two cups, and sat on the log bench underneath the one apple tree on the property. "Join me, Chepi. Lita made us coffee. It appears all our guests and residents are in bed with the lights out. Let's take a break."

"Thank you. Coffee smells good." Chepi sat and looked up. "Looks like someone needs to pick some apples. This tree is loaded. Tanzi makes fried apple pies that'll make a chipmunk spit in a chimpanzee's face."

"That good, you say? I'd like to try one of those. This is our only apple tree, and we treat it like royalty. The apple picking should be within the week. I'll make certain you and Tanzi get some." Alo poured a cup and offered it to Chepi. "Hope you like it straight. It will warm us. Must be fifty degrees and dropping. Rain coming in a little later."

Chepi took the cup. "Straight is good. Never had time for cream and sugar." He took a sip. "Tanzi told me that you were a breathing barometer and a self-taught meteorologist who never misses."

"Tanzi's been spending too much time with Lita. Cannot say that I was self-taught. I grew up in these mountains and spent most of my childhood with my grandfather. He taught me the Hopi ways—how to move through the forest without being heard or leaving a trail, how to track animals, how to read the signs for weather, and how to be a good steward of the land—but he never taught me how to deal with someone who would want to hurt Silas."

"If you don't mind my asking, how did you come to live at Grey Sage?"

Alo knew Chepi was Hopi and wanted to hear his story. He took a long, deep breath and spoke in a raspy voice just above a whisper. "Silas delivered our first daughter, a difficult delivery, and I had little money to pay him. I offered my work as a handyman and a construction worker to pay off my debt. They had just bought this property, and Maude had big dreams for it, adding on to the small cottage and creating a real home for them. She was looking for someone to help her stay true to the local architecture and someone who knew something about building adobe structures. That happened to be my line of work. Her big dreams of having an art studio and other buildings on the property and land management soon turned into full-time work. That was nearly forty years ago."

Chepi did not respond or ask another question as they drank their coffee. In the silence, he began to hum.

Alo closed his eyes and listened. The tune was familiar. When Chepi stopped humming, Alo said, "My grandmother sang that song to me when I was a child. Don't know the words."

"Neither do I. My grandmother sang it to me, too, but I'm embarrassed to say I don't speak my ancestral language."

"Our Hopi ways are being lost, Chepi. Lita's tried to pass some of them on to our girls, especially the cooking and crafts. And I spent many hours every day with Elan when he was a small boy teaching him what my grandfather taught me. Silas was so busy taking care of sick people, leaving early and coming home late day after day, and I was here. He was a good, good father, but when Silas was working, Elan was my shadow. That boy could mimic bird sounds like no one I ever heard. We made games out of tracking each other through the forest. He was better at it than I was. Elan knew every square inch of this property and loved it as much as Maude and Silas do. He would have been a good Hopi." Alo paused and poured them another cup of coffee and closed the thermos. "I think if Elan had lived, he might have been a doctor. He had a heart for helping and rescuing animals and people. That's how he died, trying to rescue a rock climber."

"Must have been hard on all of you to lose him so young."

"It was. Still is. Nothing natural about losing a child. You'll understand better when you have one of your own."

"Tanzi and I hope to have children. She wants to finish school first." He hesitated before continuing. "I've seen death. Saw a kid gunned down on the street. A teenager mangled in a car wreck during a storm. A young girl raped and strangled. No words for those images, and no words for the hurt I've seen on the parents' faces." He paused before asking, "Silas and Maude are good people?"

"The best. They're family. Silas has given his life to taking care of people, mostly people who couldn't afford the care. And Maude . . . Why, she's given so many kids free art instruction. And no one knows, not even Maude and Silas, how many students were able to go to college because of their generosity. It's goodness that you don't see in many folks. They deeded us the property down by the stream, and we built ourselves a casita. In almost forty years, we've never had a cross word. I'd give my life to protect theirs."

Downing the last of his coffee, Chepi stood from the log

bench. "Well, you won't be doing that. My buddies and I will see to it. I hope you don't mind that I'll be loaning Chief a handgun. She requested one, and I told her I'd bring her one tomorrow."

"I have no problem with that. I trust her judgment and yours." Alo stood and took the paper cup from Chepi.

"Any other guns on the property?"

"No handguns. Silas and I both have hunting rifles and shotguns, but we've never needed a gun for protection. Chepi, you've been out here this afternoon. You've heard all the details of these events. You've seen the property. You've heard Sarki. Who's doing this? What are your real thoughts?"

"Nothing much more than I reported to the group. My gut tells me Silas's life is not in danger, but I won't bet on it and leave him unprotected. Sounds like somebody just wants to scare and torment him and Maude. I think Chief's first instinct is that it's someone who has lost a child and wants some kind of vengeance because Silas was the doctor. All indications point to that. Nothing's missing. Nothing's destroyed—other than the painting, which can be fixed. But he . . . or she is sending a message. Time will tell." He paused. "Alo, this is my job, not yours. I appreciate your company, but it's nearly two o'clock. Go home and get some sleep. Relief will be here at six. Maybe I'll see you before I leave."

"Lita and I are staying here tonight. We both prefer it in case we're needed. There's a bathroom in the far corner of the barn. And next to it, there's a small workroom with a heater. It won't warm you like a fire or a hot shower, but it'll knock the chill. I'll bring out a cot before I go to bed."

"Thanks. No need for a cot. When we're here, we're on the job. See you in the morning."

Alo watched Chepi walk away in the darkness.

Walk softly. Careful. I see him, but he doesn't see me. He's walking softly. Watch for the stones. There it is. My spot by the tree. I can see everything from there. No lights in the windows. Everyone is asleep. No sleep for me. Bright light at the barn. I'll wait. I wonder what time it is. Can't use the flashlight. The walker might see me. I'll wait. Don't fall asleep. Just wait and watch. She told that story. I heard her story. I think she knows me. I think she told that story for me.

I saw you, my little white dove. You came to me. Once I held you in my hand, felt your softness and heard your coos, I was never the same. But then you flew from my hand. You were flying so high, so close to the sun I feared your feathers might become flames.

They said you were gone forever, but I waited down by the river where you first came to me. I waited for you to return. Every day, from my waking moment until the darkness poured over me, I waited. I waited so long.

Then one day I heard you. I couldn't see you. Maybe I didn't hear you. Maybe it was the wind in the pines or the water flowing over the stones.

But I felt the whir of your wings and heard your soft, mournful coo. I held my hands high in the air, waiting for your return. Hours, maybe days, I held them there, hoping you would come. I could sense you, but I could not see you.

Wait, this wasn't part of her story. I can tell the story. Maybe she didn't know this part.

Then in the dark of the night, as I slept by the river with a cold stone for my pillow, you came to me. You moved in silence, making no sound to wake me, but I knew you were there. When I opened my eyes, you were close, your white feathers glistened in the moonlight. I stared at you, feeling myself growing smaller and smaller until you flew just above me and with your wing swept me onto your back. We were one as we flew into the boundless abyss of the night sky.

Senseless stories. No white dove. No flying away into the sky. No coming back. I killed a bird. Now only blood and pain and emptiness and sorrow. You can't fly. You're gone, gone from me forever. But I still feel you, like I would feel the phantom pain of a missing arm. Real but not real. No one believes me.

I heard you that night. You were whimpering. I couldn't reach you. I tried. Then you stopped whimpering. Or I stopped hearing you. But I could feel it like the tide, the water, or maybe the wind. I don't know. Whatever it was was pulling us apart. I knew you were leaving me.

I told him. I told that man in white. I told him over and over again. I screamed at him, but he just wouldn't listen. He will listen now. I will make him listen.

The wind. I'm cold, and it's so dark. The walker is still walking. I can see his shadow in the moonlight. I can't breathe. He's close and could hear me. He's looking for me. I must go. I don't know if I can find my way home in the dark. The darkness is so thick I can touch it.

You're not coming back to me. You have another home, but I will come back to this place. It's an inn. They have guests. They won't know it's me. I will make him, the one in the white coat, the one with the Eye of the Medicine Man, I will make him listen this time.

Chapter Fourteen

Wednesday morning

Alo put on his slicker and went to the barn at five thirty. He opened the barn doors and stepped inside out of the drizzle. No sign of Chepi. Thinking that he might be patrolling the grounds, Alo flipped the outside light switch three times, turning the light on and off. In the vast darkness, even one barn light flickering would be a signal to get Chepi's attention. Alo had no reason to look in the workroom. He knew he would not find Chepi asleep on the cot he had brought out before he went to bed. Alo took off his slicker and waited just inside the barn door.

In less than a minute, Chepi stepped out of the darkness. "Good morning. You're up early."

"I rise early every day. It seems we're the only ones awake to greet the morning. Even Lita is still asleep. This drizzle and the wind in the pines make for good sleeping."

"You must have dressed in the dark. I haven't seen a light on anywhere on the property. I figured it was you with the barn light."

Alo stepped farther back into the barn to avoid the drizzle. "Come on in. How was your night?"

Chepi joined Alo inside the barn and brushed the water from his rain poncho. "Cold, wet, and quiet. Didn't see or hear anything unusual. I came to the barn about three thirty to warm myself for a few minutes. Did you get some sleep?"

"Would have slept better in my casita, but yes, I slept a couple of hours. I'll take over now. You can go on home."

"No sir, my buddies are to let me know by six what their availabilities are for the next few days. I'll get a schedule prepared for Chief this morning. She wanted to see me at six thirty, and she'll want you there too. After my meeting with her, I'll go home for a couple of hours of shut-eye before I go to work at ten. Would you like a copy of the schedule when I get it made?"

"Yes, I would, please. What have you told your guys?"

"I had to tell them enough to let them know it was a serious job. They know about the break-ins and a stalker who seems to come and go unseen in the daylight and the darkness. Not too many details, but they understand the threat."

"No police uniforms, I hope."

"No, sir. They'll be dressed like hikers and hunters, and they know to steer clear of guests and to try to remain unseen. But they will be armed. These are good men, highly trained, and you can count on them. I'll give you their names and numbers with the schedule. I'm working to get both of them out for an hour at the same time so you can walk the property and give them the lay of the land."

"I stand ready to do that."

"With their shifts, that might not work. If it doesn't, it would still be good if you could check in with them when they arrive and do a walk-around. I'll be here at night. Between you and me, we can make certain the doors are locked and the inn and perimeters are secure. My guys will be on patrol in the daylight hours." Chepi reached for his phone in his pocket. "Give me your email, and I'll send you the schedule when I get it made."

Alo hesitated. He didn't want to tell Chepi that he had no email address. Email was the last thing he had resisted.

He had tried it for a while, but it was unnatural and annoyed him. He left the emailing up to Lita and Maude. "Just send the schedule to Sarki. We'll get them printed for Silas and for me. Two printers in the library. I want Silas to know what's going on and to feel safe."

"Will do. I think with you and my two buddies and myself, we can keep things covered round the clock for the next few days."

"Not so worried about the next couple of days with possible rain. I'm thinking the group won't be making any outings, so the inn will have people moving around. Lots of activity. I'm more concerned about the weekend. Most of the guests will be leaving on Friday. I think we'll be more vulnerable when there's less activity around the inn."

Chepi nodded in agreement. "We'll figure ways to give the appearance of activity, and we'll keep Dr. Thornhill safe." He paused. "Do you think the Thornhills would consider going away for a few days, take a trip, a vacation maybe? It would give Chief time to get to the bottom of this without having to worry about the doctor's safety."

"That's a good thought, but you won't get Maude and Silas away from here now. We still have three other guests who will be with us through October. I can mention it to Silas and assure him that Lita and I can take care of things here with the guests, but I might as well be asking him to walk a tightrope across the Rio Grande Gorge. This is their home. Besides, you can't always run from trouble. He knows that. Trouble has a way of following you. We can keep him safe here."

"You're right about that. And trouble has a way of hanging around and circling back."

"You may not know, but Sarki is with the group that will be leaving on Friday. Going back home to Chicago."

Chepi's head dropped as though he had been dealt a

blow. "You mean Chief is leaving day after tomorrow?"

"Haven't talked to her about it. But she's traveling with the group, and it's a safe assumption she'll be going home."

"Maybe, but Chief doesn't strike me as the kind who'd be going anywhere until this case is solved. I'll ask her myself. If she's leaving on Friday, I need to make some arrangements and get ready."

"I guess we'll know the answer to that within the hour. Let's get to the kitchen and make some coffee. I'll turn on all the lights and start the fire. Glad I loaded up with dry wood yesterday. A fire will warm your bones like nothing else." Alo looked at his watch. "Lita and Maude will be starting breakfast in about half an hour. You got dry clothes?"

"Yes, sir, in my car. I'll get them and meet you in the kitchen. I'll have time to dry out before I meet with Chief. Thanks."

"You're welcome. I'll leave the mudroom door open. Just come on in." Alo put on his slicker and walked away.

Maude poured maple syrup into small pitchers for warming in the microwave. Talking was an effort, so she was more quiet than usual.

Lita was at the griddle, flipping sweet-potato pancakes. "If I make it through this week, I'll be bingeing on nightshades the next few days, and I may never cook another sweet potato again. At least the colonel is easy to please with his sugar restrictions. But honestly, I have this desire to cook a whole eggplant with tomatoes and smother it with so much cheese that Sarki would never recognize it. I want to know what happens to her when she eats it."

"Lita, there's nothing about that you need to know. You have fed her well, and everyone else too. Besides, we don't need Sarki to be ill or unhappy, for obvious reasons."

Lita flipped another pancake. "I know. She's supposed to be on retreat, and she's running this investigation. I'll just keep feeding her sweet potatoes and lettuce. Got to keep her healthy and out of the bathroom."

"Shush, Lita. She'll be walking in here any minute to meet with Chepi."

"All right. When you finish filling the syrup pitchers, would you mix up a bit of sour cream with brown sugar and cinnamon? Oh, and grab the bag of pecan pieces out of the fridge in the mudroom. Thought I might serve an alternative topping for the pancakes this morning. We're running low on maple syrup, and I get stingy when there's less than two gallons."

Maude had returned with the pecans when Lily glided into the room with the sleeves of her zebra-striped silk kaftan flowing behind her. "Good morning, Lily."

"I suppose it is. Where's the coffee?"

"Silas's caffeine sludge is at the coffee bar over there, and the coffee urn in the dining room should be ready. Take your pick."

"I'll help Silas out. He shouldn't be drinking that elixir alone."

Maude watched Lily float to the coffee bar in the kitchen. "Seems you were up late last night."

"No, not as late as I would have liked. You and Silas just turned in early." Lily returned to the island where Maude was stirring cinnamon and brown sugar into the sour cream. She perched herself on the bar stool.

"What's that 'as I would have liked' supposed to mean?"

"It means that I waited rather impatiently to have a few private moments with Noble by the fire. Instead, I listened to cloyingly sweet Reba with her psychological jargon and stiff-necked Noble talk without breathing about the four basic personality types and how he could have used those in his hiring practices at the bank."

"So now, Mr. Possibility has turned into . . ."

"Reba's project. But he'll tire of her. She's boring and predictable." Lily was making a three-sixty on the swivel stool. "Look at these stripes, Maude. I look like a whirligig."

Maude knew Lita was about to explode in tetchiness or laughter. "Lily, stop. You're making me dizzy. And it might be a good idea to turn down your volume knob and slow down on the coffee. Sarki's talking with Chepi in the gathering room."

Maude saw Lily's raised eyebrows. "Anything going on I need to know about?"

"No. No real developments, but security is in place." Maude poured two cups of pecan pieces into an earthenware bowl that matched the syrup pitchers.

"I actually came in here to talk to you about evening plans. We'll be leaving on Friday, and you know we usually have a show-and-tell on our last night. Think we're still on for that tomorrow night?"

"Of course we are. Nothing to keep us from our tradition. I was even thinking that maybe Clara might do an improvisational story-telling linking all the paintings. We could put the easels with the paintings in front of the fireplace for viewing as she tells the story, and maybe Kyah could provide background music with her guitar. That would be after the others had opportunity to talk about their paintings and their experience here." Maude took the two pitchers of syrup to the microwave for warming.

"Well, my friend, talking about their paintings shouldn't take long. It'll be only Reba, Noble, Bea, and I don't know about Henry. I think he's given up on his painting. I'll know today, and if Clara can weave Bea's peonies into a story with the other southwest landscapes, then we should give her another award. And you know that Laura just quit. Q-u-i-t, quit. She suddenly felt the lure of baking again. So, she's moved from the studio to the kitchen. It's her time and money if she'd rather sift flour."

"Cut Laura some slack, Lily. Maybe she'll create something fabulous in the kitchen that will be her contribution to the evening. And there's your painting. You must unveil it and talk to us about it."

"Yes, my painting. It will be fabulous. I'll show Noble and that shrieky shrink a personality type neither of them has ever seen. And it won't be boring." She grinned so widely her top and bottom teeth showed. "And don't you have something for unveiling?"

Maude put the syrup pitchers, the sour-cream mixture, and the pecans on a wooden tray for transporting to the dining room. "I did. I mean I do, but I'm not certain this is the time for the unveiling. So don't count on me. Maybe I'll do an unveiling in the studio before the group leaves on Friday." She paused. "I do need to ask your opinion about something else."

"You know me. I've never been short on opinions or quiet about them either. So, ask. If you don't ask soon, I'll start spouting off opinions on things you couldn't care less about."

Maude hesitated. "I was thinking about asking Boots and Drake to speak after dinner tonight and talk about their work. They've become friendly to the group. Do you think that would be interesting?"

Maude watched Lily's eyes roll. "A scholar who pushes his glasses up on his nose at least every twelve seconds talking about all things Native American?"

"Native American folklore, I think. And his research led

him to this area. Might be interesting to learn more about the culture of the Pueblos and the Hopis."

"That sounds a bit more interesting. And what about the greasy-haired fellow who hasn't changed his shirt since we've been here? Sort of gives me the shivers, and I'm still not convinced he's not behind this . . . this thing. What's he working on?"

"A screenplay. A Western of some kind. I know Boots is consulting with him on the project. What do you think? Yes or no?"

"Might be interesting, might not. Guess you could give them an hour, and then if folks are engaged and asking questions, or if Alo gets involved, let them continue."

"I like that idea. A specific amount of time and just see how things go. I'll ask them."

Lily lowered her voice. "You know, I hate leaving you and Silas like this. So many unanswered questions. Maude, I can stay if you like."

"Oh, I'd like you to stay, but Reba's headed to Albuquerque, and I just learned a few minutes ago that Sarki might be planning to stay here for a few more days. It's probably best if you travel with Henry and Bea back to Chicago. And with Reba headed in another direction, you can have Mr. Stiff Neck all to yourself."

"Not even certain I'd want that. I just don't like to be bested, especially by a milk-toast, middle-aged prude. But I will stay if you say the word. Or I can always come back."

"And I would call you to return if I needed you. Silas assures me this matter will be solved and taken care of quickly. I don't know if he truly believes that or if he's trying to relieve my worries. Maybe when all of this is over, we can take a trip somewhere together to get Silas and me out of these doldrums. Seems our grief over Elan has returned like this looming gray cloud that enshrouds us."

Maude put a spoon in the bowl of pecans on the tray.

"Maude, let's go to Jackson, Wyoming. The Arts for the Parks competition is over, but the art is still on display for another couple of weeks. I could meet you there next week. Jackson Hole is fabulous in September, and we could stay out at Teton Village, maybe take a drive through Yellowstone. I haven't done that in years. Silas could even go fly fishing. Let's do it."

"That's tempting, Lily, but I'd just as soon stay here until the problem is solved. I don't want to go away fearing that the problem would follow us or still be waiting on us when we return. But it does sound inviting."

Lily slithered off the stool and put her arm around Maude's spindly shoulders. "Will you at least think about it?" She paused. "And Maude, you need to gain some weight. You're getting too thin. Trust me, plumpness will get rid of some of those wrinkles."

"Why thank you, Lily. Another one of your opinions. I'll give that some thought when I know Silas is safe and my appetite returns. And while I'm checking on my weight loss, maybe you should be checking on the tremor I noticed in your right hand as you were painting yesterday."

She noted Lily's surprise. "Already done that. It's fine. Hereditary."

"Good. Just keep a watch on it. You can always talk to Silas." She handed the tray to Lily. "How about taking this to the dining room? You can put it on the sideboard where Lita will serve our breakfast buffet." She intentionally and playfully coughed. "I fear I'm too frail to lift it."

She winked at Lily, her signal she had taken no offense. They had always understood each other—no pandering, only compassionate honesty. As different in their personalities as red and blue, but together they made a rich purple. They had appreciated and learned from each other's differences through the years, and their passion for art and beauty had been one cord that had bound them for decades.

Chepi went over the schedule with Sarki as Alo and Silas listened. "Covered twenty-four seven for the next week, Chief," he finished up. "And I have another couple of officers who can step in if we need them."

"Understood. Thorough job. But neither of them has been on the property yet, correct?"

"No, ma'am. But Alo will walk the property with them when they arrive. Then I'll be here for the overnights."

"You have a day job, don't you?"

"Yes, ma'am, I do. But I can handle both. I operate well on four to six hours of sleep, and this is temporary. If at any time I don't think I'm alert enough to do the job, I'll send in another man." Chepi caught himself. "Pardon me, Chief, I meant to say another guard. But honestly, we don't have many women in our department here. These guys are buddies that went through training with me, and I trust them."

"Understood."

Alo added, "Everything here is covered. But I'm interested in knowing what will take place in the investigation today."

Sarki responded quickly. "We know the prints won't be of any help. I spent some time last night researching the names of your patients on the list you gave me, Silas. After breakfast, I'd like us to sit together with your files and go over them one by one. I've eliminated a few of them already. They just don't fit the profile, and they don't live in the area. But you have experiential knowledge that I cannot get from my research."

Silas had been staring at the schedule and now raised his head. "Yes, I can do that. Odd thing, even with a bit of forgetfulness these days, I have vivid memories of my patients. Hopefully, I can be of help."

"I'm certain you will." Sarki looked at her notes. "I'm waiting to hear about the symbols on the papers. I gave the investigator a couple of tubes of Maude's red paint. May or may not be significant. Whether the perpetrator brought the papers already painted or painted them here gives us some insight into his thinking. Every particle of information, when pieced together, will give us a better picture."

Alo raised a hand. "Remember, if you need more information about the symbols themselves and why the red color might have been used, you can speak to Chooli, the director at the Museum of Indian Arts and Culture. She has offered her services to help. Silas delivered her in a difficult birth years ago, and she figures she owes him her life."

"I may take you up on that, but first things first. I want to have some time with Silas this morning."

Chepi folded his notebook. "Chief, I know you're traveling with a group that will be leaving on Friday."

Before he could say more, Sarki interrupted. "Correction. I came with a group who will be leaving on Friday. I'll be speaking with Maude earlier this morning. I won't be leaving with the group unless we have solved the case."

"Yes, ma'am. I figured as much. You're like an eagle who grabs a trout on the surface of shallow water. His talons won't let go until he has that fish on dry ground. I didn't see you as one who'd leave until the perpetrator is in custody and this case is in the files as solved. Thank you, Chief."

"Hopefully, we'll get this case solved sooner rather than later. Alo, should I want to talk with the director of the museum, is it possible to get me there this afternoon?"

"Possibly. From my end, yes. I'll call to see if she's in her office today."

"Let me know. That's all for now." She turned to Silas. "Where shall we meet after breakfast, Silas?"

"Would the library be suitable for you? I think most of the guests will be in the studio today."

"Understood. Library immediately after breakfast."

Raining. Last night's cold still in my bones. I'll go back today. I can't stay here. It's not home. Got to get inside where he is. All those people may still be there. I don't care about them, only the man in white. Not sitting in the woods in the rain. Not today. No more just watching and waiting. Paper and paint, where are they? I'll smear with my finger like last time. Head. Large red eyes. Wings folded. Smudge the feathers. Feathers don't matter. There it is. The owl. The omen. Bad omen. The man in white will know what that means. Now, where will I put it? He has to be the one to find it. I'll know when I get there. I'm tired of pacing but I can't be still. I must do this thing. I must finish what I started.

Chapter Fifteen

Silas opened the double doors between the library and the office he shared with Maude. He unlocked the desk drawer to retrieve the ledger of the patients he had lost. It would be ready for his conversation with Sarki. He heard her enter the library and stepped from the office to greet her.

"Could we meet in here? That way, if someone strolls into the library, we won't be disturbed."

"Understood." Sarki followed him into the office and held her stack of files while she waited for Silas to close the door. "The table next to the window suitable for you?"

"Yes. Would you like a cup of coffee or a glass of water?"

"Thank you, but no. Let's get right to it."

He picked up the ledger from the desk and joined Sarki at the table. "I see you have the files. I hope they were helpful."

"I am hoping the same. It was helpful that your doctor friend released them so quickly. I put them through the sieve last night."

"Sieve?"

"Just what I call getting down to the fine details, a sifting of information to eliminate some possibilities. Elimination is a significant part of the investigative process. Probably the same in medicine. You only gave me six names, and I have eliminated four. But I'd like to know how you came up with these six names."

He pointed to his ledger. "I've kept a list of patients I have lost during my years as a practicing physician. No one has ever seen this before. Not even Maude. She didn't even know it existed until last night. I needed these names as a reminder."

"Maybe it would have been a good thing to keep a ledger of all those patients you were able to help."

"You sound like Maude. These names were important too. In looking through them, I did a bit of sifting myself, assuming whoever is doing this is someone with fresh grief. So, I only looked through the past five years of my records to find these six."

He noted Sarki's puzzled expression.

"You said fresh grief. Five years is fresh grief? Seems like a long time."

Silas slowly opened the ledger. "You've never lost a child. Seems the grief is always fresh. But you indicated this person was probably young and a parent who lost a child, so I didn't look at the older records."

"Makes sense. I've read every word in these files, including your handwritten notes, and I've eliminated four." She handed all six files to him. "I know you've read these, but could you look over them again and see which ones you might eliminate?"

Silas took the files and opened the top one. He took his glasses from his shirt pocket and began to read. A deluge of vivid memories of each case, each injury, each illness, each child, and each parent filled his thoughts. He browsed the files quickly and created two stacks.

"That didn't take long."

Silas tapped his temple with his index finger. "Some things you don't forget, and you only need the files to help recall the situation." He slid his two stacks of files across the table to Sarki.

Sarki fanned the two stacks of files on the table like a hand of cards and shifted her eyes to Silas. "Explain."

"The four on your left I've eliminated. The two on your right—the Borden and Jemez cases—I believe to be viable."

"We must have used the same sieve. Tell me why you did not eliminate these two cases." Sarki moved the files, opened her notebook in front of her, and pulled out her pen.

"Can't say exactly. Just something visceral about these two. I remembered some feelings I had about the parents. The Bordens took their daughter's death hard. They were poor, lived up in the mountains. Liliana was four when she got sick. They took her to a medicine man who treated her with what he had—herbs and tribal medicine—which works sometimes. He gave her nothing harmful, but he robbed her of time, valuable time, when she needed treatment for an aggressive leukemia. She was near death when they brought her to the hospital, and there was little to nothing curative we could do at that point. Our job was to keep her comfortable."

"How long?"

"Only six days after she came to us. She could hardly swallow water and had not eaten for several days before they brought her to the hospital emergency room. Her fever was high. Her skin was covered in bruises from the internal bleeding, and her frail body was riddled with infection."

"Did you pursue charges of some kind against those parents? Wasn't that neglect or child endangerment?"

Silas hung his head. "They were poor and did the best they could. Besides, they had other children at home who needed them. What good would piling on more trouble do? After Liliana died, her mother asked me if anything could have been done. I was honest and told her that specialized treatment might have helped. Their guilt was punishment enough."

Sarki lifted her pen and looked at Silas. "Did they threaten you?"

"No. It wasn't a threat. Just anger at losing her. They accused me of charading as a medicine man and even went so far in the conversation as to accuse me of using bad medicine and killing her. But they never threatened me. After she died, I never heard from them again."

"What about the Jemez case?"

Silas shifted in his chair. "That one was different. I was the doctor on call at the hospital the night they brought Nodin and his mother, Semi, in by ambulance. They were in a head-on collision up in the mountains during a snowstorm, and the boy was thrown from the car. He was a beautiful lad. Eight years old. This situation necessitated a judgment call, the kind no doctor likes to make.

"Nodin had massive head injuries and was bleeding internally from other injuries. He had been exposed to the cold for possibly an hour before anyone got to him. That exposure caused hypothermia, and like little Liliana, he was too far gone when he came to me. I made the decision to care for his mother, who was seriously injured herself but had a chance of survival. She was hysterical about the boy, wanting me to take care of him and not her, and wanting me to leave her there with him. As it turns out, he died within fifteen minutes of his arrival at the hospital, and because of her internal injuries, we had to perform emergency surgery. In the surgery, we discovered she was pregnant. Lost the baby, and we came close to losing her."

"That was a tough one."

Silas looked beyond Sarki. "Yes. A tough one, but tougher for her. She had months of healing and physical therapy while grieving the loss of Nodin and a baby girl she never got to hold. And with the surgery we had to do, she could no longer have children. Too much heartbreak for a young woman. When she woke from surgery and learned what had happened, she refused to let me treat her and asked for another doctor. Said she couldn't bear to look at me. All she could see was the man who took her son away. I stayed in touch with the doctor who treated her."

"What about the fathers? You've only talked about the mothers?"

"As I recall, Liliana's father was a very quiet man. Not unusual for that culture. But the Jemez father, Juan, was neither quiet nor calm. He wasn't so angry at me as he was at his wife for driving in the snowstorm. In his grief, he laid the guilt on her. Not a loving, nurturing man, at least not to his wife, and I suspect not to his son. But I don't recall any sense of his threatening me."

"He's out of the picture now."

Silas came forward in his chair. "What do you mean?"

"Divorced. According to the research I did last night, they're both still in Santa Fe, but not together."

"I see. That often happens when a couple loses a child. Their relationship just can't weather the sadness."

"You used the word *visceral* earlier. So, what does your gut say?"

"I just don't have a clear read on which one of them could do the things that have been done around here. I suppose if you pinned me down, I'd say it was the Jemez man."

"Understood. I'll give the captain a call and see if he's willing to do more in-depth investigation based on the information we can give him. He has access to records that would tell us where they are and if either of them has been in trouble with the law. It's our best lead in light of having no prints or DNA."

Sarki closed her notebook. "Is there anyone at the hospital who might tell you if either of them has been hospitalized in the last couple of years?"

"I think I can get that done with one phone call. If I can't, I'll make two calls."

"Understood. And you feel absolutely certain in your elimination of these four?"

"I don't feel absolutely certain about much these days. Let's just say I'm comfortable with all I told you."

Sarki stood. "I'll get right on this. I prefer having my next conversation in person with the captain. I'll get Alo to drive me to Santa Fe to speak with him and with the director at the museum. I have a sense we're getting somewhere." She took the two files with her and walked out the office door.

Silas stacked the other four files, closed his ledger, and sat for a few minutes, gazing out the window. Shafts of sunlight like laser beams pierced the gray clouds, flickering through the aspen limbs that quaked in the morning breezes.

A shadow. A man in fatigues walking at the edge of the forest near the creek bed. Silas was startled until he realized it was one of the guards. He was unaccustomed to armed men patrolling Grey Sage.

Maude opened the studio doors, wishing the weather was warm enough to open the portales doors. She put on her painting apron and went to the cabinet to get paints. She rarely painted in acrylics, but oils, taking so long to dry, were not an option for guests attempting to finish a painting in less than a week. She gathered the paints and distributed them as she thought needed. As she did, she glanced at Bea's painting of the peonies, recognizing she would have to work on this one again if it was to be finished.

As she was turning on the music, the group began to gather. Like school children going to their assigned seats, they returned to their work areas and began to prepare their palettes with the paint Maude had placed at their stations.

She watched as Bea flitted from one station to another with each of the guests, pointing the way to her painting. Finally arriving in front of the peonies, Bea asked, "Where's Lily? And that snarky lady, and the baker woman—the one who made the chocolate cake?"

Maude answered carefully, "Well, you know Lily. She will make her entrance soon, and I think Sarki is planning to go into Santa Fe this morning, since she wasn't able to go with us yesterday." She hated misleading, but she wasn't lying. "Laura will be in later with a surprise. How nice of you to notice they were missing."

"I'm not being nice," Bea stated. "I'm just wondering why I have to paint and they do not."

Before Maude could answer, Lily breezed through in black yoga pants and turtleneck minus her zebra-print kaftan and grabbed an apron. "I'm present, Bea." Without another word, Lily took her palette and brushes and began painting feverishly.

When everyone had begun to work, Maude announced, "I can hardly believe this is our last full day of painting. We must finish as much as we can by noon tomorrow so that we can set up your paintings for our traditional presentation tomorrow evening. And we have another surprise or two. So, let's get to work."

The right side of Maude's brain wondered about the conversation Silas was having with Sarki, and the left side evaluated the paintings as she visited each station. The time for instruction was over. Only hints and suggestions could be given at this stage of their work.

She saw that Bea was perched on her stool, staring at her painting, but she had not picked up a brush. Maude walked over. "Bea, I'd give a penny for your thoughts."

"I'll tell you what I think, and it will cost you nothing. I do not like this painting. There are no ballet slippers like you mentioned, and this painting says nothing about me and means nothing to me. It could be a frivolous purchase in a five-and-dime."

Maude swallowed her chuckle. "Well, Bea, I really don't like to disagree with you, but you could not be more wrong."

"Whatever do you mean?"

"Why, these delicate peonies speak volumes about you! And the contrast of the soft colors and that vibrant blue velvet cloth do too."

"Tell me more."

"The peonies are flowers that are given on special occasions to bring immense joy, like you and your dancing. The blossoms symbolize love and beauty and happiness and romance. They're you, completely you, Bea. Your dancing has brought all those things to so many people through the years. You're so delicate like the peonies, and yet you have this strong passion, evidenced in the strong blue you've painted here." Maude pointed to the velvet cloth. "And that vivid blue symbolizes royalty and elegance, just like you, Beatrice Caldwell. So do not tell me this painting says nothing about you."

Maude noticed Bea's head lifted a bit higher.

"I suppose you're right. With that, I must finish it. Move, please, so I can get to work."

"Certainly, and you can tell the other guests about these symbols tomorrow night when you present your painting."

Bea just stared back at Maude without saying a word and then picked up her brush and palette, which Maude had already prepared.

Maude walked to the far corner where Lily had isolated herself as she stood and painted on her large canvas. There was a marked difference in this painting. Maude did not know if it was a conscious decision on Lily's part or if it was a compensation for the obvious tremors as Lily held the large brush. The detail that was signature Lily was missing in this painting, but her colors and textures made up for the lack of fine brush strokes.

Lily stopped painting as Maude approached. "Did you get Bea settled down?"

"Momentarily. Don't let me stop you. Keep painting."

Lily laid down her brush and wiped her hands. "I don't think I'll finish this before we leave. What would you say if I left it here and came back in a couple of weeks to finish it and to have a good visit?"

Maude took a deep breath and hugged Lily. "I think that would be just what I need. We had such a good time last month when Kent and Emily got married, but we were all so busy with the wedding that you and I had little time to talk."

"Yes, and this visit has given us even less time. So at lunch time, what do you say that we look at our calendars?"

"Mine is clear. You just take a look at yours. Hopefully this situation, whatever it is that's going on around here, will be over by that time. We can really enjoy ourselves, just the two of us. And Silas, of course."

"Actually, that sounds better than going to Wyoming. We could drive up to Taos and spend a day, do some hiking on the warm days, and we can paint whenever we like. And maybe Silas or Alo could take me fishing. I haven't fly-fished in far too long." Lily picked up her brush again.

"I don't imagine it would take much persuasion to get either or both of them to do that. So, it's decided then. Just let me know when you're coming."

Lily laughed. "If I'm not in jail, I shall return soon."

"You planning to rob a bank or commit a murder?"

"Murder's more likely. I'll just plead insanity." She leaned in. "You know I love Bea, but Bea is a lot, and I mean a lot. We've had so little time to talk, I haven't told you what she did in the airport. You know me, Maude, and I'm not embarrassed easily, but . . ."

"Go on."

"During our stop in Denver, all the ladies went to the bathroom. Sarki and Reba left us and went on to the departure gate, but Laura and I were stuck waiting on Bea, who was still in the bathroom stall taking her own sweet time. All of a sudden, she said in this loud voice, 'Lily, those are the ugliest red shoes I have ever seen. Someone should tell you that with your big, unsightly feet, you shouldn't be wearing red shoes.'"

Maude laughed out loud. "Don't tell me. The lady in the next stall?"

"Yes. Laura and I were standing at the washbasin. And then Bea and the woman in the next stall opened their stall doors simultaneously. If looks could kill . . . Bea saw me and looked down at my feet. Then she looked at the lady beside her, who was wearing a loose-fitting, floral dress that could have been made out of old draperies. And she had on matching red shoes."

"What did you say, Lily?"

"Believe it or not, nothing. I pretended not to know Bea and quickly ducked into an open stall. I heard Bea apologize to the lady, telling her that she thought her friend Lily was the one wearing red shoes. Then she said, 'It wasn't Lily, so I guess it was you. Anyway, it doesn't matter. No one with feet like that should wear red shoes.'"

Maude laughed again. "Bea. No one like her."

"I tell you, Maude, the woman has lost all, and I mean all, inhibitions. And decorum? Gone. And sweet Henry? Well, he just pats her hand and changes the subject. He has a compassionate heart. And apparently, I do not."

Maude took Lily's arm. "Yes, you do, or you wouldn't keep bringing Bea with your traveling group. Her life of dance, romance, and privilege has spoiled her a bit, and we will just keep spoiling her. Her dips and dives in and out of reality certainly keep things interesting when she's around."

"That's one way to say it, my friend. I'll just say that twee thing's cup runneth over with her inflated self. Maybe Sarki will accompany her to the restroom on the trip home."

Maude had assumed Sarki had spoken with Lily. She hesitated. "Maybe Sarki hasn't had a chance to speak with you, but she told me at breakfast she was definitely planning to stay until this issue is solved and resolved, if we didn't mind. So, she won't be returning with the group."

"I didn't know. But it's no real surprise. I'll handle Bea. It eases my mind that Sarki will stay. She will solve this. She'll find this evil person and put him away. She always does."

"I pray so, and I pray that it's soon. I've lived with sadness but never with fear, and I don't like it." Maude caught herself. "Best stop this conversation right now. You keep painting, and I'll do what I do."

Maude walked to where Noble and Reba were painting and made a few comments. She then complimented Henry on his perspective and color choices. Amazed at the detail, she was studying Sarki's unfinished painting of the red cliffs when Laura walked in carrying a tray of warm snickerdoodles with Lita behind her balancing a tray of coffee and juice.

"Ah, now we know where Laura's been this morning. She has brought us some of her sweet treats. Let's take a break."

When everyone had finished snacking and had started painting again, Maude took a cup of coffee and a cookie and walked to the large windows overlooking the slope down to the creek bed. She dunked the cookie in her coffee and took a warm bite. Leaning against the window frame, she watched the aspens shimmering in the streams of light across the arroyo.

A shadow. A man with a hiking pole, dressed in fatigues, walking along the edge of the creek. Her breathing grew shallow, and her heart raced.

Chapter Sixteen

Wednesday afternoon

Sarki and Alo entered the mudroom door, Alo cautiously carrying Elan's portrait. Lita was in the kitchen beginning the preparation of the evening meal with Tanzi. Silas sat in his favorite chair in the gathering room with his study materials spread out on his lap board and his habitual cup of midafternoon coffee.

Lita approached Alo for her customary welcome-home kiss as he and Sarki entered the kitchen. "Welcome back, and I see you have brought the portrait home. That will make Maude's day. Did you have lunch, or could I prepare something for you quickly?"

Sarki answered before Alo could. "Ate in town. Where is everyone?"

"The writers are away from the inn doing research. Not sure where, but they should return by four o'clock to prepare for this evening. The artists are in the studio, where they've been all day except for a quick lunch on the portales. No siesta today."

"Could you get Maude to leave the studio without drawing much attention?" Sarki asked Lita. "Ask her to meet us in her office."

"Certainly. Do you need Silas too?"

"He looks busy, but he does need to join us."

Alo nodded in agreement. "I'll get Silas. We'll meet you

in five minutes."

As Sarki walked briskly out of the room, Lita asked Alo, "What's going on? She seems wound more tightly than usual."

"Just frustration, I'm guessing," Alo whispered. "She's accustomed to making things happen, and they are not happening on her timetable."

"I'll get Maude." Lita laid down her apron and left the kitchen.

Sarki was already in the office, sitting at the table near the window, when Alo and Silas arrived. Silas took the same seat where he'd met with Sarki earlier this morning. Alo turned Elan's portrait around and propped it against the wall next to the stone fireplace. It still bore the red image, which he didn't want Maude to see again—at least for now. Alo had wanted to get the painting cleaned up in town at one of the galleries before bringing it home, but he'd decided against it. He thought Maude was the better one to do the job because it was her painting, and it would satisfy her soul to restore it.

Alo positioned himself in front of the portrait so that Maude would not notice it when she entered the room. He had given Silas a brief report on their walk to the office, so no one said anything until Maude and Lita arrived moments later.

Alo motioned. "Maude, you sit with Sarki and Silas at the table. She has a bit of an update."

He nodded for Lita to join him. He noticed in Maude's slow movement that she expressed no eagerness as she pulled out the oak straight chair and took her seat at the table. Alo had sensed her reluctance for several days.

Sarki began. "I have nothing new, really. I was able to speak with the director at the museum, but she had little to add that Alo had not already told me. But it did confirm that the perpetrator has knowledge of these symbols, which gave me more insight into his mind. I was able to give that information to the investigator."

"Any more information about the paint used?" Silas asked.

"Yes. It was confirmed that the paint was from Maude's studio—the very tubes I gave the investigator. They lifted prints, but still no matches in the system. It would appear the perp did the work here in your studio. As I said before, that's bold."

Alo barely heard Maude's whisper. "Or demented."

Sarki's head snapped around in surprise. "You're right, Maude. Or demented. Hard to determine if the perp had a plan before he or she arrived and knew that he would find what he needed in the studio or if the thought came to him while he was on the property and went into the studio to get the job done. My gut says the former."

Silas inquired again. "Any more background information on the Borden or Jemez families?"

"Not conclusive, as the investigator hasn't finished the research yet. We do know that none of them have police records. We know where they live, and we know the Bordens had another child, and they still live in a small town up in the mountains. I asked the investigator and the captain about surveillance for all four for a few days. They don't have the manpower, but the captain agreed to assign someone to keep an eye on Juan and Semi Jemez, since they're here in Santa Fe. They're still trying to get a definitive address on her. But again, no criminal records on any of them."

Maude spoke again, louder this time. "That could be good, I suppose. We're not dealing with hardened criminals."

"Maybe, but not necessarily. Could be they just haven't

been caught," Sarki responded. "Regardless, we're not about to relax."

Alo stepped forward. "Maude, we did bring home Elan's portrait. It hasn't been cleaned, as I thought you would know best how to clean it without damaging it." He stepped aside. "It's right here when you're ready. Thought you might prefer to wait until our guests leave on Friday."

The light in Maude's face lifted his heavy spirit. He took Lita's hand and squeezed it.

"Yes, thank you, Alo. I would prefer to be the one to restore it, and waiting until the weekend is best. It will take some time, but I will be glad when Elan is above the fireplace again. This room's not the same without him."

"I'm assuming the guard has been on duty today."

Alo found Sarki's abruptness distasteful but said nothing.

Silas answered. "I know that Alo walked the grounds with him before you left for town. I didn't meet him, but I did see someone in fatigues walking in the edge of the forest earlier. I'm assuming it was the guard."

Beside him, Maude took a breath, then nodded as if she'd realized something. She had seen the guard too.

"Good." Sarki stood from her chair. "I'm headed to the studio to put some more paint on my canvas. I ponder when painting." She started to walk away and then turned back. "I almost forgot. We did learn one other thing from Chooli at the museum. The Jemez boy's name was Nodin according to your records. It means 'wind.' Probably irrelevant, but I found it interesting."

Maude closed the studio around five o'clock and encouraged

her guests to put on a jacket and take a short walk before dinner. "Breathe some fresh air and stretch your legs. And don't forget to stretch your eyes. They've been fixed and focused for hours today, so look far into the mountains and take in the last light and color of the day. Dinner at six thirty."

She met Alo on the portale as she walked toward the kitchen. She had no need to ask. He was headed to the studio to make certain all the doors and windows were secure.

Tanzi and Lita were moving around the kitchen as though their steps were choreographed. Maude entered, hoping they did not need her help. "I smell something that has the promise of being delicious."

Lita answered. "Guarantee on the promise. Mustard-glazed chicken. One of your favorites."

"Could I be of any help?"

"No." Lita was emphatic. "We have it covered. Why don't you take a breather? You've been at it all day. Go rest your eyes and your legs."

Relief. "That sounds like a prescription, and I think I'll take you up on that."

Maude walked straight to her office and headed for the portrait like a homing pigeon heads for home. She picked it up, turned it around, and stared at Elan's face, smudged and streaked with blood—red earlier but now almost brown after two days of drying. The only cleaning she had ever done to a painting was a light dusting. Since the painting was oil and had been sealed, she was hopeful the iron oxide from the blood would disappear with water and a light detergent.

She put it away in the closet until she could spend more time with it and went to her suite to lie down for a few minutes before dressing for dinner.

Maude was usually energized by artist retreats, but this one had drained her. She lay quietly with her thoughts. If she could only hold her breath and force her smiles until Friday, she would be able to breathe again when the inn was quiet. The writers were no bother, as they were usually out and about and were only seen at mealtimes, and sometimes not even then. She could manage better when she had no public responsibilities.

She closed her eyes and slipped into a light sleep, only waking when Silas kissed her cheek.

"Wake up, my dozing dear. You don't want Lily sitting in your hostess seat, do you?"

She roused and looked at the clock. "Thank you for waking me. Ten minutes to dinner. And speaking of Lily, she's coming back in a couple of weeks. Only Lily. No traveling companions, and I'm actually looking forward to her visit. She wanted to know if you might take her fly-fishing."

She did not know why that was her first thought upon waking. Maybe because Silas mentioned Lily or because she desperately wanted things back to normal. She rose quickly to freshen up.

Silas was changing his shirt as Maude brushed her hair. "Maude, you do remember the last time I took Lily fly-fishing? Bordered on a disaster for me—and the fish. We'll see. Depends on the weather. Could be really cold in another couple of weeks."

"Not to worry. Lily and I always find something inter-esting to do." She paused. "I'd like you to check out her tremors. She's been to a doctor, but that's all I know."

"I noticed the tremors too. Could be a number of things. Let's leave that be until she returns. Right now, we are spinning enough plates."

"As Sarki says, 'Understood.'"

They finished their freshening up and arrived in the dining room five minutes before dinner, which was sumptuous. Mixed salad greens with radishes, jicama and tomatoes, mustard-glazed chicken served over saffron rice with side dishes of a trio of sauteed peppers, fresh roasted asparagus and beets, and Laura's dessert of lime pound cake with a mango sauce and whipped cream. After dinner, the guests moved to the great room for an evening with the writers.

Boots and Drake had been receptive to her invitation of giving them an hour to do their presentations. Boots had asked for a screen to show photos, and Drake asked only for a stool where he could sit to read selections from his novel, which he was adapting into a screenplay.

After Maude's brief introductions, Alo slid the screen from the corner and placed it next to Boots. The professor began. "For Native Americans, the physical world where we humans live is actually a world of illusion and shadow. Reality for them is in the spiritual world, the world where the Creator lives. There is a belief that we are all connected and that everything in this earthly existence holds a deeper meaning."

He paced slowly in front of the screen as he spoke of how Native Americans through the centuries had woven cultural symbols and their stories into their art and how the meanings of the symbols were a part of the wisdom and culture of Native Americans.

"For example, the eagle holds great symbolism." He flashed the pictogram onto the screen. "But you must understand the symbol of the eagle represents much more than just the raptor itself, such as its relationship and place among in the world, its environment, what it communicates—its language so to speak, and what that eagle means to all other living things."

Boots continued with images of many of the symbols and then examples of how those symbols were used in pottery, weaving, baskets, and jewelry. "For many these symbols have power. Take this one for example."

Suddenly the screen was filled with the symbol of the Eye of the Medicine Man.

As Boots began to explain its significance and showed a silver belt buckle almost identical to the bolo Maude had given Silas years ago, Maude froze, as though everything and everyone in that room had been suspended in time. Images and thoughts flashed and ricocheted in her mind.

Why would he choose that symbol when there are so many others? What is Sarki thinking right now? And what about Alo? Is this a mere coincidence, or is the perpetrator among us? Maybe Lily was right after all. Sarki's theory could be all wrong.

She looked at Sarki. She sat as still as a totem, stone faced, not a muscle moving, and intensely staring at Boots.

Maude returned to the moment only when Boots asked Alo to remove the screen and everyone began to applaud. Boots closed by saying, "Friends, it has been my pleasure to speak to you this evening about some things that have stretched my mind and thinking through the years. Learning about other cultures has a way of doing that. Native Americans would read much more into our gathering here this evening than we do—the fact that in this moment of time, we, coming from many different places, are gathered in this room. I close with an ancient thought prevalent across many tribes of Native Americans. It goes something like this: When you came into this world, you cried to catch your breath, and the whole world rejoiced. Now go and live your lives so that when you breathe your last breath, the world will cry, and you will rejoice as you join the great Creator, the Great Spirit, in the world where it is eternal summer and there is always plenty."

With another round of applause, he made his way to take his seat next to Clara. On the way he tapped Drake on the shoulder with his folder. "Drake, my boy, you're up."

Drake, dressed in a clean shirt but still mop headed, took a seat on the stool Alo had provided. "I'll be doing readings from two of my novels, one for which I am writing the screenplay during my stay at Grey Sage. After Boots' presentation and my reading, it will become clear to you why we are here together. He's my professor and my constant source of wisdom, especially when it comes to native folklore. My novels draw heavily from what I have learned from his research."

He then set up the background for the scene he was about to read. Maude heard none of what he read, instead trying to connect the many dots of the events over the last several days. Most of those dots included Boots and Drake. The timing. The symbols. The library incident. It was far too much to be coincidental.

She was only jarred from her thoughts when Silas tugged at the sleeve of her sweater and whispered, "Drake's finished. Don't you think you should say something?"

Maude stood from the cuddle chair she shared with Silas, unsure that her legs would hold her up. She slowly made her way to the front of the room and delivered a few gracious comments about the presentations.

"I do believe that Laura has made another batch of cookies, and perhaps Boots and Drake will linger in the great room, if any of you have questions and would like to have conversation with them. We are all so busy during the day that we have little time to do that. Enjoy. Breakfast will be in the morning at seven thirty, and we have another lovely evening planned for tomorrow."

Maude took the deepest breath she had inhaled since the

presentations began and walked to where Silas was standing. Alo had gotten to Silas before she did.

Alo has the same questions I have.

It's here in my pocket, and it's the last one. The last message before I do what I must do. An omen of what's coming. I have to get it to the man in the white coat. It's time he suffered. They're all in that room again. I can see from the lights. They're living it up not caring about the hurt he caused. He doesn't deserve to live. I must get in, but everything is locked now. I saw the Indian locking doors and checking windows. I cannot spend another night in this damp cold. I'm going back. Where's my bag? No. My red bag? Where is it? I had it. I always have it. Did I drop it? It could be anywhere, but I must find it. I'll never find it in the dark. I can't use the light to search. I can't let the Indian or the walker see me. Not until I am ready. Tomorrow. I'll do it tomorrow. I'll come back. I'll walk the same path. I'll figure a way. I must find my bag. It's my life. It's my story.

Chapter Seventeen

Thursday

*A*fter an early-morning private briefing with Chepi about his night's surveillance, Sarki joined the others for breakfast. Chepi's report of a quiet night did not settle her spirit as she hoped it would. Something was needling her, and she didn't know what. She had that familiar yet uncomfortable feeling bedeviling her, like she was on the verge of something. Not really expecting any news from the investigator but merely to prod and remind him of her expectations, she made a couple of quick calls after breakfast. With nothing new to report, she joined the others in the studio to avoid any further suspicion about her continued absence and because she wanted to have something decent to show in the evening's presentation.

Sarki strode into the studio like a woman on a mission. The Indian flute music filled the quiet corners of the room, and the air was scented with cinnamon from the diffuser on the desk. Lily, moving with weird contortions, was in the far corner painting something on a canvas the size of a wall panel. All the others were at their stations. Maude was leaning over Bea's shoulder, guiding the paintbrush in her hand as one teaches a child to form letters. Clara was walking from station to station, eyeing each painting as though she were trying to memorize the scenes. Everyone was engaged. Without notice Sarki took her place and began. She painted and pondered, backing away at times and squinting her eyes. Other times, she leaned in close for fine brush work.

Sarki was cleaning her fan brush when Kyah came in and whispered something to Noble. She watched as Noble put down his brush, wiped his hands, removed his apron, and followed Kyah out of the studio. Maybe a business call. She hoped it was not a family emergency.

Maude approached her and spoke quietly. "You have made so much progress, Sarki, even with losing a good portion of the day yesterday. It is certainly presentable for tonight, and you will have a few more days with me after the others leave tomorrow to put on the finishing touches."

Sarki pitched her voice low and soft. "Not that I don't want to spend more time here, but I'm hoping that my stay will be short." She looked over her glasses at Maude. "For obvious reasons."

"Yes, for those reasons. But I'd really enjoy taking you back out to the red cliffs for another *plein air* session in the late-afternoon light. Sometimes we capture a scene in one light, and it looks so different with light from a different angle."

Sarki's antsy feeling returned. "Why do I think that you're not talking about my painting? You're talking about the presentation last night, aren't you?"

Maude leaned closer. "Not really. I was talking about your painting, but now that you mention it, I was jolted off center last night when Boots put up the pictogram of the Eye of the Medicine Man. And honestly, in thinking through things, I did wonder if perhaps our assumptions in looking at this situation are blinding us to the more obvious right here all along."

Sarki continued to paint. "Understood. Possible but not probable, unless there's some unknown mysterious connection between Boots and Silas. I know the timing is suspicious, and my antennae were waving last night, but I truly think we're on the right track. I did make Chepi and Alo aware of this development this morning, so they are alerted and will be vigilant."

Maude nodded, then backed away and spoke loudly enough for the others to hear. "Stunning choices, Sarki. Just keep at it."

"Thank you, Maude. I'm really on to something here."

Only moments passed before Laura came in with another tray of her baked treats. "Warm butterscotch bars right out of the oven, and Lita's coming with coffee and a pitcher of ice-cold milk. Coffee's good, but I recommend milk with these. It will take you back to your childhood."

During the break, Clara made her rounds to ask questions of each artist, gathering information for her storytelling this evening.

As the group was enjoying the treats, Noble returned to the studio. Sarki approached him. "I saw Kyah call you away. I do hope all is well. An emergency or problem back in Chicago?"

Noble swallowed. "No. No problem at all. Just an odd and most interesting thing. Do you remember Sunday afternoon when the young woman showed up and needed assistance with her car troubles?"

"You mean when you pulled out a three one-hundred-dollar bills to pay for her car repairs and restored my faith in bankers?"

"Yes. That pitiful woman—the one who looked like her hair had been chewed off. Well, she came by to repay me. She only had two hundred and said she would be back with the other hundred later."

Sarki's antennae were waving stronger. "Did she know your name?"

"No. She had described me to Kyah, and Kyah figured it out. Guess I can't help being a tall, slender, distinguished, handsome gent. I didn't want to take the money back, but she insisted. I told her just to pay the other hundred forward because I'd be leaving tomorrow."

"Can't recall that ever happening before. Was she driving?"

"I assume she was, but I can't say for sure. She was standing in the entrance hallway waiting, and I had no reason to think about a car. She really caught me off guard."

"I suppose it would. Well, we'd better get back to painting."

The butterscotch bar churned in Sarki's stomach. She left the room abruptly and walked through the portales to get a look at the driveway. No car in sight and no dust on the lane from traffic. She went to the entrance to see if the woman might still be inside speaking with Kyah. No sign of her.

She saw Kyah in the hallway and approached her. "Did the woman who just spoke with Mr. Sinclair leave?"

"Yes, ma'am. Right after speaking with him."

"Was she driving a car?"

"I wasn't paying close attention, but I didn't see a car. But she could have parked it where I couldn't see it from the front door."

"So, she rang the front doorbell?"

"Yes, ma'am, she did."

"Okay. Thank you, and if she returns, please let me know. You know where I'll be."

Stomach still churning, Sarki returned to the studio.

Silas was grateful for a few moments alone as he entered the office and closed the door. He was especially glad Maude and Sarki were in the studio and that Alo had gone to pick up another load of firewood. He sat at the desk, reading the Jemez file again while waiting for the call from the hospital. The administrator had reported yesterday that someone from the records department would call at ten o'clock this morning with the information he sought.

Normally a sound sleeper, he'd been restless through most of the night. He and Maude had talked over Boots's presentation for more than an hour. Maude was puzzled and disturbed, thinking maybe the recent threats had nothing to do with his treatment of a former patient. She had been unable to convince him that it could be Boots, even with a complete recounting of his possible involvement in every incident. But after the discussion, his thoughts continued to rumble long after Maude was asleep. He finally concluded Sarki was on the right track. Boots had no known or sensible motive.

The phone rang. He picked it up on the first ring. "Hello."

"Dr. Thornhill, this is Monica from the records department at the hospital in Santa Fe. How good to speak with you this morning, and I do hope you and Mrs. Thornhill are doing well. We all miss you around the hospital—not only the patients you cared for, but the nursing and administrative staff. They just don't make doctors like you anymore."

"Thank you, Monica. You sweetly made this old relic of a doctor's day. I'll try to drop by just to walk the halls and see everyone soon. I might even put on my white coat again."

"Let us know, and we'll put out the welcome mat." She paused. "I was able to locate the information you requested. Regarding the Bordens, Mrs. Borden was the only family member admitted here since their daughter died. She gave birth to a healthy baby boy about two and a half years ago."

"Oh, I'm so happy they had another child. Not that this boy would ever replace the daughter they lost, but I'm still happy for them. What about Semi Jemez?"

"That one is another story. She's been seen in the emergency room twice in the last two years. My guess from reading the records is that it was from physical abuse, although she would not report it as such. As usual, she reported a fall, but the abrasion and contusions told another story. Additionally, she was admitted for a psych evaluation eight months ago, but we could only keep her for forty-eight hours. Nothing since."

Silas searched the desk drawer for paper and pencil. "What about a current address for her?"

"Yes. Her latest address is different from the earlier address. Her 124 Sycamore Street address in Santa Fe is on the record of her latest visit. No telephone or email listed."

"Thank you, Monica. I really appreciate this, and I appreciate your confidentiality."

"Yes, sir. Always. But I must admit I am a bit curious as to why you need this information."

"I can imagine that you are, and I simply ask you to trust me for now. Maybe one day soon when I show up for a visit at the hospital with a tray of Lita's cookies, I'll be able to tell you. But for now, I am most grateful for this information."

Silas said his goodbye, leaned back in the chair, and gazed out the window. He closed his eyes and tried to remember the details of the night Semi and young Nodin had been brought to the hospital. He recalled that Semi was of slight build and that the surgery was especially difficult upon discovering she was pregnant.

He remembered praying for her during surgery and

before telling her about Nodin's death the next morning. He had asked her nurse to accompany him when he told her. He could still envision the nurse leaning over the bedside stroking Semi's hair—lustrous and sable and still blood-encrusted in places from the lacerations. When she learned of her son's death and the loss of her unborn child, Semi had screamed and become inconsolable. She'd sent him away.

He remembered instructing the nurse to remain with her. After that, Semi would not allow him to care for her or even to come into her room.

He closed the file. Maybe after lunch, he could brief Sarki on what he had learned. The Bordens were no longer suspects. If the perpetrator had some relationship to his medical practice, then it had to be Semi Jemez.

Alo had returned to Grey Sage and was unloading and stacking the wood when the guard approached him. "Morning again, Mr. Loloma. I'm glad you're back."

Alo stopped what he was doing, dropped the piece of wood on the truck bed, and removed his gloves. "How's the morning, Robert? Just call me Alo. Everyone does."

"Yes, sir. I thought you should know we had a visitor this morning. I haven't reported to the chief yet. Thought you should know first."

"A visitor or an intruder?"

"Not sure. She came in on foot from the highway and walked the lane to the front door. I spotted her when she was maybe seventy-five yards from the inn—a slight young woman. I watched her but observed nothing I'd call suspicious. She appeared to know exactly where she was going. When I could see she was ringing the front doorbell, I ran around to the mudroom door and went in just to be cautious. Probably gave your wife a fright when I ran through the kitchen, but I wasn't taking any chances. I remained in the hallway out of sight."

"What was she doing here?"

"Kyah let her in. I talked to Kyah later, and she explained that the woman showed up a few days ago to use the phone. Her car had broken down, and one of your guests had given this woman some money to help with the car repairs. She returned to repay him."

"That sounds legitimate but a bit out of the ordinary. Never have I had that happen before."

"I thought so myself. I was about to lay it all to rest, but then I found this." He pulled a red bag made of a thin fabric from his pocket. "I watched her when she left through the front door and walked the lane back to the highway. But before she got to the highway, she left the lane and took a trail through the woods. She was headed in the direction of the main road, so I thought maybe she was enjoying a walk through the forest. It's a perfect time for that. But I followed her anyway to where her car was parked under some trees just off the road. I thought it unusual that she wouldn't just drive in. And why would she park where she did? I didn't get close enough to get her tag number before she drove away, but I did get the make and model."

Alo felt the wrinkles in his brow deepen. "So, what about the bag? How did you come to have it?"

"After she drove away, I walked through the woods to get back to the inn. Just thought I'd take a different route. No trail, just through the trees. This red bag caught my eye. It was lying next to a tree down near the stream. The ground and the bag were damp and mostly covered in aspen leaves." He handed the bag to Alo.

Alo took the bag. "What's in it?"

"See for yourself, sir."

Alo loosened the drawstrings and spread the bag open to look inside. His brows met in the middle. "Hair?"

"Yes, sir. Just hair. I didn't want to handle the bag too much, but I think that's all that's in it. Do you think we should get this to the chief?"

"I most certainly do. Fine job." He closed the bag and handed it back to Robert. "Here. Take this and go to the barn. I'll get Sarki and meet you there."

Alo walked briskly away toward the mudroom door trying to figure out how to get Sarki out of the studio without causing too much attention. He stopped, spun on his heels, and returned to the barn. "Robert, you got a cellphone?"

"Yes, sir, right here."

But Alo had thought of something else. "Never mind. She might not recognize it's you. I'll use my phone. Texting is not something I usually do." Alo texted a brief message to Sarki.

In less than two minutes, Sarki joined them in the barn. "What's up?"

"Could be nothing, but when Robert gave me the report from this morning, I thought you should be aware of it." He turned to Robert. "Tell the chief what you told me."

Robert repeated his story almost verbatim to Sarki, stopping just short of telling her about the red bag. Alo watched her. She hardly batted her eyes while she listened intently.

When Robert finished, Alo asked, "What do you make of this?"

Sarki's head waggled. "I know this woman to came to see Noble today. He told me. I didn't see her this morning, but I did see her Sunday when Noble gave her the money.

These kinds of coincidences are rare, so I'm curious."

Alo turned to Robert. "Show her the bag."

Robert handed her the bag as he told her where he'd found it.

She opened the drawstring bag. "Red silk organza." She looked in without touching the contents. "What is this? Hair? Just human hair?" Confusion spread across her face.

"Did you see the woman's hair?" Alo asked.

"I did. Short, almost boyish, and a dark sable color. As Noble described it this morning, it looked like a dog might have chewed it off. Not styled, just cut short in gaps."

Understanding dawned. Alo took the bag from her. "It's hers. It's her hair."

"What makes you think that?"

"I don't know how I know, but I do." He pulled the drawstrings closed and held up the bag. "It's another sign, a message of sorts."

Alo removed his hat and ran his fingers through his shoulder-length hair, also sable-colored but streaked with gray. "In our culture, hair is a symbol of strength and connection to our ancestors. Sort of like the story of Samson in the Bible. We cut it to mourn the loss of a family member. Some say the hair holds memories, and cutting it is a way of letting go of the grief and pain. Others think it's a symbol of a new beginning. Hard to be certain why she would do this."

Sarki nodded in agreement. "Understood. Could Chooli tell us more about this belief and custom?"

"I can give her a call. And the professor might have knowledge of this custom."

"I'm not ready to involve the professor." She looked at Robert. "Tell me again about where you found it."

"It was next to the trunk of a tree down by the creek bed. Partially covered in aspen leaves. And you can tell the bag's still damp."

"Yes, and that tells me it was not left there this morning. It was left earlier. Could be damp from yesterday's rain or this morning's dew. Take me where you found it. Do you remember?"

"Yes, Chief. I even took a picture of it before I picked it up." He showed her the photo on his phone.

"Good work, young man. You'd make a fine FBI agent. You have the nose for it. Lead the way." She followed him a few steps then paused. "Let's keep this to ourselves for now." She looked at her watch. "It's almost lunch time. Robert, you keep close watch on this property. Maybe stay nearer the house, but still out of sight, until Chepi gets here later. Alo, you and I'll brief Dr. Thornhill after lunch, and hopefully he'll have new information for us."

They walked in silence down the hill and followed the creek to the tree where Robert found the bag. He pointed at the base of the tree trunk.

"You two stay here," Sarki barked. "Don't move."

Alo watched Sarki as her eyes shifted from side to side before she carefully approached the spot, avoiding the disturbance of even one leaf and walking slowly around the tree in about a five-foot circumference. "She's been here. She didn't drop the bag. She's been sitting here."

Chapter Eighteen

$\mathcal{S}$arki called the inspector before lunch for an update. She gave him the morning's report and the make and model of the car involved and asked him to do what he could to see if the car was connected to Semi Jemez.

Following that, she joined the group in the dining room. She had no need to eat, and her frustration mounted as she listened to their chatter about the coming evening's activities. She hadn't participated in a show-and-tell since third grade and wasn't keen to do so again. But she knew her frustration was about more than the evening's plans. She had often been required to hide her activity when she was working under cover. She hadn't liked it then and liked it even less now, but it was necessary to keep down the furor it would cause with the other guests.

Trying to motivate Silas to eat quickly, she whispered about having new information before taking her seat at the table. His response that he too had information almost kept her from swallowing the morsels of fruit, cheese, and fresh bread on her plate. When the others dispersed back to the studio and to their suites, she went with Silas and Alo to the office.

They had barely closed the door when she said, "You first, Dr. Thornhill."

She followed Silas to the table, and they took their unassigned but customary seats. This time Alo joined them at the table. Silas pulled a piece of paper with his hand-scribbled notes from his shirt pocket. "I received a call from the hospital records department this morning. We can rule out the Bordens. The only one in that family who has been hospitalized in the last three years was Mrs. Borden giving birth to another baby. Sadness and goodness ran in their veins. I can't believe either of them is capable of these acts of desperation."

"Desperation? Understood. You offer grace. I offer justice. And what about Semi Jemez or her husband?" She watched every muscle in Silas's face.

"Nothing discovered about her husband, but Mrs. Jemez is another matter. Hospitalized twice in the last two years for accidents, but due to the injuries, hospital staff thought it was more likely physical abuse. When they questioned her, she covered for her husband as the abused often do and refused help or to press charges. But just eight months ago, she was admitted for forty-eight hours for a psych evaluation. She was found in a church where she had slept overnight. She was delusional, but the tox screen showed no use of street drugs, only prescribed meds. She had not committed a crime and seemingly posed no danger to herself or others, so they had to release her."

Sarki spoke. "I believe her to be our perp." She recounted the details of the morning.

"You mean she was here?" Silas asked when she finished.

"Possibly. I know you had limited experience with her after the wreck, but do you remember how she looked? Would you recognize her? Was she slight of build with short very dark hair?"

Silas looked out the window. "I think I would recognize her. She was a small woman, frail almost, and her hair was dark, long, thick, and shiny. I was recalling earlier this morning the day after her surgery, going into her room to check on her. She was still under the effects of the anesthesia but wanted to know immediately about Nodin. I had to tell her about his death and also the loss of her unborn baby. She became hysterical and sent me away and told me never to come back. It was my colleague who had to deliver the news that her internal injuries meant she would be unable to have more children. Her past and future had been snatched from her. All of that was quite a blow to a young woman."

Sarki noticed Silas's speech slowing and growing softer. He gazed out the window, and it seemed to her that he had drifted to another place and time. She let him ramble without interruption.

"I think I would recognize her. I remember going in to see her in recovery. Her hair was quite lovely, but one side of her face and hair had not been cleaned from the accident. We had rushed her into surgery late, and cleaning her face was not high on our agenda. We were trying to save her life. I asked the nurse to clean the blood away. Funny the things we remember."

"Yes. But your memories are helpful. She fits the description of the woman who showed up here this morning. Only the hair is different. Her hair is very short now, but she left this." Sarki pulled the red bag from her jacket pocket. "Robert found this in the woods this morning. I believe after seeing where it was found that she has spent time there, maybe waiting and watching. I don't know if she intentionally left this or if she dropped it. Makes no difference in the outcome."

She turned to Alo. "Would you mind explaining the significance of the hair to Silas?"

Alo gave a sensitive explanation of the ritual of cutting hair to mourn and rid oneself of the pain. He expressed his agreement with Sarki that Semi Jemez was the perpetrator.

"We won't know for certain until we know," she said. "But with these leads, I believe this will be over very soon."

Silas's voice was stronger now, almost as if he were delivering a diagnosis. "Semi Jemez is in deep grief. She has suffered great loss, and we have no idea what she has suffered at the hands of her abusive husband. This kind of stress and grief could have led to psychosis."

Sarki took the bag from the table and returned it to her pocket. "We have physical evidence now. DNA. We are fairly certain she's been here twice under the guise of car troubles, and we're nearing certainty that she's been the one who is responsible for the notes and the break in. It will be simple now to bring her to justice."

Silas stood from his chair. "It may be simple to bring her to justice, but justice isn't what she needs. And I can assure you that Maude and I want no part of justice that would bring more pain to this woman's life. She needs help, and the kind of help she needs won't be as simple as justice. Restoring her mental health and giving her hope and a reason to live again will take time." He walked quietly out of the room.

Sarki's eyes locked with Alo's. When she was certain Silas could not hear her, she said. "I've been in some form of law enforcement thirty plus years, and I cannot recall ever having heard that kind of response from a victim."

In Alo's stoic way, he responded. "That's Silas. He has the hands and heart of a healer. He knows about grief, the paralyzing kind of grief. Silas does not consider himself the victim here. For him, Semi Jemez is the real victim."

No lunch in the dining room today. Maude had asked Lita

to prepare a salad and sandwich smorgasbord to be served on the portale outside the studio. The bell was rung when lunch was ready. The guests ate at their leisure, but most did so hurriedly to return to the studio.

Maude checked on Sarki when she didn't come out to eat. She had been in and out of the studio most of the morning but had focused on her painting for the last hour. "I noticed you've been coming and going this morning. Could I bring you a sandwich and some fruit?"

"Thanks. I'm busy. Not hungry."

Maude was about to walk away when Sarki said, "We're close to solving this case. I know that will bring relief to you on many levels."

Maude smiled for the first time all morning. "Really? Is Silas safe now?"

"Our job is to keep him safe, and we will continue to be cautious until the perpetrator is in custody. I think you can relax, Maude. You have planned quite an evening for all of us. Now just enjoy it."

"I think I'm more likely to enjoy it with this news. I've always considered these evenings as the benediction for a week of work and pleasure as we have feasted on everything that appeals to our senses—the autumn colors, the feel of a brisk morning breeze, good food, music and conversation. And we always give thanks for getting acquainted with those guests who are here, because they are the ones who are supposed to be here for whatever reason." Maude smiled big again. "Like you, Sarki. You were supposed to be here this week—not last month, not next month, but this week. And I'm grateful you are here. I will find a way to make up tenfold for the week you've had."

"Are you saying I am a welcome visitor?"

Maude paused before answering. "No. You're not a visitor. You are a guest, a welcome guest. There is a difference, you know. Not all visitors are welcome as I have become painfully aware in the last few days."

"I'll ponder that while I finish painting the bark on this aspen tree. It's almost there."

By four o'clock, the studio smelled of sealer and turpentine, meaning the painting sessions had come to an end and the brushes were being cleaned. Maude had always been particular about brush cleaning and taught her technique to all who entered her studio. She hastened to help Bea and Henry when she observed the near destruction of the brushes they had used.

Kyah had been a great help in setting up easels in the great room and gathering the unveiling panels. Maude noted Kyah's excitement in the way she moved and related to all the guests.

Maude had undeniable pride in providing opportunities for would-be artists, be it those who painted or those who performed, and tonight six artists would step from the studio into the limelight with their work. Clara had assured her that she was now familiar with each painting and how it would fit into the story she would weave.

Maude reminded Kyah and handed her a note. "Remember, as we set up the paintings, Clara wants them in this order. We must be certain that she can remove the unveiling drapes very easily. And we might need a larger easel for Lily's painting. I'll get Alo to move that one if Lily decides to unveil it, but I think you and I can handle the rest. We'll wait until the studio is clear."

"Yes, ma'am. I will be most careful. But what about Miss Bea's painting?" Kyah asked. "I don't see her peonies on the list."

"Good observation. I will check with Clara about that. We had some conversation about Bea's painting. A still life of peonies on blue velvet would certainly take a right turn in a story weaving these southwest landscapes together. She'll find a way to make Bea feel unique."

Kyah took the last easel from the closet. "Yes, ma'am. Miss Bea is unique and maybe deserves her own story. I've never known anyone quite like her, and I've grown so fond of her this week." Kyah giggled. "She has told me so many stories. You wouldn't believe. Some of them are like fairy tales. I'm not sure they're all true, but they are to her, and she made them real to me. I do hope she'll return. I'd be sad to think that I might never see Miss Bea again. Anyway, I've written a song about her."

Maude's heart warmed. "How thoughtful of you, Kyah. I will let Clara know that. Your new song may just be her answer." She looked at her watch. "We must get these artists out of here so we can finish up."

Maude stepped to the door. "It's time, my friends. Make sure your brushes are clean, and just walk away from your painting. We paint in acrylics during these retreats so the paint will dry quickly. And with a spray of sealant, they'll be ready to show this evening and for your travel tomorrow. When you can return and spend a couple of months with us at Grey Sage, we will paint with oil. But for now, go take a rest and get cleaned up for our special dinner and evening. Kyah and I will finish up here, and the next time you see your painting will be when Clara pulls the drape off as she tells her story. I am looking forward to a fabulous evening."

Sarki took a walk down to the stream and stood on the bridge taking it all in. The angle of the late-afternoon light casting shadows through the forest. The whisper of a cool breeze against her cheeks. One of Laura's pumpkin cookies in her hand. She finished the last bite of cookie, stretched her arms high above her head, and then leaned forward to touch her toes. There had been no time all week for her normal yoga sessions or morning runs, and her tight muscles were screaming.

But Maude was right about one thing. In spite of the unexpected call back into the role of a law officer and not having the time she had counted on for creating, rest, and reflection, Sarki had found sanctuary at Grey Sage. The experience had provided a feast for her eyes and for her soul. Even as close as she was to closing the case, she was uncertain she'd be leaving tomorrow with the group.

After inhaling autumn and exhaling her stress, Sarki walked back up the hill and went to her suite. She stood at the window, looked out at the mountains, and called Chepi. "Dinner is at six thirty. Can you meet me at six o'clock?"

"Yes, Chief. I'll be there. Robert filled me in on the morning's events, and I just called the investigator for an update. I'm up on everything."

"Understood. Sounds like they've linked the car Robert saw this morning with Semi Jemez, but they've not located her."

"Not yet. Just a matter of time, though."

"And not much time, I'm thinking."

"Yes, Chief. We'll get her before she can hurt anyone if that's her intent. At least we have a better sense of who we're dealing with now."

"Maybe. We have her identity, but what we don't know is her intent or how unpredictable she is. I know you'll be here all night, but I have requested a local officer to be on surveillance with you. He's meeting Alo at five thirty to walk the property in the last bit of daylight. Then we'll meet with both of them at six sharp. This woman's behavior and activity have escalated, and I do recall what happened

Monday evening when we were all gathered in the great room. We do not want a repeat."

"As you say, Chief, 'understood.'"

After ending the call, Sarki lay on the bed and looked out the window, ruminating over the day's activities and conversations. Silas's comments had echoed through her thoughts all afternoon. She intended to ask him, when the time was right, why he did not see himself as the victim. How he could be so full of compassion and understanding and grace was a puzzle to her.

She'd had a successful career in solving cases and catching criminals. But at the root of it all, Sarki realized she had been searching her whole life for the one who murdered her mother and robbed her of her family. Similar to Silas's log of patients he had lost, she'd kept a list of her cases. The ones she had solved went in the green book, and the ones still open were in the red book.

She was beginning to understand that during her career, every victim had been a stand-in for her mother, and every criminal had been her mother's murderer.

Victims. She'd thought she understood victimhood until hearing Silas this morning. He was a compassionate, purposeful healer who comprehended human behavior from a perspective different from hers. She had comprehension but little compassion. She had purpose but no peace. She solved crimes without considering the human condition.

Having created a list of questions, she longed for a contemplative conversation with Silas, a conversation with someone like she'd never known before. Maybe Silas, with his wisdom, would help her solve the riddle of her own life. The hope of that conversation might keep her at Grey Sage for a few more days.

My red bag. It's gone. No time to find it. That army man was walking around again. He was up to no good. He didn't know it, but I saw him following me.

I gave the money back to the tall man. He didn't want to take the money and told me to pay it forward. I won't be here to do that. I made him take it. I didn't give him all of it. Now I can go back there again. The tall man said they were getting ready for something tonight. I don't know what.

Maybe that woman will tell another one of her crazy stories. She thinks she's telling my story, but she has no right to tell my story. No one knows my story but me. What she says isn't true. She lies. That bird never comes back. Every time I feel the wind on my face, I think it's Nodin. I named him after the wind, but he doesn't come back to me, not even in the wind.

I don't have my red bag, but I have scissors. I'll cut more hair and make another bag. The man in the white coat. He'll get the owl picture and the red bag. He'll know what it all means. And when he does, I'll do what I must do. Then maybe I will be free.

But free for what? I am alone, all alone. Nodin is gone. That man in the white coat took him and my baby girl and made it so that no babies will be mine ever again. No family. All I wanted was my family. I have no family. I'm tired. I can't do this much longer.

Cannot quit now. It's almost time, almost done. Where are my scissors?

Chapter Nineteen

Thursday evening

𝒜aude stood at the end of the dining table and watched as the guests, dressed for a special evening, gathered in the dining room for their final dinner at Grey Sage. Lily, looking like a floating flower garden in her duster of orange poppies on sheer black georgette crêpe, sidled next to Maude and whispered, "Look at Bea. Why she probably thinks this dinner is in her honor, and if she had a tiara, she'd be wearing it."

In layers of peony pink, Bea made an entrance like a grand dame on Henry's arm as the last guests to enter the room.

"If it makes Bea happy, let her relish these moments. They don't last long."

Lily continued her commentary as though she were a reporter on the red carpet at the Oscars. "And would you look at Drake? First time I've seen that mop of gorgeous waves clean since I've been here. I suppose his father never taught him to tie a Windsor knot—or that paisley ties do not pair well with plaid shirts."

Maude smiled genuinely this time, not the forced smile of the past few days. "He's always intense and focused on other things, but let's give him a break, Lily. At least he's honoring the evening with cleanliness."

"I think I'll shock him and everyone else and take the

seat next to him tonight. That chair's been empty since we got here."

"Your pleasure, my dear. We have no place cards or assigned seats, but you know you're breaking tradition."

Lily winked. "So, what's new?" She sashayed around the table and took the empty seat next to Drake.

When everyone was seated, Silas stood for his customary blessing. Lita and Tanzi, dressed in clean aprons stood, at the end of the table for Lita's announcement of the evening's menu.

"Tonight, for your final dinner at Grey Sage—" She chortled. "Well, maybe not your final dinner, because we do hope you will return. But for our final meal of this retreat, we will begin with a bowl of roasted pumpkin soup, followed by a kale salad with crisp apples, dried cranberries, and walnuts and dressed in warm vinaigrette. Your main course will be pork piccata served over herbed polenta with glazed carrots and sauteed zucchini ribbons. As always, there is a basket of fresh bread with tonight's fragrant rosemary-lemon butter. And just for this dinner, Tanzi has created a perfect dessert for such an autumn evening—her Brown Butter Bourbon Pecan Pie."

Everyone applauded, after which Bea stood and said, "I'll have my pie first, please." She sat down as though she had just pronounced an edict.

Maude watched Lita's eyes smile as a low rumble of laughter rolled through the room.

As always, there were a number of interesting exchanges around the inn's dining table, but Maude ate quietly without entering into conversation. Most of the week, although she had been seated at the table, she had not been truly present. With her secret always looming, it was an effort to be the hospitable hostess and protect her guests from alarming information. But tonight she was truly present and soaking up every bit of the essence of what Grey Sage offered—a place where strangers could become friends and a place where guests felt safe to create, to converse freely, and to explore new ideas.

When dinner had been consumed, the guests once again took their seats in the great room. Alo had built a roaring fire, and the draped paintings, lined like wooden soldiers in front of the fire, awaited the unveiling. Maude scanned the room, noting that Chepi was seated on the edge of his chair alone in the farthest corner next to the window. Alo was not in his usual seat with Lita but in a chair he had brought in and placed near the entrance to the foyer. Silas awaited her in their cuddle chair.

Maude made her traditional final evening remarks and ended by saying, "Where could you go to experience what we have experienced this week? We have had splendid autumn days, warm sunshine, gentle rain, and many hours of creating. After five-star meals, we have been mesmerized with Clara's storytelling, and Kyah's music, and such remarkable presentations by Boots and Drake. And tonight will be the finale. No, it will be the grand finale. Our artists' works will be unveiled as Clara spins her yarn to link all these stunning landscapes. Usually, each artist presents his or her own work, but our artists have chosen not to do that tonight, preferring to hear Clara's interpretation of their works through her intriguing storytelling. Our own Bea expressed herself on canvas not in a landscape but in a still life. So, before Clara begins, we have the unveiling not only of Bea's painting but also the premiere of Kyah's original song."

Before Maude could finish, Bea stood from where she was seated next to Henry, curtsied, and then joined Maude in front of the paintings. "Yes. I painted peonies, and I would have put ballet slippers on the table with the blossoms, but Maude had none for me to see. She did say that the peonies were symbolic of me—graceful, romantic, delicate, and vibrant. Let me show you." In a perfect arabesque, Bea lifted her right leg through layers of sheer pink fabric, extending it backward in the air at a ninety-degree angle to her left leg. Supporting herself on one leg, and as delicately as though she were plucking a petal from a peony, with her extended right hand she slid the drape from the painting, letting it float gently to the floor.

Aahs echoed through the room. Maude was certain their response was less about the painting and more an expression of surprise that an eighty-plus-year-old woman could assume and hold this position so perfectly.

Bea gracefully lowered her leg and her arms and turned to the face the group. After a deep bow, she took her seat.

"Bea, what grace and beauty. Thank you. I should have asked you to dance this evening. But we do have a musical surprise. Your beauty, your love of ballet, and your painting have inspired Kyah this week, and she has written a song just for you. She has entitled it 'The Porcelain Ballerina.' Listen to Kyah as she sings the story of the porcelain figurine who magically pirouetted herself to life and danced until resuming her beauty as a porcelain ballerina. And when Kyah is finished, Clara will begin."

As Kyah picked up her guitar and took her seat on the stool, Maude joined Silas. From where she sat, she could see that Tanzi, anxious to hear her sister, had taken the seat next Lita. She felt Silas reach for her hand as they waited.

Kyah strummed her guitar as though it were a harp, the resonance of the strings painting a picture of the ballerina as she came to life. Then with the purest soprano voice, delicate and flutelike, Kyah sang the story of the porcelain ballerina, her performance nothing less than artful and enchanting. Just like her singing earlier in the week, there was that moment of holy hush when she finished. No one wanted to disturb the magical spell that Kyah had cast, but Bea stood and led the group in applause.

Kyah acknowledged her audience and took the stool away while Clara returned the drape to cover Bea's painting since it was not a part of her story. Maude held her breath, hoping that covering the painting would not incite Bea. She wanted nothing to destroy these mystical moments.

Dressed in black and in vintage fashion, Clara stood, her hands clasped and her head bowed slightly until the only sound in the room was an occasional crackling of the fire. With no need to hurry, she slowly lifted her head and began.

"Sshh." Silence.

Again, "Sshh."

She stepped closer to her audience, leaned forward, and closed her eyes. "Sshh, can you hear the silence?" She paused. "Listen. Can you hear the river?" A mesmerizing stillness loomed in the room. Clara gave them time to eavesdrop on the silence and to imagine.

"Sshh, now listen for the whir of the wings of the white dove."

Maude was pulled from her quiet imagining by a sudden rap at the door. Not the bell, but a rap. Like a streak of lightning but without the thunder, Alo left the room for the foyer.

Alo unlocked the door. As though they had anticipated what might happen, Chepi had moved from his chair when Alo did and was only a few feet away, assuming his position behind the door. He nodded at Alo. Alo slowly opened the door.

A diminutive woman with a one-hundred-dollar bill in one hand and a red bag in the other stood in the near darkness. She was dressed in ragbag clothes and had the look of someone dirty with shame or sadness.

After a quick look at her, Alo turned to Chepi, nodded his head, and lowered his hand to signal him. Chepi moved closer to be prepared but was standing down as Alo had communicated.

Alo asked quietly, "How may I help you, miss?"

The woman raised her near-shaven head. Her sunken eyes were outlined in black, her cheeks pale with dried, smutty tears. In a weak voice, she answered, "I came to pay back the tall man. He loaned me money."

"That's kind of you. I will gladly give the money to him."

A bit more agitated and louder, she said, "No, I don't know you. I must give him the money." She paused and listened. "What are they doing in there?"

Alo watched her eyes as they looked beyond him. "It's a special evening for our guests." He stepped toward her. "Miss, why don't we talk outside so as not to disturb them?"

He stood, awaiting her response. As he could see both her hands, he did not perceive her as a threat.

Her voice grew louder. "No, I don't know you."

"Miss, please step back, and let's continue this on the porch."

"No. I hear her. She's telling that story again. I heard her tell that story before. She's lying. The dove never returns." She held out her right hand holding a red bag. "You don't understand. I have to give this to the man in the white coat. He lives here."

Alo stepped closer to the door, entering her space and forcing her to step backward. He placed his hand on the door facing to create a barrier. "Miss, I am not allowing you inside. Step back, please, and let's talk outside."

Chepi stepped nearer.

In a surprising flash, the waif of a woman darted under Alo's arm and bolted through the foyer and into the great room. She stopped as she entered the room filled with people all surprised by her presence. Alo and Chepi rushed to her, one on each side, and took her arms. Before they could remove her, she began to scream. "She's lying. That story is not true. The dove never returns. He never comes back." She continued her outburst, but her voice faded as Alo and Chepi gently but forcefully dragged her out the front door onto the porch.

They were joined within seconds by Silas and Sarki. Alo and Chepi continued to subdue her by holding her arms. Silas was silent, but Sarki spoke up.

"Semi Jemez. No question. We have her. A weapon?"

"Not in her hands," Alo responded. "Only a hundred-dollar bill in one and the red bag and piece of paper in the other. She's not a physical threat."

Sarki patted her down as Semi continued ranting. "How did you know my name?" she screamed.

Sarki moved close to Semi's face. "We know a lot about you and what you've been doing. We just don't know what you intended to do, but you won't be doing it."

Silas stepped forward and almost shoved Sarki away. "Mrs. Jemez, I believe I'm the one you wish to see. Am I right?"

Semi quietened and seemed to fold right before their eyes, slumping into Alo's arms.

"Take her around to the infirmary," Silas instructed. "I'll let you in through the mudroom door."

Alo took the young woman in his arms and carried her to the back entrance. Sarki and Chepi followed. As he walked, Alo listened to Chepi's explanation.

"Sorry for the scene, Chief. Alo did his best to calm and control her, even moving her out onto the porch, but she just bolted."

"Everyone's safe and everything's under control," Sarki barked, "but the room is in pandemonium now. They have no idea what's happening. Lily's in an uproar and blowing that whistle around her neck as though that will bring the cavalry. Bea's somewhere between screaming and whimpering. Noble's telling everyone he's seen the woman before, and I don't know about Maude. I'm going back in. Can't hide this any longer. I'll do some explaining and hopefully satisfy them so the evening can continue as planned. Chepi, you call the investigator and stay with Alo and Silas until I get there. Take notes of anything she says."

Sarki entered the great room through the dining room. She could see that Maude had replaced Clara in front of the group, and she could hear Maude beginning her effort to console them. She stepped to Maude's side. "Maude, with your permission, I'd like to offer an explanation to your guests."

Sarki noted the relief on Maude's face as she stepped aside.

"First, everyone is safe and everything's under control, and there is no danger. Hear me: you're in no danger. I will tell you that what you witnessed is a disturbed young woman who has been somewhat of a nuisance to our dear Silas for the last several days." She saw no purposeful reason to communicate that Semi's actions had been dangerously threatening.

"You should give thanks to Maude and to Silas for their

commitment to keep you safe and not to disturb your beautiful days here. They have hired round-the-clock security. They have allowed me to be their liaison with local law enforcement, and all have done a stellar job. The woman was quickly identified, and now she will no longer have opportunity to disturb the serenity of this sanctuary at Grey Sage. There is no reason that we cannot continue this beautiful evening."

Maude stepped forward. "Sarki, thank you. And I agree about not allowing this disturbance to rob us of this evening. Clara, you had just begun your story." She looked to where Kyah was seated in the corner. "Kyah, could we ask you to return to the front and play and sing something for us? Maybe something calming that would take us to another beautiful place as you did earlier. And then, Clara, would you be so kind as to start your story again?"

Maude moved back to her seat.

Sarki agreed. "Yes, please continue."

She stayed for a few moments until the hush had settled once again in this hallowed room. Then she moved with purpose to the infirmary to join Silas, Alo, and Chepi.

Silas sat on his rolling stool at the end of the examination table. Refusing to lie down and still clutching the hundred-dollar bill and red bag and paper, Semi sat at the end of the table, her short legs dangling, her frail body weaving at times. Alo and Chepi took their places standing slightly behind her on each side of the table.

Silas watched as Semi's tears created blackened tracks down her sallow cheeks. She had almost lost her breath from crying so deeply the last few moments. But now she was calmer.

Silas began to speak quietly. "I hope that you will allow me to speak to you. Semi. I know you're hurting deep down inside. I know your heart is broken because Nordin died and you lost your baby."

Sarki's entrance distracted him. He looked at her and shook his head, hoping to keep her quiet or keep her from advancing to the table. He preferred handling Semi alone.

He looked back into Semi's face and felt her penetrating stare.

"Don't you even speak my son's name," she spat. "I begged you to save Nodin and leave me be. Instead, you took my son and my unborn daughter, and you might as well have taken my life. You left me with nothing but sadness."

Semi threw the red bag and the paper into Silas's face. "I have tried and tried to rid myself of this sadness. I cut my hair like the medicine man told me, and still the sadness won't leave. I give it to you now. I want you to know my sadness and my fear deep in your bones the way I feel it."

She stopped to wipe her tears with her sleeve. Silas offered her the box of tissues from the shelf. She refused to take them from his hand.

"I wanted my son to live. He was a good boy, and I'm no good. You could have saved him, but you wouldn't listen to me. You were the last one to hold my son and my baby girl. Not me. I never held my baby, and I didn't have a chance to say goodbye to Nodin. He's never, ever coming back. You held his body, and you were a medicine man who could have made him better."

Giving her words time to settle, Silas waited before saying, "Semi, I don't know if you can really understand what I'm about to say. But I ask you to listen. Yes, I held your son, but I was only holding his lifeless body. God was already holding your boy in His arms as He welcomed him into heaven. There was no way to bring him back. And yes, I chose to save you because you are worth saving. I had no way of knowing that you were pregnant until your surgery, but your internal injuries had already taken the life of your baby. God was holding her too. She and her brother were together with the One who made them." He paused. "Words will never be enough to say how sorry I am that all of these things happened to you, how sorry I am that I was not a miracle worker. This is your sorrow, and no matter how sorry I am, I can never know the depths of your pain."

"Yes, it happened to me. To me. Not you. And you live in this beautiful big house, and you have so many friends and you have a son. I saw his picture. If the same thing had happened to him, you would have saved him."

Silas closed his eyes for a moment. "Semi, I told you that I cannot know your sorrow. But the boy in the portrait you saw? Yes, he was my son, and I held his lifeless body in my arms just like I held Nodin's. My son died in an accident, and I couldn't save him either. That was twenty-three years ago, and I still miss him every day. I trust that Elan is with the One who made him, just like your son and daughter. And I believe I will see him again."

Semi started to cry again. "I don't know if I believe you. Everyone lies to me. I can't trust anyone. Life is one big painful lie."

"I understand, Semi. It's difficult to trust when you've been hurt so badly. But as one who has grieved the death of a child, I want to help you out of this dark place. I know I must earn your trust."

Silas saw Sarki motion for him. He rose from his stool. "Let me get you a cool, clean cloth for your face. Would that be all right?"

Semi nodded in agreement.

Silas went to the shelf, grabbed a clean cloth, and went to the sink. As the water warmed and he dampened the cloth with it, Sarki joined him. "Police are on their way."

"I'm not pressing charges," Silas quickly retorted. "She's not going to jail. She is going to the hospital where she can begin to get some help. No jail. Do you understand?"

"If you don't press charges, then there will be no jail."

"No charges. Get Chepi to call an ambulance. I'll call the hospital."

He returned to Semi and handed her the cloth. She took it and began to wipe her face.

"Semi, I will be honest with you." He pointed to Sarki. "The woman at the door is a law officer. You have broken laws, and you could go to jail for what you have done. In fact, the police are on the way to take you there. But I do not believe you belong in jail, so I will not be pressing charges. I cannot bring your children back, but I do want to help you. I want you to learn to trust again, and you can start by trusting me."

Semi whispered under her breath, "I don't want to go to jail. I'm already in a prison of sadness. I just want to die."

"I am so sorry you feel that way, but trust me when I say there is help for you so that you can feel better and have hope again. I have asked the officer to send the police away and instead to call for an ambulance to take you to the hospital. Right now, you need sleep and care. I want to help you. I want you to have the help you need so that you want to live again. Could we start there?"

"I have nowhere else to go. I just want to go to sleep."

"Yes, Semi. Rest and sleep are good. And tomorrow, my wife and I will come to visit you in the hospital. You will like my sweet wife. She was a mother, too, a mother who lost her only son. She is a gentle person. I know you don't trust me now, but would you give my wife and me a chance to become your friends?"

Silas watched her rigid body relax.

"Grab that pillow, Alo." He positioned it under Semi's head and helped her lie down.

"You just rest. You're safe, and you are not alone. The people who are here and the people at the hospital only want to help you and make you feel better."

The room remained quiet. Chepi left to meet the ambulance outside. He had instructed no sirens.

Within fifteen minutes, Semi was on her way to the hospital. Silas had called in a favor to get her admitted and explained he would take responsibility for payment.

Without any further words, Sarki, Alo, Chepi, and Silas walked back into the great room just as Clara finished her story.

"Sshh," she said. "Can you hear the silence? Do you hear the whir of the white dove's wings as she flies away? Keep listening. The dove of peace always returns."

Silas watched as Clara bowed her head and took one step back. He prayed she was right—that the dove of peace always returns.

Chapter Twenty

Friday

The buzz of normal activity reverberated through the halls at Grey Sage. Maude and Lita were in the kitchen preparing breakfast. Kyah was assisting the guests with their bags. Alo was packaging the artists' paintings for their airplane trip home. Silas was on the phone with his colleague at the hospital.

Lita hummed a happy tune as she rolled out sweet-potato biscuits, and Maude sensed Lita's cheerfulness meter was ticking in the red zone.

Lita stopped humming. "Life's getting back to normal around here today," she stated. "Mystery solved. This is the last meal with Lily's traveling crew, and as I said before, I am done with sweet potatoes. Don't want to eat one. Don't want to cook one. Why, I don't even want to see one until Thanksgiving. With Sarki gone, I'll be gorging on night-shades."

Maude was tending the Canadian bacon. "About that. You know, Lita, Sarki only had a couple of days here before she put on her law officer hat to help us. She's been working nonstop. To say thank you, Silas and I have invited her to stay as our guest for a few more days."

Lita stopped rolling out the biscuits and rolled her eyes. "How long?"

"I don't know yet. She'll tell us this morning. I've asked

Alo not to pack her painting until we know. It's the least we could do."

"More sweet potatoes."

"And something else you need to know. As soon as Alo leaves to take the guests to the airport, Silas and I will be going into town to see Semi Jemez. He needs to make some arrangements with the hospital, and he wants to see Semi to follow through on his promise."

Lita started rolling out the biscuits again. "Maude, do you think she would have ever hurt Silas?"

Maude turned over the last of the Canadian bacon and put the tray back under the broiler. "I don't know. I've asked myself that question. From what Silas reported, she's very disturbed and distraught, but that doesn't mean she's capable of hurting someone. Silas says she just needs help, and he's committed to getting her what she needs."

"Silas. He's always fixing people, trying to make them better."

Silas took that moment to walk into the kitchen to get his coffee. "I heard that. We're all fixing or making something, Lita. Alo makes repairs. You make biscuits. Maude makes me happy, and she makes appealing art. Besides, I feel I must help this woman get her life back on track."

It had been days since Maude had felt such relief. Lita was back to her jolly self. The muscles in Alo's face had relaxed, and Silas had a new project. "Let's get this breakfast served and these travelers on their way. Can you imagine the stories they will tell their friends when they get back to Chicago?"

Lita chimed in. "I can hear Lily, now exaggerating it all like this woman was a serial killer on the loose. Just so you know, I came close to choking Lily with that chain around her neck when she started blowing her whistle last night.

That woman's got more than her share of bats in her belfry. What good did she think that would do? Just added to the chaos." She shook her head. "I guess they'll all have their version of what happened. That is, except for Bea. She just won't remember."

Silas went to the fridge for the pitcher of cream. "Have you two noticed how chaos seems to follow Lily to Grey Sage? Think of the fiasco last Christmas. The accident on the road because she wouldn't listen to Alo about the weather. Stranded here for days because of the snowstorm. Then Jedediah was attacked by the wolf. And then think about all the events of this week. Enough to make someone's hair gray." He ran his fingers through his wavy, white hair. "Maude, if Lily calls again to book the inn for a retreat, maybe you should think long and hard about that one."

Maude sighed. "I suppose that's one way to look at it. But think about this: last Christmas was wonderful, our first real Christmas here since Elan died. If they hadn't been here, we would have been all alone since we couldn't make our planned trip to Curaçao because of the storm. And we made so many new friends. Kent and Emily fell in love while they were stranded here and returned in August for their wedding. And think about this week: Sarki, a former FBI agent shows up just when we needed her. I think Lily brings us great friends and good fortune just when they need to be here."

Silas sipped his coffee. "Only you, Maude."

"And besides, she's asked to bring the group back for Christmas, and I've already said yes."

Lita plopped the last biscuit onto the baking sheet. "With Tanzi in the picture, I think I'd best have a conversation soon with Doli and Catori to let them know we'll be visiting them this Christmas."

Alo walked in and joined the conversation. "Maybe not.

Our girls and their families weren't here last year. I missed them, and they belong at Grey Sage for Christmas, and so do we."

"Then we need to have a conversation with Tanzi. She's been great help this week, and she and I have some creative ideas about what we can do here at Grey Sage."

Silas chucked. "Oh, the last time you came up with creative ideas, Lita, our family home became an inn. I'm not sure I'm ready for another one of your ideas."

Lita put the biscuits in the oven. "Oh, this is a good one, a way to transition me into retirement and still keep things in the kitchen running smoothly. I had dreamed that one day one of our daughters would return with her family to Grey Sage, and we could all retire. But that's not going to happen. Tanzi came up with an idea of offering theme dinners on the weekends. Sort of private fine dining for limited guests willing to pay a premium. She'll be the chef, and we won't need to have as many retreats."

"So now, we've become a restaurant?" Maude asked. "And you'd stay out of the kitchen?"

"Didn't say that. But we figured by offering these dining opportunities on occasion, it would help increase the revenue to cover her salary with a minimum of work."

Silas nodded. "Smart. At least someone is thinking about the business side of things."

"And Chepi could work part time to help Alo."

Alo scoffed, albeit mildly. "And who decided I need help?"

Maude intervened. "Let's face it. Silas is the only one around here who has transitioned into retirement. It's high time we all thought of doing the same. And what another wonderful gift Tanzi and Chepi have been to us this week. And there's Kyah. We should take a look at these fine young people. I don't think their appearance is just serendipitous."

Lita started cracking eggs. "Sounds like the four of us have a lot to talk about. Let's get this breakfast on the table, and our guests on their way, catch our breaths, and I'll have us a pot of chili for our evening meal. Trust me, I'm loading it down with peppers. And we'll have a family meeting around the table."

"I'll look forward to that," Maude said. "I'll tell the writers the kitchen is closed. We've provided them far more meals than they have requested. We deserve the rest of the day off."

Immediately following breakfast, as the other guests were packing and getting ready to leave for the airport, Sarki requested to speak with Maude, Silas, and Alo. They met around the breakfast table in the kitchen.

Before Sarki began, Maude spoke up. "Sarki, will you be taking us up on our invitation to stay on a few days? I feel that you've been robbed of your time here."

"Understood. More on that later. I thought you would want to know that I've spoken with the locals. I explained the situation and how you preferred not to press charges against Semi Jemez. However, I was told that since they have been involved with the investigation and there was a break-in, they can proceed with charges without you. I explained further, and they're leaning toward honoring your request. I questioned them hard about why they would choose to add more to their workload and add another case to a system that is already overloaded. And I explained that in your medical opinion, Ms. Jemez is disturbed and in need of psychiatric help, and you are willing to see that she gets it."

"Exactly right," Silas responded. "As always, you are thorough and accurate, Chief."

"Thank you. I have made my plea, but if you have any friends in the system, you might want to give them a call. Speak with care. Often, when one refuses to press charges, the officials understand your refusal to mean you will not cooperate with them in prosecuting the perp. Sometimes they don't take too kindly to that. But in this case, I think if you make your appeal as a doctor who wants to keep her out of a legal system where she can't get the help she needs, you might be more successful."

Maude watched an impish grin spread across Silas's face. "Oh, I may know a couple of folks who might think I was able to help them at some point. I'll make the calls this morning before I visit Ms. Jemez. So will you be staying on with us?"

"I will not. I have some prior commitments back in Chicago, and although I would much prefer staying here for a few more days, I should get home for now. I will return if for nothing but one conversation with you, Silas. I want to know more about what makes you Silas."

"That will be a short conversation, Sarki. But I promise we'll have it whenever you return."

Sarki smiled and nodded. "Lily has told us that she's planning to return for Christmas with a group. Maybe I'll return then or later in the winter. I'll do almost anything to escape February in Chicago. There is no cold like the cold wind coming off that lake."

"I don't want to discourage your return," Alo said, "but February can be cold here—and with snow. Not as cold as January, though. The animals are telling me that our winter will be colder than last."

"So, you're talking to the animals now, Alo?"

After a week of serious tension, Alo smiled broadly.

"No. They talk to me. I do not talk back."

She nodded in agreement and stood from her chair at the table. "I'm not certain when, but I will return to see you again. Please give Chepi my highest regards. It was a pleasure to work with him. I could make one fine FBI agent of him."

Alo got up from his chair. "I'll be certain to do that. He'll feel honored to hear your evaluation of him, but I'm thinking we have other plans for him and his wife. Then, if you're not staying with us, I should go and pack your painting for your travel. Everyone else's is ready. Please excuse me, ladies"

Maude and Silas joined Sarki as she walked out of the kitchen. Silas said, "Please know how very grateful we are for all your help this week. Seems God sent you when you were needed most. And through you, we've made a new friend in Chepi. When you return, I hope you'll be seeing more of him around here for some other plans we have in mind. And know that when you return, you return as our most welcome guest. So don't you let Lily wrangle a thin dime out of you if you return with her." He turned and hugged her.

She paused before walking away. "You're right. Lily's a wrangler."

Lily's whistle echoed shrilly through the adobe walls of the inn. Her travelers gathered. Alo was loading the bags and paintings for the drive to the airport.

Maude joined Lily with the others in the great room. "We have two things to do before you leave," she said. "Those of you who've been here before know what they are.

Follow me."

Maude led them through the great room, across the portale, and into the studio. "On the table over there, you will see three trays of thinned paint. If you look on the north wall, you'll see handprints of guests we've had through the years. Handprints now on top of handprints, but what a stunning kaleidoscope of colors, memories, and people we have enjoyed. So have at it. Grab a pen, dip your palm in the paint, and leave your handprint on the wall. Underneath please write your name and date and anything else you'd like to say. You can clean up at the sink."

Maude laughed, but Lily guffawed when Bea refused to put her hand in the paint. Instead, Bea removed her shoe and sock and instructed Henry to bring the paint tray to the corner. She delicately dipped the sole of her foot in the pink paint and pressed her foot against the wall, then hobbled to the sink and lifted her foot to wash it. That done, she returned to scribble something beneath the print.

As the group finished and began to leave the studio, Maude said, "Let's go see what she wrote."

There, on the wall, Bea had signed, "Madame Beatrice Caldwell, Ballet Artiste."

Maude and Lily just looked at each other and chuckled. "Better watch her in the airport bathroom," Maude said. "I think it's one of those days."

They followed the others back to the great room. When the group had circled, Maude announced, "Now, for our last tradition. Silas will lead us in prayer for your safe travels."

Silas stepped to the center of the group and pivoted to look at each traveler. "Normally, I'd ask you to bow your heads for prayer, but I want to see your faces as I pray this morning." With a nod, he began. "Lord, we welcome every guest into our home as we welcome You into our hearts. We have delighted in their presence this past week as they have joined us around our table, as they have spent time enjoying Your creation, and as they have spent time creating. These wonderful folks have given back to us much more than we have given to them, and we thank You for bringing them our way. They have left their handprints on our walls and their soul-prints in our lives. We ask You to guide them in the paths they should take, and may they travel safely today as they take their memories of Grey Sage back to their everyday, walking-around lives. Amen."

Silas, Maude, Alo, Lita, and Kyah stood at the door to say their personal goodbyes as the guests departed. Maude walked arm in arm with Lily out to the van. As Lily raised the whistle to her mouth, Maude grabbed her arm. "Maybe you can wait until you return to blow your whistle again. It could be worn out from last night." Then Maude reminded her. "Let's talk next week about your return. We can enjoy our time together in peace. Until then, I am planning to enjoy these autumn days in quiet and solitude. As Clara said, I'll be listening for the whirring wings of the dove of peace to return to Grey Sage. I think I hear them. So goodbye…for now."

LITA'S GREY SAGE CASSEROLE

Ingredients

3-4 medium-sized zucchinis, sliced in ¼" slices

½ cup chopped onion

¼ cup finely chopped deseeded jalapeño

1 cup canned tomato sauce

1 cup salsa (either homemade or a jarred salsa from the
    grocery shelf)

2 cups frozen whole kernel corn or a 15-oz can of whole
    kernel corn

½ teaspoon ground cumin

½ teaspoon cayenne pepper

½ teaspoon garlic powder

1 teaspoon chili powder

1 tablespoon white vinegar

3 cups crumbled tortilla chips

Salt to taste

1 cup grated mozzarella cheese or cheddar

Garnish: chopped green onions, a dollop of sour cream, and
    a couple of tortilla chips

Directions:

- Preheat the oven to 350 degrees. Grease a 9"x13" baking
  dish and set aside.
- Prepare the zucchini. Either cook in the microwave or
  steam on the stovetop for 5 minutes until about half

done. The zucchini should not be mushy.

- In a large mixing bowl combine the onion, jalapeño, tomato sauce, salsa, corn, spices, and vinegar.
- Stir in the zucchini and tortilla chips and mix thoroughly.
- Put in the 9"x13" greased baking dish. Top with grated cheese.
- Bake covered in a 350-degree oven for 25 to 30 minutes.
- Garnish with chopped green onion, a dollop of sour cream, and tortilla chips.

Note: 6 fresh tortillas fried in a skillet or air fryer and crumbled can be used in place of bagged chips.

TANZI'S SALAD

Ingredients:

1 heart of Romaine lettuce, finely chopped

1 medium carrot, coarsely grated

2 green onions, green part only, sliced

Blue cheese dressing (a bottled dressing or see the recipe below for a lighter version)

1 cup pickled beets, cut into small pieces

Blue cheese crumbles

Directions:

- In a large bowl, combine the lettuce, carrots, and green onions. Toss with the dressing.
- Plate the salad onto 4 plates. Sprinkle the pickled beets and crumbled blue cheese on top.

BLUE CHEESE DRESSING

2 tablespoons mayonnaise

¼ cup low-fat buttermilk

¼ cup plain fat-free yogurt

1 tablespoon white vinegar

½ teaspoon sugar

⅓ cup crumbled blue cheese

Salt and freshly ground pepper

Directions:

- Whisk the mayonnaise, buttermilk, and yogurt together until smooth.
- Add the vinegar and sugar and whisk until well combined. Add the crumbled blue cheese, and salt and pepper to taste.

Note: If preferred, the yogurt can be drained and thickened by putting paper towel in a small colander or mesh strainer. Spoon in the yogurt and allow to sit in the refrigerator for 15 minutes.

BUTTERSCOTCH ICEBOX CAKE

(with variations)

Ingredients:

1 (12.2 oz) box graham crackers

1 (3.4 oz) butterscotch instant pudding mix or 2 (1 oz boxes)

2 cups milk

1 (8 oz) package cream cheese or Neufchatel

2 (8 oz) tubs frozen whipped topping, thawed

Brickle bits

Directions:

- Arrange a single layer of graham crackers across the bottom of a 9"x13" dish or plastic container.
- In a large mixer bowl, beat together the pudding mix and milk until thickened, then add the cream cheese and one tub whipped topping. Mix thoroughly.
- Transfer half the mixture to cover the graham crackers, spreading it to all the edges.
- Arrange another layer of graham crackers on top of the pudding and spread the rest of the pudding mixture over them.
- Place a final layer of graham crackers on top, and cover with the second tub of whipped topping.
- Sprinkle with brickle bits.
- Cover and refrigerate for 4 hours before serving.

Variations:

- VANILLA: use vanilla pudding and follow the above directions.
- CHOCOLATE: use chocolate pudding and top the last layer of whipped topping with chocolate shavings (optional)
- COCONUT: use vanilla pudding and add 1 cup of sweetened shredded coconut to the pudding mixture, and then sprinkle the top with toasted coconut.
- LEMON: use lemon pudding and sprinkle lemon zest on top

PHYLLIS'S BLACK AND WHITE CAKE

Cake Ingredients:

2 cups all-purpose flour

2 cups granulated sugar

¾ cup cocoa powder

1 teaspoon baking powder

2 teaspoons baking soda

1 teaspoon salt

1 cup buttermilk

½ cup vegetable oil

2 eggs

1 teaspoon vanilla extract

1 cup hot coffee (can be made using instant coffee or espresso granules)

Cream Cheese Filling Ingredients:

½ cup heavy cream

1 teaspoon vanilla extract

1 cup powdered sugar

¾ cup cream cheese, room temperature

Chocolate Mousse Ingredients:

4 ounces dark chocolate, chopped

1 cup heavy cream, divided

1/8 cup powdered sugar

1 teaspoon vanilla extract

Chocolate Ganache Ingredients:

1 (8 oz) bag semisweet chocolate chips

½ cup heavy cream

1 teaspoon Karo syrup

½ teaspoon instant coffee granules

1 tablespoon Kahlúa or other liqueur (optional)

Directions:

Cake:
- Preheat oven to 350 degrees.
- You will need 4 cake pans, each 8 inches in diameter. Cut out 4 parchment paper circles that will fit inside the cake pans. Place the parchment papers in the pans and use melted butter to butter each pan well.
- In a large mixer bowl, add the flour, sugar, cocoa, baking soda, baking powder and salt. Using the paddle attachment, mix on low speed until well combined.
- In a medium bowl mix together the buttermilk, oil, eggs, and vanilla.
- Add the wet ingredients to the dry ingredients and mix.
- With the mixer on low speed, slowly add the coffee and continue mixing until everything is well combined. Scrape the bottom of the bowl with a spatula and mix as needed.
- Pour the batter equally into the 4 prepared pans.
- Bake the cake for about 35 to 40 minutes. Do the toothpick test—insert a toothpick in the middle of the cake and if it comes out clean, it's done. Let the cake cool in the pans for about 30 minutes then turn them out onto a cooling rack or a cutting board and cool completely.

Cream Cheese Filling:
- In a mixing bowl, place the heavy cream and mix until the cream has thickened and it forms soft peaks.
- Add the remaining ingredients and mix until the cream cheese is fully incorporated into the whipped cream. The mixture should be thick enough so that it's spreadable.

Chocolate Mousse:
- Into a heatproof bowl, place the chopped dark chocolate and set aside.
- In a small saucepan, heat 1 cup heavy cream over medium heat until it begins to simmer.
- Pour the hot cream over the chocolate and let it sit for 2 minutes. Stir until smooth and let cool to room temperature.
- In a separate bowl, beat 1 cup heavy cream and the powdered sugar and vanilla until stiff peaks form.
- Gently fold the whipped cream into the cooled chocolate mixture until smooth and creamy.
- Cover and refrigerate for at least two hours or until set.

Ganache:
- Into a heatproof bowl, place the chocolate chips and set aside.
- In a microwave-safe bowl, heat the cream and Karo syrup in the microwave until steaming. Add the instant coffee granules to this mixture.
- Pour the hot cream over the chocolate and let sit for 1 to 2 minutes. Stir the chocolate and cream together until smooth and well combined. Add the Kahlúa if desired.
- Note: Pour mixture over cake while still a bit warm.

To assemble:

- On a cake plate, set the first cake layer, then top with chocolate mousse.
- Add the second cake layer, then top with cream cheese filling.
- Add the third cake layer, then top with chocolate mousse.
- Add the fourth cake layer, then top with cream cheese filling.
- Pour warm ganache over the top of the cake and allow to drip down the sides.
- Refrigerate to allow the mousse and ganache to set.

About the Author

Phyllis Clark Nichols's character-driven Southern fiction explores profound human questions using the imagined residents of small-town communities you just know you've visited before. With a strong faith and a love for nature, art, music, and ordinary people, she tells redemptive tales of loss and recovery, estrangement and connection, longing, and fulfillment ... often through surprisingly serendipitous events.

Phyllis grew up in the deep shade of magnolia trees in South Georgia. Born during a hurricane, she is no stranger to the winds of change. In addition to her life as a novelist, Phyllis is a seminary graduate, concert pianist, and cofounder of a national cable network with health- and disability-related programming. Regardless of her role, Phyllis brings creativity and compelling storytelling.

Phyllis currently serves on a number of nonprofit boards. She lives in the Texas Hill Country with her portrait-artist, theologian husband.

Website: PhyllisClarkNichols.com
Facebook: facebook.com/Phyllis Clark Nichols
Twitter: twitter.com/PhyllisCNichols